Secrets From A Misty River

J.D.Missen

All rights reserved. No part of this book may be reproduced in any form on by an electronic or mechanical means, including information storage and retrieval systems, without permission in writing from the publisher, except by a reviewer who may quote brief passages in a review.

Copyright © 2024 J.D.Missen

This is a work of fiction. Names, characters, places, and incidents either are the product of the author's imagination or are used fictitiously. Any resemblance to actual persons, living or dead, events, or locales is entirely coincidental.

Published 2024 by Carrot Press
Book cover and image design by Carrot Publishing

ISBN: 978-1-7384353-5-7 (paperback)
ISBN: 978-1-7384353-6-4 (hardcover)
ISBN: 978-1-7384353-7-1 (ebook)

Also by J.D.Missen

Fiction
Confessions from a Fractured Mind

Poetry
Love, Death and Madness

Childrens
The Little Spider
The Little Mole

For my children, Daniel and Chloe

Deben Quay Riverside

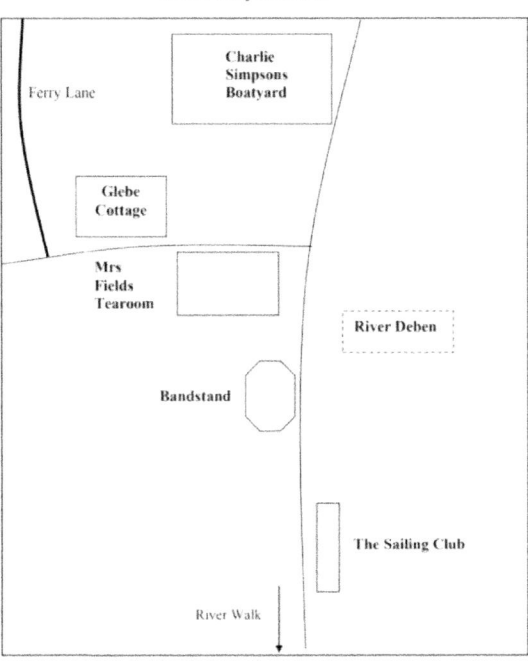

Ferry Lane

Charlie Simpsons Boatyard

Glebe Cottage

Mrs Fields Tearoom

River Deben

Bandstand

The Sailing Club

River Walk

THE SUFFOLK TIMES

Saturday, 21 February, 2006

Rubbish Collection Strike Fiasco
by Phil Wattle

A strike by Council workers has led to a build-up of rubbish on the streets of Deben Quay. Rubbish was not collected on either Thursday or Friday due to a walk out by staff over the promise of a pay rise less than the increase in the cost of living. Difficulties in the economy, caused by the collapse of the sub-prime market in the U.S. have been blamed for the lack of resources. Council workers will be back at work on Monday, but refuse will not now be collected until normal collection days, leaving many households with twice the usual amount of rubbish to store. For more information on when your bins will be emptied contact Deben Quay Council Office: 2562 or see their website: http://WWW.DebenQuay.gov.uk

Woman's Whereabouts Unknown
by Caroline Woods

A local woman from the Deben Quay area has been reported missing after not being seen for several months by her family. Lucy Mortimer is 23, slim with shoulder-length brown hair. She is thought to have moved away from the away from the Deben Quay area in September last year but has not contacted her family since. If you know of her whereabouts, please contact Deben Quay police.

More Snow Predicted
by Russell Carter

Further snow showers have been forecast for this week and may become heavy, leading to widespread disruption to services and transport links. Council gritters will be out in force to salt and grit main roads before nightfall, but police warn that minor roads may still be icy and drivers should avoid travelling.

Speeding Drivers
by Leah Hart

Three motorists were stopped last night, for driving over the speed limit in Deben Quay town centre. A woman and two men were fined for driving over the thirty mile-per-hour speed limit.

DEBEN BUTCHERS
For all your local meat supplies.
Tel: 27435

CHAPTER 1

It is a bitterly cold, damp February morning the day the body is found. The early morning sun remains hidden behind a blanket of cloud as a bone-chilling mist, which has been slowly rolling out across the river since dawn, begins to sweep onwards towards the quayside buildings that stand proud along the river's edge. The maltings that overshadow the far end of the quay were once used to store that coal that was offloaded from barges that were moored there. Now the buildings stand derelict, redundant of their former use in the once vibrant port but not deemed important enough to repurpose into something more meaningful than a place for the local pigeon population to reside.

Leading away from the quayside is a thin narrow path that runs alongside the river Deben. The original dirt track was used as a tow path for the barges so that the heavy horses, who lived in the nearby fields, could pull the boats down the river at low tide and onwards to the small hamlets of Kingsfleet and Bawdsey – the last two villages before the river flows out into the cold North Sea. Almost ten years ago, a local councillor decided to use his locality budget to create a more user-friendly concrete path, seemingly without concern for the environment but never-the-less it had the desired outcome in encouraging residents to venture out of the town centre and partake in some gentle exercise in one of the most serene parts of the County.

In the warmer months this particular stretch of the river is often frequented by both regional and visiting sailing clubs, whose small dinghies and sailboats cheerfully litter the old harbour. During the winter season though it is more often visited by local residents on foot; resilient joggers and keen dog walkers who brave the biting breeze to amble along the narrow picturesque path, along with the occasional birdwatcher who can be found standing at the water's edge, observing the wading birds with their long legs sunk into the low mud flats that meander along the river's edge.

On this day though there are only a few isolated people dotted along the narrow path adjacent to the riverbank; out for a bracing stroll that is guaranteed to redden their cheeks and burn their lungs on such a crisp morning. They are seemingly unaware of the young woman's body that is caught up amongst the reeds and tall bullrushes. She has been dead long enough for the advanced stage of decomposition to cause her body to refloat. Her bloated youthful face is partially covered by her bedraggled shoulder-length hair; her clothes are dark and sodden, skinny indigo jeans stuck fast to her rigid body. One plimsoll is missing, the other is still tightly laced to her right foot.

There is nothing to indicate how she died - no obvious injuries that could have been noticed by a vigilant passer-by who might have spotted her trapped amongst the vegetation by the incoming tide. Instead, it is a small fawn-coloured terrier, happily taking advantage of the low tide to ferret around the mudflats, who stumbles upon her remains.

The mongrel's owner, Mrs Fields, is standing on the coastal path just above the mudflats, waiting as patiently as she can in the freezing cold wind that is blowing up the river and buffeting the woolly hat she fastened tightly around her steely grey hair a little while earlier. Mrs Fields nose is just beginning to numb from the bitter chill, when she is jolted from her thoughts by the sound of frantic barking coming from the riverbed below. The elderly widow reluctantly withdraws her attention from the landscape of the peaceful river, curious as to the root cause of her dog's state of great excitement. Gingerly she crouches down as far as her aging knees will allow, her gaze drawn downwards towards the cluster of rushes protruding from the mud flats below. It does not take long for her to spot the body.

First to arrive at the quayside is PC Barnaby, one of the recent intakes of newly qualified police constables who was, albeit reluctantly, assigned to the small, rural police force. It is not usual practice for an inexperienced officer to be assigned to such a case, and certainly never usually alone, but the call handler was convinced that the report of a body by an elderly lady who is known for her forgetfulness, would turn out to be far less sinister than it appeared. In fact, only last year a similar call was made about a 'body' in the same location, which turned out to be nothing more than a discarded dolls head.

As PC Barnaby fights her way through the bitter wind to reach the location described in the phone call, she cannot help but wonder why it is that any sane person would want to walk their dog here at this time on a Sunday, let alone in this foul weather. It does not take long for the police officer to spot the elderly lady, who is still valiantly standing on the river path, being battered by the strong westerly breeze that is now rushing up the river from the nearby coast. It is fortunate that Mrs Fields lives close by, as the river path is still largely absent of any other people who could have provided her with assistance - it had taken Mrs Fields only minutes to return home to phone the emergency services after recovering from the shock of her dog finding a dead body.

If there had been anyone else nearby then they would have been sure to notice PC Barnaby struggling to comfort Mrs Fields, who is by now beginning to realise the seriousness of the situation, whilst attempting to abstract information from the petite woman and simultaneously trying to keep the overly excited Jack Russell at bay.

Nutmeg is of course completely unperturbed by the goings on and is instead immensely enjoying the unexpected attention being lavished upon her.

'So, Mrs Fields,' PC Barnaby reiterates, holding a notebook in one hand and a biro in the other, which she waggles in the air to prevent Nutmeg from grabbing hold. 'So, you were walking along the river path earlier this morning, when your dog disappeared amongst the reeds. Is that right?'

'Yes, that's right dear. Nutmeg jumped down onto the sand to sniff about like she always does. I don't mind waiting for her, I've always loved looking out across the river, even in winter and anyway, Nutmeg does love to ferret about on the riverbed. It's all the new smells you see and being a terrier, she just has to follow her nose. She'd been gone a little while when I heard her barking. I was worried she might have injured herself as she doesn't normally do that, so I looked down the side of bank to see what she was barking at,' Mrs Fields says, closing her eyes. The frail woman takes in a deep breath then exhales steadily; a trail of vapour momentarily spreads out in front of her before dissipating into the mist. When she re-opens her eyes again, Mrs Fields turns away from the officer, quite lost in thought, staring out across the river. Her tired grey eyes comb the tranquillity of the slow-moving water, drinking in the gentle lapping sound of the tide, which is starting to come in. When she returns her gaze to the police officer, her eyes are sparkling with moisture.

'And after you found the body, what did you do next?' Barnaby asks, trying to sound as if she knows how to question a witness who has just found a dead body on her morning walk.

'Well, I put Nutmeg back on her lead and went home to phone for the police, then I came back to show you where she is….' Mrs Fields voice trails off, her face crumpling at the intrusion of the unwanted memory.

Sensing that little else will be gleaned from the witness in her current state of shock, Barnaby says 'Thank you Mrs Fields, shall I take you back home now, before you catch a chill?'

Mrs Fields nods enthusiastically, she does not need to be asked twice. Her teeth begin to chatter, as if suddenly noticing the cold for the first time and her thin shoulders start to visibly shake. She stoops down to deftly snap Nutmegs lead back on, then without so much as a glance at PC Barnaby, Mrs Fields begins to gingerly make her way back up the river path as quickly as her frozen stubby legs will allow. Nutmeg, enthusiastically straining at the leash, pulls the elderly woman towards Glebe Cottage, as if she too, is eager to reach home.

As they reach the front doorstep of the tiny cottage, Mrs Fields unclips Nutmegs lead, then turns around to wave to Barnaby, who is waiting politely at a distance on the path that joins the quaint cottage to the river path. Then the elderly woman plunges a trembling hand into her coat pocket, fumbles about for a moment and extracts a set of keys. She picks out the blue yale key from the bunch and shakily thrusts it into the brass lock. Turning the key firmly clockwise until it clicks, she pushes the heavy oak door inwards. Mrs Fields pauses for a moment, allowing Nutmeg to push past her, eager to be first into the warmth of the front living room, then follows behind as swiftly as her achy limbs can move. As the front door closes behind her, the elderly woman pauses on the terracotta tiled hallway floor and exhales audibly. She has never felt so relieved to leave the quayside that she has loved since she was a child.

Chapter 2

Detective Inspector James Morgan has been lying in bed wide awake for the past half-an-hour, trying to motivate himself to get up. As the alarm clock bleeps again, having set to snooze for the third time, he sighs loudly in the hope that someone might notice his displeasure. With no reaction forthcoming, Morgan curses quietly then reaches across the small bedside table to turn off the alarm. He switches on a small beige lamp then pulls back the duvet, involuntarily shivering as the cool air reaches him; he has yet again forgotten to change the timer on the central heating. Steeling himself against the chill, Morgan gingerly places one foot then the other onto the carpet, then hauls his slight frame out of bed. With both feet firmly planted onto the carpet, he twists around to fumble across the floral-covered duvet for the dressing gown that is now inexplicably hanging off the bottom of the bed.

Morgan had set his alarm clock to awaken him early with the intention of heading out for a morning run, something he has been promising himself that he would do for many months but has not yet actually achieved. Pulling back a corner of the bedroom curtain though reveals an uninviting damp mist curling around the windows - not the most inspiring weather for a run, though in all honesty, it takes little to put him off these days.

Grateful for the excuse not to head outside, Morgan pads across the pink deep-pile carpet that his wife insisted on when they first bought the house, towards the ensuite wet-room that he only finished decorating the previous weekend. He pauses momentarily as the door shuts behind him, hoping that the feint noise does not awaken Celia, then patters across the room to switch on the newly installed power shower. As he waits for the water to warm up, Morgans thoughts turn to the day ahead; he cannot decide if he should be looking forward to the couples planned lunch with friends or feel irritated at the intrusion on a sacramental day off from work.

The tendrils of steam creeping around the edges of the shower curtain spur Morgan into action again. Discarding his dressing gown and pyjamas onto the cold floor, Morgan pushes aside the curtain and steps inside. Ten minutes later, he is feeling wholly revitalised, albeit slightly guilty for yet again not going for a run. Turning off the steaming torrent of water, Morgan strikes out a hand, curling it around the curtain to locate one of the large fluffy towels that are always neatly folded on the heated towel rail. Tucking the towel around his waist, he wanders back into the bedroom to find his clothes that his highly organised wife has no doubt retrieved from the floor where he left them the previous night and hung up in their wardrobe. There, just as he expected, a pair of dark grey trousers and a pale blue shirt are nestled amongst the neatly ironed clothes.

Standing at the bottom of the bed, Morgan watches Celia, who is still gently snoring, flat out on her back with the duvet pulled up under her chin. He still recalls the first time he watched his wife sleep all those years ago, when they were considered barely adult enough to marry and the sense of pride he felt when he finally got to call Celia his wife. That first flush of romance has now long gone, but still, they are content in their own way.

The shrill ringing of the telephone squashed between a squat brass lamp and a small plastic alarm clock on the bedside table, jolts Morgan from his thoughts. He watches as Celia groans, sleepily strikes out a hand, picks up the phone then gingerly holds it to her ear. Although Celia resigned herself to the demanding nature of her husband's job many years ago, he expects that she will feel fully justified in being a little annoyed at being woken at such an early hour on a Sunday, especially when he is rostered off. Morgan watches as his wife's hazel eyes slowly open then search around the room until she locates her husband, whom she glares at.

'James, it's for you,' Celia mumbles, slamming the handset down onto the bed side table, then turning over and closing her eyes again.

Quickly Morgan traverses the room to pick up the abandoned receiver and listens carefully to a clipped voice on the other end.

'DI Morgan? Sorry to call you on your weekend off but a body has been found in the river. Unfortunately, there's no one else senior enough who can attend.'

Groaning inwardly, Morgans face scrunches up into a grimace that he is certain the call handler will expect from him, given the interruption to a rare weekend off. He is now seriously regretting his decision not to take Celia to Norwich for a trip to the theatre, which she had suggested when they first discovered that he was not rostered on for the weekend, but the thought of traipsing around endless women's clothes shops had prompted him to turn it down. Of course, if they had gone and stayed overnight then he would not have been at home to receive the phone call that effectively means his weekend is over - instead he will need to go to the quayside to investigate.

'Sorry, Celia,' Morgan says softly as he gently replaces the receiver onto the aging corded phone that Celia refuses to replace for anything more modern.

Celias eyes remain firmly shut, but a subtle flickering below the lids reveals that she is awake and listening as her husband finishes dressing then moves out of the bedroom. Her eyes remain firmly closed as she hears his footsteps heavy trip down the stairs, two at a time. As soon as the front door slams shut however, she opens her eyes again and sighs dramatically. She will need to set about cancelling their lunch plans; it looks as if she will have to endure yet another day on her own.

It takes a little under ten minutes for Morgan to reach the quayside, despite being handicapped by only having the use of one hand - the other is occupied holding a bacon sandwich that he purchased from a petrol station enroute. Even though it is not his first case as a newly promoted Detective Inspector, it is the first one where he is the most senior officer at the scene. It is not often Morgan wished that his line manager had not decided to take time off from work but he would have preferred it not to have been this particular weekend. Still, it gives Morgan the opportunity to prove that he was the right choice for the job.

     A jolt of excitement surges through him as he pulls the car up onto the grass verge that runs along one side of Ferry Lane. Slamming the door shut behind him, Morgan moves to the rear of the car and flips open the boot, where he delves in to locate crime scene overalls. The detective momentarily looks at the greasy bacon sandwich that he is still holding in his left hand, then having thought of the task ahead, he deftly tosses the object into a nearby shrub. He pulls on the protective clothing as quickly as his shaking fingers will allow, whilst chastising himself for his nervousness at being in charge.

Fighting to steady his heart rate, Morgan stands next to his car and surveys the scene ahead of him. He has parked at the end of a tarmac road, which abruptly ends as the pathway evolves into a narrow dirt track. From there he will need to walk the rest of the way down the path to the river. He takes another deep breath then begins to make his way up the bridleway that is still littered with debris from the previous summer tourists. The narrow strip of land is almost entirely covered by overgrown weeds that are so enormous they are almost taking over the unmade track. Yet another casualty of the town council's cutbacks in road maintenance, Morgan grumbles to himself as he trudges down the track.

The quayside is already alive with a hive of activity – with all available police officers from Deben Quay Police Force having been directed to the area. A police cordon has already been set up at the start of the concrete quayside path to prevent anyone unauthorised from entering the area; it is vital at this early stage to gather any evidence just in case the death turns out to be suspicious. As he approaches the cordon, Morgan flashes his ID card at the officer standing just inside the taped off area and is immediately greeted with a grunt, followed by the tape being lifted just high enough for him to duck underneath.

Just as the detective is stooping under the tape, a deep, booming voice barks to the police constable to hold the tape up a little higher. A little portlier than his police counterparts, Dr Len Bootle, the only full-time pathologist based at the local hospital, exudes a rare air of cheerfulness as steps across to the far side of the cordon.

'Well, it's certainly a chilly start to the day,' Dr Bootle says conversationally as he looks across the river before dramatically inhaling several deep lungsful of the brisk morning air.

Morgan grunts, then returns his focus towards the concrete path that runs alongside the tidal river then leads away from the town before disappearing into the encroaching mist. He sets off at pace, striding off down the path, then feeling a little guilty at his haste, pauses briefly to allow Dr Bootle to catch up. They hurry along the overgrown path side-by-side, with the river on the left of them and on their right, a sharp drop onto marshy farmland below. Walking briskly, they soon move away from the small group of onlookers who are now gathering girth on the other side of the cordon.

Ahead of them in the distance, a cluster of police officers are standing idly on the exposed path. As the two men approach the grassy inlet where the body lays, one of the officers peels off from the group and begins striding towards them.

'She's down there, Sir.' A constable shouts to Morgan, pointing towards a cluster of reeds and bullrushes nestled between the water and the steep bank below the river path.

'Let me have a look first, if you don't mind,' Dr Bootle says officiously, placing a hand on Morgans arm and gently moving him aside.

Morgan shuffles backwards towards the edge of the path, almost toppling down the grassy slope before moving deftly back into the centre of the path again. It is only then that he notices how bitter the wind is, not helped by the damp chill that is beginning to penetrate up his legs from the concrete path. Resisting the urge to jump up and down to warm himself up, Morgan re-focuses his attention onto Dr Bootle, who has now dropped down onto the small area of sand and shingle exposed by the high tide with surprising agility for a man of his age and stature. Perhaps the aging pathologist's weekly rounds of golf are better exercise than Morgan had previously given credit he decides, as he watches Dr Bootle manoeuvre around the body, visually inspecting it from various positions.

The pathologist is careful to touch the body as little as possible as he makes his initial examination. 'Well,' Dr Bootle begins, then pauses to raise his gaze upwards towards Morgan, to ensure that he is listening. 'The body is obviously a young female, probably in her early twenties. Even from this awkward position, I can see that rigor mortis is present throughout the body, indicating that death occurred sometime within the last thirty-six hours. There is no obvious injury, so it's likely she drowned, but of course a more accurate cause and time of death will have to wait for the postmortem.'

'When will you be able to do the PM?' Morgan says as he too jumps down onto the riverbed, his shoes sinking into the soft sand. He is glad that he had the foresight to grab shoe covers from his car boot as can imagine only too well Celias displeasure if he returns home with sand stuck between the treads of his best pair of suede loafers. Morgan neatly moves towards a spot alongside Dr Bootle, leaving a trail of footprints behind him, which are immediately filled with river water.

'I don't think it looks suspicious, so I'll do it tomorrow. Now if you don't mind, I'm going to enjoy the rest of what should have been my day off,' Dr Bootle barks as he hauls himself back onto the path, niftily gathers up his equipment and strides back up the river path.

From his lowered position, Morgan can just about make out the rotund figure disappear into the mist at the end of the quayside path. Dr Bootle will no doubt be heading towards the nearby Deben Golf Club, to finish off the game he would have started earlier that morning, as was his usual routine. Even so, he is a little taken aback by the pathologist's brusque manner. Perhaps it is time for Dr Bootle to retire and focus on his golf handicap, leaving the grisly business of pathology to someone who possesses a little more enthusiasm and a little less despondency.

As the pathologist disappears entirely from view, Morgan returns his focus to the female lying prone in front of him. It is not the first body he has seen as a police officer but even so, the detective is a little perturbed by her bloated appearance - she has clearly been in the water for some time. Frustratingly, Dr Bootle's cursory search yields no ID on or near the body; there is no purse, phone, or handbag present. At this precise moment there is literally nothing to help identify her.

Morgan continues to stare at the body as if willing it to reveal its secrets. She is not wearing a coat, which seems a little strange given the time of year. It is possible she had been drinking at one of the pubs in town and slipped unnoticed into the water – something that has happened to many other youngsters across the country. Perhaps she had been carrying her coat and handbag and they were carried away by the tide, whisked away down-stream to the sea?

Although Dr Bootle made it clear before he left that he believes the death to be accidental, it is still necessary to ensure that all precautions are taken and correct procedures followed, just in case the cause of death is later revealed to be more complicated than initially thought. Morgan shouts up to the three officers who are still waiting on the concrete path above him in the freezing mist and gives them instructions on how to secure the area as a potential crime scene, ignoring the snigger that comes from one of the constables and the exchange of looks between the other two. Perhaps he is telling them to do a job they already know how to do, but it's his first time in charge and he is going to make dammed sure he does not mess it up.

After taking a final look at the scene, Morgan pulls himself up onto the path again, where he immediately spots Dr Bootle's assistant Harry Turner, who is perched close by at the river's edge. Harry is looking down into the river below, a thermometer dangling from his left hand to record both the ambient and water temperatures, which will help to determine a more accurate time of death. Morgan smiles tight-lipped at Harry then begins to make his way back up the river path towards the town. He often wonders how Harry has managed to cope with working with Dr Bootle for so long; perhaps the exuberant salary makes up for the unsociable hours, grisly work and over-bearing boss. Then again, his own superintendent is not much better. Morgan strongly suspects the two men may have gone to school together - the old boys school closed down years ago, but many of those who held powerful positions in the town had been pupils at the establishment. Sometimes it is a case of *who* you know, not *what* you know, which paves the way for a career in a small town.

Morgan quickens his pace as he strides towards the quay, passing by a small team of forensic officers who are just arriving. Closely following behind them are two men in dark grey suits, who appear to have been tasked with collecting the body. Moving onto the grass verge to allow the entourage to pass, Morgans eyes automatically follow as they make their way up the path towards the body. One of the scenes of crime officers jumps down onto the riverbed and begins expertly photographing the cadaver, whilst her colleagues begin searching amongst the plants surrounding the body, moving outwards in a fan shape as far as they can go without getting their feet wet. The team will be all too aware of the pressing need to search the area before the incoming tide washes away any evidence and are working at an impressive speed.

      In the distance, a little way off behind the SOCO team, a small group of police officers can just be seen through the dense mist. They are meticulously combing the river path and nearby grassy areas, searching for anything that could have belonged to the deceased. In particular, they will be looking for the dead woman's lost shoe as well as a handbag or the contents of it, which could have been stolen and dumped amongst the tall grass. Finding these items are a priority in helping to establish her identity, as well as in indicating whether or not she may have fallen into the water from the river path by accident, or if something more sinister could have occurred. Unfortunately for Deben Quay Police Force, this area is very popular and there will be a plethora of rubbish and personal items that will need to be sorted through, collected, tagged and bagged, ready for forensics to examine.

Morgan stops to observe the hive of activity that has infiltrated the normally quiet ambience; downstream, the body, which has been carefully extracted from the reeds and zipped into a black bag, is making its way through the mist towards him on the narrow path. Morgan follows the mournful procession as it sashays awkwardly towards the quayside, then leaves the sombre entourage to continue unaccompanied on its journey towards the private ambulance waiting in nearby Ferry Lane.

Chapter 3

A group of local journalists are beginning to gather girth on the far side of the police cordon, trying to glean any titbits of information that can be colourfully transformed into a semblance of a story. Amongst the journalists is Phil Wattle, the editor of the local paper - The Suffolk Times. Phil Wattle stamps his feet against the concrete path trying to rid himself of the insidious chill that is creeping into his legs, whilst continuing to chat to the other journalists standing next to him, who are all trying to ascertain what is happening further up the river. The group jostle into position to photograph the body bag as it is carried past them. Phil Wattle, who has spent many years chasing far less exciting news stories, is at the front of the crowd, seemingly having decided to take a personal interest in this particular story - a job he would normally leave to the more youthful members of staff.

'Anything you can tell us constable?" A short, stocky man at the front of the group shouts to the officer standing at the cordon.

'Sorry lads, you know I can't comment. You'll all have to wait for the press release.'

'When will that be then? We could be here all day freezing our bits off,' retorts another journalist, who is also stamping his feet against the cracked concrete path. Others around him echo their discomfort, as they move about, trying to keep warm as the freezing mist rolls across the water towards them.

The tide has now come in further, leaving only the tops of the reeds visible where the body came to rest. Trying not to shiver in the penetrating damp air, Morgan scribbles into his notepad, noting the weather conditions and sketching a brief map of the surrounding area, adding reminders to check on river tides and weather patterns for the last few days. A shadow across the page informs Morgan that he is no longer alone. The police officer who was first on the scene has arrived after escorting Mrs Fields home.

'PC Barnaby, I hear you were first to arrive?' Morgan barks officiously.

The constable pulls out a notebook from her handbag and flicks through to the page where she made notes. 'I was the first to respond to the emergency call and arrived here about twenty past nine this morning. The body was discovered by a Mrs Fields and her dog at about 9.A.M. Mrs Fields was very distraught, so I quickly interviewed her at the quayside before taking her home. She lives at Glebe Cottage behind the tearoom.' PC Barnaby points in the direction of a small cottage, which is almost entirely hidden by an enormous willow tree.

'Thanks, you might as well go back to the station. We can get a formal statement signed by Mrs Fields tomorrow,' Morgan says.

PC Barnaby does not need telling twice. She too is beginning to feel the cold and is glad for the opportunity to head back to the warmth of the station.

Ignoring his sensible inner voice instructing him to find somewhere to shelter away from the cold, Morgan walks back up the path again to the spot where the body was found, to take another look at the river and the surrounding area. On the other side of the river path is a marshy field containing a few sheep and a couple of cows, beyond that, a small, wooded copse. Morgan makes a note in his book that this area will need to be checked in case the young woman came through the woods. Morgans many years of experience have taught him to explore all avenues as often it is the simplest of explanations that turn out to be the truth of the situation. It is possible that the woman had not been alone, perhaps she had gone to the woods for sex with someone she had met in a bar then she had wandered off to the river where she fell in. They will need to check CCTV cameras in the town centre as well, in case they can shed any light on that particular theory. There are other possibilities though and as yet, they need to keep open minded as they do not know when or where she died. The answer to some of those questions will have to wait for the postmortem.

Almost out of view, Morgan can just make out a small group of police officers conducting a finger-tip search of the area close to where the body was found. They begin to move away from him, focusing on the grassy bank and fields furthest from the river path. Morgans eyes move past them and back towards the river path where he can see the outline of a dilapidated boat shored up on a sand bank, covered in grey-green algae and peppered with gnarly limpets. The vessel is lying on a sharp bend just before the path snakes out of sight, twisting away from the town and towards the sea, which is hidden from view by the dense mist that is still shrouding the river.

Suddenly the detective's attention is diverted by shouting in the distance. One of the officers searching the ground around the water's edge, is gesturing towards the riverbank, shouting something that is not quite audible. Morgan hurries along the path as quickly as his frozen limbs will allow to discover what the men are looking at; a kayak bobbing about in the shallow tidal water. The vessel looks fairly new and is upside-down, rhythmically bumping against the river wall at regular intervals. So, this must be how the girl has come to be in the river Morgan deduces, baldly ignoring the fact that the girl was not appropriately dressed for a boat trip on the river. He runs back up the path to recall the SOCO team, who are just about to leave the freezing quayside. The kayak will need to be forensically examined and photographs taken of the boat in situ.

Fifteen minutes later, with a plethora of photos taken, the kayak has been hauled up over the river wall by a rather wet and very cold police constable, who reluctantly volunteered to step into the icy water to retrieve it. The forensics team quickly set to work, eager to get out of the chilly air and back to their warm, dry laboratory. In no time at all, the boat is carefully wrapped and ready to be moved to the unmarked van that is already parked nearby in Ferry Lane.

At that exact moment when the kayak is being removed from its resting place, Chief Superintendent Bennett chooses to descend upon the quayside. Morgan tries but fails to hide his displeasure as he watches the rotund chief of Deben Quay Police Force striding purposefully up the path whilst winding a stripy scarf around his jowly neck. Bennett immediately spies Morgan and heads straight for him.

'What's the situation Morgan?' Bennett barks.

'Good morning, Sir. A woman's body was found in the river at approximately nine o'clock this morning by a Mrs Fields, who was walking her dog in the area.' Morgan half-turns to point further downstream to where the body was discovered. 'Dr Bootle has already inspected the body and it's been removed and taken to the morgue. The forensics team managed to complete an initial search of the area before the tide started to come in and we've got another team conducting a finger-tip search of the surrounding area.'

'Any name for the deceased yet?' Bennett asks, pulling his grey overcoat more tightly around his round girth.

'Not yet. There wasn't any ID on the body and so far, we haven't found anything to help identify her,' Morgan admits. His attention is momentarily diverted from the conversation as he needs to move aside and allow the kayak, which has now been wrapped in something that looks like cling film, to be hauled past him.

'What has that kayak got to do with the investigation?' Bennett says, rubbing his hands together, a stream of vapour trailing as he speaks.

'We found it downstream, close to where the body was found. It could be connected so SOCO are taking it in.'

'Any initial suggestions to the cause and time of death?' Bennett asks.

Morgan shakes his head. 'Nothing definite. There's no obvious sign of injury. Dr Bootle thought that the body could have been in the water for a day or so. He seems quite certain that we're looking at an accidental drowning.'

'Right, well we'd better do a press release sooner rather than later, I see they're champing at the bit for information already.' Bennett looks towards the group of journalists, who are waiting further along the path. 'We can turn this to our advantage to help identify the body if need be.

Tell them we'll speak to them later this afternoon and treat this as an accident until we hear otherwise. When's the postmortem?'

'Tomorrow sometime. It seems that Dr Bootle didn't think it was urgent enough to cancel his round of golf.'

'Quite right. Ok Morgan, I want you back at the station for a briefing at one PM this afternoon.'

'Yes Sir. I'll let the journalists know about the press release.'

By lunchtime, the mist is beginning to recede a little. The damp chill however has left Morgans clothes thoroughly saturated, leaving him with the doubtful feeling that he will ever feel warm again. Hunger is also beginning to gnaw at his stomach, affecting his levels of concentration. Leaving a few of the officers at the quayside, he decides that it is time to leave, with a stop off to pick up a sandwich from a nearby newsagent, enroute to the police station.

By the time Morgan has purchased and digested a chicken salad sandwich, the incident room has already been set up in one of the larger offices at Deben Quay police station. He arrives just in time to hear Bennett barking instructions at the team on how to proceed next with the investigation.

'Our main priorities are to identify the body found in the river and of course to determine cause of death. The postmortem will be carried out tomorrow, but until we hear otherwise, we are treating this as an accidental death.' Bennett says as he struts up and down the room in front of an oversize whiteboard that is covering most of one wall. 'A kayak has also been found downstream of the body, so we've got a possible link to work on and in case you haven't yet heard, there will be a press release this afternoon. Only the bare facts though, I don't want to see any details in tomorrow mornings paper. DCI Cook will be leading the investigation as soon as he returns from leave.'

As if hearing his name being mentioned, the door opens and in strides DCI Tom Cook. Cook is Morgans closest friend and has been ever since they first met during police training, when they were both just eighteen. They have remained firm friends ever since, despite their differences over work ethics and Cooks recent promotion to the rank above Morgan.

'Thank you, Sir,' Cook says as he removes his heavy overcoat and walks purposefully across the room to take centre-stage. 'Morgan, I want you to go to the sailing club tomorrow morning and ask about the kayak, see if it's one of theirs. Hopefully by then forensics will have emailed us some photos, so you can take those with you. We need a statement to be signed by Mrs Fields, Fallow and Barnaby can handle that one,' Cook nods towards the youngest members of the force. 'They can also ask around for any witnesses who might have been in the quayside area over the last couple of days. We're going to need to check all of the CCTV cameras along the quayside and in the town centre,' Cook concludes, ignoring the quiet groans that are resonating through the room. Searching through endless CCTV footage, scrutinising grainy picture after grainy picture, trying to make sense of the fuzzy images in front of them, is one of the most tedious and disliked parts of the job.

'Today though I want you all to concentrate on identifying the body. We need to go through recent missing person files and see if any of the descriptions match our body. If we have no luck there or with the DNA and fingerprint results when they're processed, then we might have to release a photo to the press. Now you all know what you're doing so get on with it.' Cook shoos the team back to their desks so that they can begin sifting through the missing person files of approximately fifteen young women that have disappeared from Deben Quay and the surrounding area during the past year.

The team set to work, methodically trawling through both digital and paper records, contacting all of the relatives and friends who filed the missing persons reports. It is paramount that they have the most recent information on file as it is often the case that the people who disappear return home but no one thinks to inform the police, so the file is still open. Keeping up-to-date with missing person files in itself is an ongoing problem and one of the issues DCI Cook often complains about. He has tried on several occasions now to persuade his superiors that they need to employ more staff just to allow them to keep up with the ever-increasing amounts of paperwork. How they would cope with a major investigation is not something Cook wishes to contemplate.

By mid-afternoon the team have worked their way through approximately half of the cases. Some will need to be left for another day as they have been unable to contact all of the next-of-kin detailed on the missing persons reports. It is likely they will receive an influx of calls from concerned relatives once the news of the body is released and pre-empting this deluge of queries could save some relatives a lot of stress and uncertainty as well as a great deal of paperwork for the team.

'I'm pretty sure this is an accidental death. What do you think?' Cook asks Morgan, who is leaning against the threshold of his office.

'It looks that way, but it might be wise to wait until after the PM before we make it public knowledge,' Morgan replies with a hint of sarcasm.

'Yes, you're right. It's just frustrating losing a day's leave if it's only an accidental death. Surely someone in plain clothes could've handled it?'

'You would've thought so, but I guess Bennett just wanted to be on the safe side. Well, we'd best get to the waiting hounds and throw them a bit of a story.'

Morgan reluctantly follows Cook down the stairs to the media room - neither of them enjoy this part of his job. A press release is often likened by the team to being thrown to the wolves and even from the safety of the corridor, the two men can hear that the gaggle of journalists are already becoming restless. It probably does not help that they have been kept waiting and are all too aware that little information is likely to be given out at this early stage in the investigation. Cook will need to utilise all of the skills he learnt on the communications course he attended last month, to field questions away from the important details they do not yet wish to release to the public.

Phil Wattle, the editor of the Suffolk Times, is sitting in the first row of grey-plastic chairs that have been carefully placed into lines by Fallow a little earlier. Cook nods towards Wattle to acknowledge that he has seen him, then confidently traverses the room to the front to take his place at the top table. Taking a deep breath to calm his nerves, Cook prepares to deliver the pre-written statement that has already drafted by the Comms team. It does not seem to matter how many times he speaks in public, it still terrifies him.

Deben Quay Police Press Release - 22 February, 2006

A body has been found in the River Deben earlier this morning. The identity of the deceased or how they died has not yet been released.

A kayak was also found further downstream from the body but at this stage a connection between the two has not been established. Any witnesses who might have been in the area during the last few days should contact DCI Cook at Deben Quay Police Force.

Cook rushes through the short statement before inviting questions from the audience. It quickly becomes apparent that no further information will be divulged, so the journalists begin talking amongst themselves, ignoring Cook who is staring at them indignantly. It is obvious that some of the theories being loudly discussed around the room will end up in tomorrow's newspaper, a notion that will greatly upset Chief Superintendent Bennett, but there is little Cook can do to stop it. He could perhaps however have a quiet word with Phil Wattle before he leaves and promise him regular updates if he reins in the story at this early stage. Wattle also seems to have had a similar thought as he waits behind after the rest of the press rabble have left, to catch Cook for a quiet word.

At the crumbling offices of the Suffolk Times, located close to the centre of the town not far from the police station, Phil Wattles small team have gathered to discuss the day's events and to decide how they are going to cover the stories. Probably most eager to cover the body story is the newest member of staff, Caroline Woods, who is an experienced journalist but has only recently moved into the area.

'I'll be covering the body story with Caroline,' Phil Wattle informs his team, ignoring the looks of disappointment on at least two faces. 'At this stage, it looks like it's an accidental death, so we won't all need to work on it. Leah and Russell will continue with the other work that we already discussed on Friday.'

The journalists nod in agreement, they all love their jobs and want to keep it that way, even if they do not approve of who is covering the respective stories.

'Caroline, I want you to start interviewing the locals and find some witnesses. Someone must have found the body. Your best bet is to try the tearoom on the quayside. Also try the sailing club, see if anyone saw anything there. If you're quick, you might get there before they close for the day.'

'Will do boss,' Caroline replies eagerly, grabbing her coat from the hook at the back of the door and heading over the threshold before the meeting has even finished. As the door closes behind her, she can hear Leah and Russell muttering to each other, discussing why it is that they have been primed with the more mundane stories yet again. Even though Caroline is used to not being the popular one, the comments still needle her a little. She shrugs the bitterness off though to focus on the task ahead and prove to the team that their boss has made the right choice.

By mid-afternoon, Mrs Fields has sufficiently recovered from the shock of finding a body on her morning walk, to open up her small tearoom. The tearoom is located on the quayside, a short distance from where the body was found and only a short distance from her cottage. At this time of year, Mrs Fields would normally expect business to be quiet, but with all the activity that is going on along the quayside, there is a plentiful supply of nosy locals as well as journalists and police officers wanting warm cups of tea and hot soup. Luckily for Mrs Fields, the building is located just outside the police cordon, so business can continue as usual even though the investigation is still ongoing.

There is a fairly constant flow of customers throughout the afternoon, keeping the elderly owner unseasonably busy. As expected, conversations in the tearoom revolve around the discovery of the body and a somewhat weary Mrs

Fields re-tells her part in the tale more times than she cares to recall. One customer in particular, a young rather attractive woman sporting a black baker hat, is taking great interest in the story. Mrs Fields has suspected that the young woman is a journalist ever since she took up residence at table 12, which is situated at the back of the small wooden framed building. Mrs Fields tries to avoid talking to her but having served all of her other customers, she can no longer avoid that particular table and reluctantly heads towards the back of the room with her order pad.

'So, you found the body then? How terrible!' The young woman's face is flushed from the moist heat of the tearoom.

'Well, that's not quite right my dear as it was my dog Nutmeg who found her. Of course, I phoned the police, Nutmeg being unable to do so. Do I know you from somewhere dear? You look very familiar?' Mrs Fields asks.

'I doubt it. I'm new to this part of the country. I probably have one of those familiar looking faces. So, it was a woman then?'

Mrs Fields smiles thinly, putting an end to the uncomfortable conversation. She takes the woman's order of a large latte and a slice of homemade flapjack, before moving swiftly away.

The elderly woman continues serving the seemingly never-ending flow of customers who are still coming into her tearoom until late into the afternoon. By the time the last customer has left, Mrs Fields feels more exhausted than she has done for a long time, prompting her to wonder wistfully if it is time to shut up shop and retire. The idea is still in the back of her mind as she locks the back door and heads out into the dark night to collect Nutmeg for their evening walk.

The terrier is of course ecstatic to see her owner, her tail wagging furiously as soon as Mrs Fields steps through the front door. Mrs Fields unhooks the lead from the coat rack and the dog begins jumping up and down, her stubby nails clacking onto the tiled hallway floor.

The air has become even colder now that darkness has descended and Mrs Fields can clearly see her breath as she exhales into the chilly air outside her home. As the quayside is still cordoned off, she divulges from her usual route and instead takes Nutmeg up Ferry Lane towards the town. In no time at all they have completed a circuit around the older part of the town and returned back down Ferry Lane.

Back home in the warmth of her cottage, Mrs Fields feeds Nutmeg with a bowl of meat and biscuits, then busies herself making a cheese and pickle sandwich with her homemade granary loaf.

She takes the meal through to the sitting room, balancing the blue China plate in one hand and an over-size mug of decaffeinated tea in the other. She places them down onto the small wooden table and settles down in her favourite armchair, that is ideally situated in front of the wood burner. The warmth of the fire lulls her to sleep and the next thing Mrs Fields is aware of is being woken up by Nutmeg, who is barking furiously next to the back door of Glebe Cottage.

It is typical of her husband to fall asleep half-way through the documentary on youth crime he insisted that they watch, Celia grumbles to herself. She would have preferred to watch something much lighter like a talent show. Celia is sitting next to her husband on the sofa, watching her husband's belly rise and fall in time with the rhythmic sounds that are periodically being emitted from his nasal passages. She cannot recall when it was that her husband gained such a protruding stomach – or began falling asleep in front of the TV, but she is certain that neither habit was present when they first met nearly fifteen years ago.

Celia sighs loudly then looks around the room, as if in hope that someone might hear. She cannot remember the last time Morgan took her out to the cinema or even volunteered to wash up after dinner. How things have changed she concludes as she reaches across her husband's rotund belly to grab hold of the remote control, which is perched precariously on the arm of the sofa. She begins flicking through the TV stations, trying to quell the feeling of irritancy that is bubbling up in the pit of her stomach. It is not her fault they have been unable to have children, so why does she always feel as if she is the one who has let the side down. Some evenings Morgan seems to barely speak to her, let alone show her

43

any of the affection she so desperately craves. She cannot help but feel disappointed with her life; it is certainly not the one she envisaged when she married the love of her life. She wonders if her husband feels the same and if so, if there is any future for them as a couple.

'Ah yes, there it is, the talent show is still on. I've only missed the opening credits,' Celia says quietly to herself. Cautiously she turns up the volume, hoping that Morgan will stay asleep long enough for her to enjoy watching her program without having to listen to his constant negative diatribe about something that is after all, just for entertainment.

This time she is in luck. Not only is she able to watch the entire program in peace, but she also has the luxury of having a whole king-size bed to herself, while her husband sleeps soundly on the sofa, a heavy blanket pulled up around his chest. Celia loves wriggling down into the cool cotton sheets, pulling the thick duck-feather duvet up around her neck. She sprawls out across the bed, her toes poking out of the covers on the other side. Her last thoughts before she drifts off to sleep with a slight smile on her lips, are that she could get used to this.

Chapter 4

Morgan is having a very strange dream, one where a fire alarm is going off and someone is poking him with a large stick, urging him to go and sort it out. He cannot work out why he should go and look, surely that should be a job for a firefighter? Shaking himself awake, he quickly realises that it is the phone that is ringing and that he is still sitting upright on the sofa where he fell asleep several hours earlier. Morgan automatically curls a heavy fist around the back of his neck to massage it, then reaches over and picks up the phone. Not quite awake, he barely registers the voice urging him to get to the quayside as quickly as possible. Eventually the words penetrate through the thick fug that seems to have descended on his exhausted mind and suddenly he is very much awake again.

It is just before one o'clock in the morning and snow is falling. Soft silent flakes are covering the tiled rooftops and car bonnets in a thin layer of white powder. There is no one else about at this time of the morning - other more sensible residents are still tucked up in their warm beds. Morgan wraps his coat around him more tightly to keep in just a little more body warmth. He too wishes to be at home, rather than being outside in the freezing cold in the middle of the night, but this is the vocation he has chosen and he has to take the bad along with the good.

Morgans boots crunch across the driveway, leaving feint indentations in the thick frost. The car windscreen is frozen solid and a blanket of snow is now settling on top of the icy layer that formed earlier in the evening when the temperature began to drop at dusk. Even the car door has frozen shut and it takes a little force to open. The temperatures inside are not much higher, leaving Morgan wondering how anyone could survive sleeping rough in this bitter weather. He hopes that the rough sleepers who are usually in the shelters on the riverside have found somewhere warmer to sleep tonight.

As he waits for his car to defrost, Morgan tries to wake himself up, which should not have been difficult given the temperature, but he feels so exhausted that he could sleep anywhere. A cup of coffee would have been very much welcomed, but unfortunately the call is urgent and cannot wait for an early morning caffeine fix, however much it is desired. Perhaps if his wife had awoken at the sound of the telephone, she could have made him a hot drink to sip as the car defrosts, Morgan considers uncharitably.

With the car finally defrosted and the windscreen de-misted, Morgan fastens his seatbelt and pulls out onto the road where there are few other vehicles on the road to hinder his progress to Ferry Lane, where Morgan pulls up onto the grass verge. Reluctantly he pushes open the car door and braces himself against the bitter wind that he knows will be whistling up the lane from the river.

The darkness at the bottom of the path is interjected only by the headlights of two local fire appliances that are sprawled across the bottom of the lane and onto the adjoining grassed area that has been churned up into frozen muddy furrows. Morgan stands at the edge of the grass verge to observe the scene before him. The fire is already an inferno; the wooden cladding of Mrs Fields tearoom has already almost entirely been consumed by the flames. The crackling and spitting of the fire can be heard above the thrum of the fire engines, which are rhythmically humming in the background. Morgan cannot help but be reminded of sitting in front of the log fire at his favourite pub, then immediately regrets the thought as it occurs to him that the building might not be the only thing that is on fire.

The ferocity of the fire has enticed a larger than usual number of firefighters from the warmth of the local station and one of them says loudly to a colleague that the inferno is by far the worst fire he has ever seen. There is little that can be done except to stand in the freezing cold and watch as the tearoom, which has been standing at this spot for nearly eighty years, continues to be consumed by flames.

'You might as well head off home for a few hours rest,' Cook shouts to Morgan as he walks up the path towards him. 'We'll close off the river path and Ferry Lane and get a couple of PCs on patrol. There's not much else we can do until the fires out and we're allowed into what's left of the building. We've sent someone to let Mrs Fields know what's happening,' Cook says, nodding in the direction of Glebe Cottage, then pulling the collar of his overcoat up around his neck more tightly.

'Thanks Tom, I'll come back first thing. Don't stay here too long yourself. As you say, there's not much we can do for now,' Morgan replies, grateful for the opportunity to go home and get back to his warm bed.

As Morgan is heading back towards his car, he notices a woman in a dark hooded coat standing close to one of the fire appliances. She must be a journalist he deduces as he casually watches her scribble into a notebook then try to catch the attention of a firefighter who is walking past. Another person who will be having a late night.

Celia is still deep in slumber when her husband returns and remains oblivious to the nights events until she wakes up a few hours later. When she enters their small but immaculately tidy kitchen, Morgan is eating a bowl of Weetabix topped with blueberries, much to his wife's approval. He finishes his mouthful then breaks the news to her as gently as he can; Celia has been working in the tearoom for the past seven years and really enjoys the job, which has given her a sense of purpose as well as regular contact with the outside world.

'Do they know what's happened yet?' Celia asks softly as she sits down on the chair beside her husband.

'We don't know yet, it was still alight when I left. I'm going back in a bit to see if there's any news from the fire investigators. Do you know if Mrs Fields is insured?'

'I'm not sure, but I can't imagine she would leave something like that to chance.' Celia nurses a mug of tea in one hand, visibly shocked by the news.

'Let's hope not. From what I saw last night it looks as if the whole building will have to be demolished. That's the problem with these wooden buildings, they go up like a bonfire.'

Morgan finishes off a piece of buttered toast then swigs down the rest of his mug of tea. Pushing back his chair, Morgan ignores Celias grimace at the sound of the wooden leg scraping across the tiled floor. He bends down and gently kisses her on the top of her head, his hand automatically squeezing her shoulder as he passes by.

The daily newspaper is lying on the front door mat. Morgan scoops it up on his way out of the house. To his surprise, an article about the fire is already in the morning paper and must have correctly deduced that the young woman at the tearoom was a journalist.

THE SUFFOLK TIMES

Monday 23 February, 2006

Body Found in The River Deben
by Phil Wattle

Yesterday morning the body of a yet unidentified person was found in the river at Deben Quay. The deceased was found early morning by a local resident who was walking her dog close to the sailing club. Police are appealing for more witnesses to come forward who may have been in the area over the last few days. As yet, no one has come forward to claim the unidentified person and there have been no reports of anyone missing in the last few days. A post-mortem will be conducted at Hemley Hospital after forensic tests have been carried out to try to establish the identity of the body.

A kayak has also been found further downstream from where the body was found. Further tests are being undertaken to establish ownership and to establish any connection with the deceased. Anyone who was in the area on Sunday morning should contact Deben Quay police station.

Building Fire in Ferry Lane
by Caroline Woods

Mrs Fields tearoom, located close to the quayside, caught alight in the early hours of this morning. The building was almost destroyed before fire crew got the blaze under control.

Anger at Snow Disruption
by Russell Carter

Recent snow showers which caused havoc on our roads, angering local residents, who felt that roads were not gritted in time despite early weather warnings. The snow is now starting to melt and the Environment Agency have issued a warning over the risk of localised flooding. Anyone with concerns over the possible flooding should contact the Flood Risk Helpline 0800 69873

Cherry Farm Shop

Locally grown and picked, fruit and vegetables. Suppliers of local meat and jams. Located at the end of Deben Quay High Road

---

The cul-de-sac is still quiet - it will be some time before many of the other residents wake up. Morgan peruses through the rest of the paper as he waits yet again for the windscreen to defrost. The fact that the car has frozen up again during the few hours he has been home, is testament to the bitterly cold temperatures. He watches as the thick blanket of condensation on the windscreen, begins to evaporate from the bottom upwards and summons up just enough patience to wait for the windscreen to almost completely clear before pulling out into the road.

The detective drives uncharacteristically carefully as he makes his way towards the remnants of Mrs Fields tearoom once again. Judging by the largely undisturbed layer of snow covering the roads and paths close to his home, there has been little traffic on the roads during the night even though there are now more vehicles about then there were last night. The nearer he gets to Ferry Lane however, the greater the disturbance; the deep furrows in the snow-laden roads haven already been churned up into a brown slush. The muddy tracks that criss-cross the grassy areas where the emergency services parked glisten with a light layer of frost.

Morgan pulls over onto what he judges to be the grass verge - it is difficult to tell as most of the area is now covered in a blanket of whiteness. He leaves the wheels at a slight angle, then pulls on the handbrake as hard as he can. Three years ago, during a particularly bad snow fall, there had been multiple accidents at the police station car park, with vehicles sliding down the shallow gradient from their parking spaces and ending up gently crashing into the cars at the bottom of the slope, despite being left by their owners with handbrakes firmly left on. Now every time it snows, Morgan recalls the nightmare of having to convince to his insurance company that his car had been accidently damaged by another parked vehicle whose engine was off and was unoccupied. In the end, as there had been several other claims from the same car park, the insurance company paid out, albeit reluctantly. It was fortunate that they had all chosen to take advantage of a special introductory offer using the same insurance company, which had made the process significantly less complex. Now Morgan half-wishes that the car had been scrapped, as it would have given him an excuse to purchase a newer model without Celia worrying about him spending money they do not have.

    The sound of the car door slamming shut echoes through the street. The noise ricochets around the nearby buildings bringing awareness of how quiet the neighbourhood is with its sparse population of residential houses. Morgan is glad that he thought to put on his thick socks and boots before he left the house, though even they cannot prevent the cold from penetrating up his legs. Nor can his thick wool gloves stop the chill from biting at his fingers as he makes his way across the crisp grass towards the scene of the fire.

    There is little left of what was once the town's only thriving tearoom. The flames had clearly been very intense and had spread rapidly, fanned by the elderly buildings wooden construction. It is also possible though, thinks Morgan as his heavy boots crunch across the grass, that the fire was started deliberately - the use of an accelerant would also have resulted in the catastrophic damage that now stands before him.

As Morgan approaches the building, he can see that the timbers are still smouldering. A small number of fire fighters are still working hard to dampen down any remaining hot spots, but there are far fewer than had been in attendance earlier. Enroute to the tearoom, Morgan had heard on the local radio station that there was now another large fire to contend with in a disused warehouse on the edge of the Foxhall industrial estate. Most of the firefighters will have been diverted to tackle the blaze, which is close to residential areas.

The front entrance of the tearoom where the majority of the shiplap boarding on the outside of the building has been completely destroyed, leaving the inside of the building exposed to anyone who might walk up the quayside path. The remnants of the interior are clearly visible; a smoke-blackened coffee machine squats on the worktop towards the back of the room; the empty cash till with its open drawer is on the counter; chairs stacked on top of tables, ready for the floor to be mopped.

Morgan steps back to allow two firefighters, who are commandeering an enormous hose, to move in front of him, then continues walking around the perimeter of the building. There is a line of footprints clearly visible on the snowy grass around the edge of the plot. He follows the tracks around to the side of the building, where the fire was less intense and more of the structure has been left intact. There, in the muddy path leading to the backdoor, are two well-defined footprints.

Morgans heart thumps as he reaches into his inner coat pocket and retrieves his mobile to request the return of SOCO, who have probably only just returned to their warm beds. Running back to his car, he retrieves some police tape and metal stakes to fence off the area as a temporary measure until the team arrive. Minutes later, with the task complete, Morgan jogs back around to the front of the building again. His pace slows to a walk as he moves purposely towards the lead firefighter who is talking loudly to a structural engineer about the condition of the building.

'I've just spotted some footprints at the side of the building, which could be of interest. Do you know if any of your team have been round that way?' Morgan asks as he approaches the two men.

"Someone will have checked that the fire hadn't spread, but otherwise we've all been at the front of the building. I'll ask the team later when we're all back at the station.'

If arson is the cause of the fire, which is feasible given the intensity of it, they will need to eliminate all those who have either worked at the tearoom or been fighting the fire, before any possibility of a suspect's footprint can be identified. He makes a mental note to also find out who made the original call to report the fire.

Morgan retraces his steps towards the back of the tearoom, stepping over the enormous hose again, which is strewn across the long grass. As he turns the corner, the sounds of the fire engines' motor diminish, along with the cheerful banter of the firefighters who are continuing to dampen down the fragile timbers still smouldering beneath the charred outer layer of painted wood.

The rear of the building is shrouded in darkness from the nearby pine trees that tower above it. The eeriness is only heightened by the flickering shadows being cast from the revolving blue lights of the fire appliances a short distance away. Morgan peers into the blackness, his eyes gradually adjusting to the low level of light. In the centre of the rear wall of the tearoom, he can see that the wooden back door is slightly ajar. Just inside the door, are several tins of paint, along with a ladder and paint brushes. It momentarily crosses Morgans mind that perhaps these could have caused the fire, but he quickly chastises himself when he realises that the area around the tins is not charred. Frustratingly it will be some time before the building is deemed safe enough for them to enter and allow a closer inspection of what is left of the tearoom.

Chapter 5

DCI Cook has already gathered his team for the mornings briefing by the time Morgan reaches the office. Morgan heads straight to the coffee machine located at the front of the room and pours himself a large cup, ignoring Cook who is waiting to speak and is openly glaring at him. Morgan blatantly disregards his friend's seniority and moves across the room so that he can stand with his frozen legs pushed up against the scorching radiator.

Cook clears his throat melodramatically in protest at the interruption, then starts his speech again. 'The postmortem will be carried out today on the woman found in the river Deben, so we'll have a better idea soon of what we are dealing with.'

A few murmurs are heard as Cook moves across the room to perch on the windowsill, his large frame blocking out most of the light from one of the small windows that overlooks the carpark at the back of the building. 'We're still waiting for DNA and fingerprint results, so until we have these, we'll need to carry on trying to identify her through the missing person files. No one's phoned in yet, but it's early days and she might not have been local. The press is also appealing for witnesses to come forward, so we can expect a lot of phone calls over the next few days. Fallow, I want you to help out with sifting through the information that comes in.' Cook looks up at Fallow and waits until he acknowledges that he has understood.

The senior detective begins to pace up and down the length of the room, stopping every so often to warm his hands on a small radiator tucked underneath one of the windows. 'You've probably all heard by now that Mrs Fields tearoom was destroyed in a fire in the early hours of this morning. DI Morgan and I were at the scene last night and from the ferocity of the fire, it looks likely to be arson. We're waiting to hear if it's structurally sound enough for us to take a look inside - it looks as if the whole building is now unstable and will need to be demolished.' Cook pauses as Morgan once again traverses the room towards the coffee machine and returns moments later with a mug that he offers to Cook. Cook grabs hold of the mug and takes a sip, wincing at the cheap, bitter liquid that Morgan has yet again forgotten to add sugar to.

'Morgan, can you go to Mrs Fields house and see if she's returned seeing as we didn't get an answer from her last night? Take a female PC with you just in case she gets upset. I'll have to do another press release about the fire, but in the meantime, I don't want anything getting back to the press.'

Morgan inwardly smirks. Cook better hope that Bennett does not get wind of his non-pc utilisation of female officers. 'It might be a bit late to be worrying about the press,' Morgan responds, waving a folded-up newspaper in front of Cooks face. 'There was a journalist at the tearoom last night - it's already in this mornings' edition.'

Cook grimaces as he places his mug of coffee down onto a nearby desk so that he can take the paper from Morgans outstretched hand. Cook unfolds it and glances through the headlines before re-folding it again. 'Damn, well we'd better do a press release soon then,' Cook says, slamming the paper down onto the desk and jolting his cup of coffee, which over-turns, its contents flooding across the melamine surface. Cook stares at the brown sticky mess as it begins to drip down the desk leg, then sighing heavily, turns to look at Morgan, who is already reaching for a box of tissues. 'On second thoughts, can you take Fallow with you to Mrs Fields house, he could do with the experience. And go to the sailing club afterwards, see if they're missing any kayaks. The rest of you can carry on going through the missing person records. We'll meet again tomorrow morning at nine, hopefully by then we'll have some forensics back and the results of the PM.'

'Yes boss,' Morgan replies cheekily as he finishes mopping up the last dregs of coffee and drops the soggy tissues into the only waste-paper bin in the room. The previous week they had all received an email informing them that Deben Quay Police Force was modernising and becoming paperless. If there was no paper, that meant there was no need for waste-paper bins and therefore no need to employ cleaners to empty them. It was not a popular decision and the team only managed to hide one bin before the rest mysteriously disappeared during the night.

DCI Cook allows the police stations heavy front door to slam shut behind him, then trips down the steps and strides off at speed up the path that runs through the centre of town. He shivers, pulling his coat around him more tightly, then shoves his hands into his coat pockets, having forgotten his gloves yet again. One of the drawbacks of having children is you often end up forgetting to look after yourself but Cook does not regret the decision to have them for one moment, especially having lost his own father at an early age.

The low winter sun is only just visible through the clouds and its weak rays do not have the strength to cut through the sharp chill that has been left by the early morning mist. One of the oddities of living near water is that the weather in Deben Quay is more likely to be determined by the mood of the river, rather than the meteorology that rarely predicts their microclimate with any significant degree of accuracy.

Cook marches quickly towards the imposing headquarters of the Suffolk Times, which is now coming into view. A symbiotic relationship has developed between Cook and Phil Wattle over the many years of them both working the same patch. Wherever possible Cook provides Wattle with information before the general press releases and in turn, Wattle passes to Cook any titbits he thinks he might like to hear. The purpose of today's visit is to find out if Wattle has received any information about the dead woman - often the public prefer dealing with the press than the police.

Suffolk House is only a few streets away from the police station, but even so, the short walk lifts Cooks mood a little. The newspapers' headquarters occupies one of the towns largest buildings, with its red-brick façade and elegant windows symmetrically lined up across the front of the building, which is neatly divided in half by an elegant front door. The building was originally constructed as a distribution warehouse for goods imported through the nearby quay but was left abandoned for many years after the decline of the port trade. It was finally redeveloped in the late nineteenth century to house the towns first newspaper - Suffolk Times. The centre of the warehouse originally contained a steam-driven printing press, surrounded by several small offices carved out from the gargantuan space. Little has changed to the internal layout since the Victorian era, with the current Suffolk Times still occupying the same space as it has done for the last two centuries and the original printing press still taking up most of the lower floor. The most visible change in recent history is to the open-plan room on the upper floor, where the typesetting would have been originally completed by hand. This has now been replaced by rows of uniform Macs and copious specialist software designed for the modern printing industry.

Cook runs up the stone steps and pulls open the heavy outer door that is framed by an ornate archway that seems at odds with the remainder of the building. Having visited Suffolk House on many occasions, Cook recalls the internal layout of the building sufficiently well to waltz past the receptionist without any preamble and quickly make his way down the narrow corridor to the small offices at the back of the building. The door to the editor's office creaks as Cook pushes it open, revealing the newspapers' aging editor inside, sitting behind a large Teak desk.

'Cook my friend, come in and shut that door, you're letting in a draught.' Wattle leaps up from behind his enormous desk and deftly extracts two stubby glasses and a bottle of whisky from the back of a large grey filing cabinet. He lines the glasses up on his desk and pours out two large measures, one which he hands to Cook, who is by now making himself comfortable on the only unoccupied chair in the room.

'So, what's happening then? Off the record of course,' the journalist teases as he runs one hand across his whispery grey, slightly balding pate.

Cook momentarily peruses the cluttered room, noting the oak shelves that are overflowing with books and the collection of framed newspaper prints that cover the entire wall behind the 1970's desk. 'Not much to tell at this stage. As you already know, we found a dead woman in the river yesterday, but until we get the PM results, we won't know the cause of death. To be honest though it looks like an accident, especially as we found a kayak not far from the body.' Cook leans back into the chair then takes a sip of the fiery liquid, feeling it burn a track all the way to his stomach.

'Any ID on her?' Wattle asks before he also takes a sip from his glass, wincing as the neat alcohol hits his inflamed ulcers.

'That's the strange thing. She didn't have any ID on her and no one's reported her missing. We're now going through missing person records, see if we can identity her from them.'

'We can have a look through our archives, see if we can find any stories about missing women, if that's any help to you?'

'That would be great, thanks.' Cook places his empty glass down onto the desk, which is overflowing with newspaper clippings and type settings, then reluctantly stands up, not relishing the thought of the cold walk back to the station. 'If you hear of anything let me know and of course we'll let you know any updates from our end.'

'Cheers Tom. I'll be down the Eels Foot tonight if you fancy a drink?'

'Not sure if I can tonight Phil, depends on how the investigation goes,' Cook smiles tight-lipped then closes the door behind him.

Morgan and Fallow would have travelled the short distance from the police station to Ferry Lane, in what would have been complete silence, had it not been for the local radio station blasting out hits from the eighties. The senior officer is finding it increasingly difficult to hide the displeasure he feels at being saddled with Bennetts nephew once again and quietly seethes as he tries to concentrate on driving and ignoring Fallow, who is nodding his head in time to the music.

As he pulls up onto the side of the road, Morgan leans over to switch off the radio. The lane is much quieter than the last time he was here, notably due to the absence of the fire appliances that had previously littered the area. The deep furrows made by the heavy vehicles parking across the grassy area are just one of the reminders of the catastrophe that occurred during the night. The other more poignant reminder is the remains of the burnt-out tearoom, which is just visible through the foliage at the back of Glebe Cottage.

The two men make their way across the churned-up grass towards Mrs Fields house. Glebe Cottage stands at the end of the lane and is the last property before reaching the quayside. It was once the harbourmasters house but was sold off many years ago when the post disappeared, along with the lucrative river-based trade that once thrived in Deben Quay.

Morgan trips up the path, cutting in front of Fallow who is eagerly trying to reach the building first, He raps loudly on the front door then waits for a moment for a response from within. When there is no movement inside the property, Morgan peers through the small sitting room window shrouded by net curtains that have turned yellow with age. There is no sign of any life at the cottage.

'Fallow, go around to the back door and see if it's unlocked,' Morgan instructs.

The young man nods, then strides off down a narrow path that is almost entirely hidden by overgrown Hebes and Hydrangeas. Moments later, Fallow returns up the path, shaking his head slowly from side to side.

'Ok well I think we have enough reason to force entry,' Morgan decides. Without waiting for a response, he heads back towards his car, the sound of Fallows footsteps following closely behind.

'Don't you think it's rather strange that she's not here?' Fallow shouts after Morgans rapidly disappearing frame, which is now trudging across the sodden grass at speed.

'Well, yes of course it's strange, especially given her business burnt down last night, never mind the fact that she found a body yesterday. That's why we need to gain entry to the property,' Morgan replies, rolling his eyes.

Morgan reaches the car first and forcefully pushes the button on the car boot to release it, then heaves open the lid. He rummages around in the mound of debris for a moment before pulling out a heavy object that he immediately passes to Fallow. Morgan tries to suppress a smile as the slim-built officer almost buckles under the weight of the hefty sledgehammer.

'Maybe she went to stay with a friend or a relative? She must've been upset about finding the body?' Fallow tries again to engage Morgan in conversation.

'She still managed to open up for business though, didn't she? I doubt there's an innocent explanation for this one,' Morgan snaps, his patience wearing thin. Without even a glance at the rookie officer, Morgan slams the car boot shut and strides back up the path.

Fallow waits a moment for Morgan to walk on ahead, then follows sheepishly behind him back to the cottage. He knows that Morgans ire for him is at least in part because of his family connections and wishes not for the first time, that it is something that he could change. He always seems to have been in the shadow of the other men in his family and his uncle getting him this job has not helped the situation.

After a great deal of sweating on the part of Fallow, the front door to Glebe Cottage yields enough for Morgan to shoulder his way into the building. Once inside, it is immediately obvious that there is no sign of either Mrs Fields or her dog.

Morgan picks his way through the cottage, trying to avoid the debris littered across the threadbare carpet. It seems that Mrs Fields has mainly been occupying the ground floor; with a make-shift bed made up in the front living room and a pile of dirty laundry on the flagstone floor in the dated kitchen. Perhaps she has begun to find the steep staircase a little too difficult to manage, concludes Morgan, as he traipses further into the poky cottage.

The first task will be for them to locate any friends or relatives with whom Mrs Fields might be staying. Celia is certain that Mrs Fields has a son, but when the couple discussed her elderly employer early that morning, Celia had to admit that she has no idea where he might live, or even if he is still in contact with his mother. Morgan doubts the elderly woman has many friends - she always seemed to him to be something of a recluse, with the tearoom providing her with her only regular source of human contact. It is still possible however that she has family and they will need to search through all of Mrs Fields personal papers to find contact names, addresses and phone numbers.

Their second task will be to find any documents relating to the tearoom. In particular, they need to locate any financial and insurance-related documentation - anything that could give them a possible motive for the fire.

Morgan sends Fallow upstairs to search through the two tiny bedrooms, tasking the youngster to gauge an idea as to whether or not any of Mrs Fields clothes and personal items could have been taken from the house. Morgan waits for Fallows footsteps to fade away, then sighs audibly before beginning to search through the more lived-in area downstairs rooms.

After two hours of sifting through mountains of newspapers, magazine clippings and an assortment of paperwork, all of which is stacked up into high piles on and around the dining room table, Morgan has managed to locate an address book and the insurance documents that he needs. From what he has found, it seems that his wife is indeed correct in that Mrs Fields does have a son, Luke. The small floral book yields an address, but no phone number and there is no indication of how recent the information is.

'Right, you might as well head back to the station then and try to locate Mrs Fields' son,' Morgan instructs, hoping rather unkindly that the tedious task will keep the young officer busy for the rest of the day and far away from him. 'I'll just wait for the door to be secured then I'll head off the sailing club,' Morgan says, tasking himself with the more interesting job.

Fallow nods to acknowledge that he has heard the instructions, then heads back up the path again with a slightly heavy heart. Morgan really could be very obvious sometimes. How long will it be before he is accepted as just another member of the team Fallow ponders, as he takes a right turn and heads towards the quayside so that he can take the scenic route back to the station.

Chapter 6

The sailing club is only a short stroll from Glebe Cottage, located in an old houseboat that is bobbing up and down enthusiastically on the high tide. It is mid-afternoon and there is little sign of any activity at the club, partly due to the time of year, but more likely, decides Morgan as he approaches the aging vessel, due to its location close to the police cordon, which has not yet been removed.

Morgan knocks loudly on the outer door to the boat then retreats to the concrete path that runs alongside the river, to pace up and down whilst rubbing his hands together to warm them a little. A few minutes pass then Morgan, deciding that the door is not going to be answered, steps across the narrow gap onto the gunwale to try the handle. It is unlocked. He pushes down on the lever then shoves open the heavy door and steps inside, allowing the door to gently close behind him. From his position at the threshold, Morgan can see there is someone sitting behind a large pine desk in an office, sifting through paperwork. A portable radio perched on the small table nearby is blaring out hits from the charts. Morgan steps across the carpeted floorboards that creak in protest at the additional weight being unexpectedly thrust upon them, then stands in the doorway to observe the young woman as she works. He deduces that the woman is probably in her late twenties, having not yet reached the age where she has lost her youthful looks and slender figure, though her natural blond hair has already begun to darken.

'Good afternoon,' Morgan says, rapping loudly on the door frame to gain the young woman's attention.

Startled by the sudden noise, Sally Stockbridge, the leader of the sailing club, drops the document she is holding onto the top of the mound of paperwork that almost entirely covers the surface of her desk. As the shock of the unexpected interruption subsides, a look of annoyance spreads across her face, her eyes hardening as she glares at the intruder.

'I'm sorry to interrupt,' Morgan says, holding up his ID card and trying not to smirk at the woman's obvious ire. 'I need information about anyone who has hired out canoes and kayaks during the last few days and if any of the boats are missing?'

'Well, that won't take long,' Sally snaps, 'Even without the quayside being closed off we're not exactly busy at this time of year. I think I would notice if any of our stock is missing.' Sally stands up and moves to the other side of the tiny office, where two well-worn metal cabinets have been positioned in front of one of the windowless beige walls. Sally pulls open the top drawer then begins to search through the sparsely populated suspension files.

Morgan smiles tight-lipped as Sally looks up momentarily from her task to glare at him again. He holds back the retort that is on the tip of his tongue and instead focuses on trying to wait patiently for her to search through the neatly organised filing cabinet. Patience is not one of Morgans strong points as his wife keeps reminding him.

It only takes a few seconds for Sally to retrieve the documents she has been searching for; a book containing the club's sales and purchases for the current financial year.

Morgan takes hold of the book from Sallys outstretched hand then shoves aside a mound of paperwork to place the item onto the crowded desk. He pulls up the chair that Sally was occupying before he arrived then opens up the hardback cover. He flicks through the book until he reaches the most recent entries, then jots down in his notebook details of all of the sales from the previous week.

Kayak and Canoe Hire February 2006			
Day	Client Name	Hire Time	Time returned
Friday	Sue Harris	10.00-11.00	11.05
Friday	Derek Harris	10.00-11.00	11.05
Friday	Charlotte Watts	13.00-15.00	15.00
Saturday	Anne Ellis	09.00-10.00	10.15
Saturday	Kate Ellis	09.00-10.00	10.15
Saturday	Paul Beckham	10.00-11.00	11.00
Saturday	Sarah Thomson	14.00-15.00	15.07

Morgan looks through the list again before handing the book back to Sally. He reaches into the inner pocket of his coat and pulls out a photo that was emailed through to the station. 'Can you take a look at this photo of a kayak, we found it near here and need to know if it's one of yours?'

Sally leans in towards Morgan to take a closer look at the photograph, brushing his arm in the process. 'It does look like one of ours, but I can't be sure. I'll do a stock take and let you know for definite if we've one missing. Although if there is, it must have been stolen as all the ones we hired out have been returned – here, you can see from our records,' Sally says, pointing to the sales ledger book.

'Here's my phone number,' Morgan says, handing a contact card to Sally. 'Please phone me when you've checked, we need to know urgently.'

Sally nods, her shoulders relaxing a little. 'Is this to do with the body that was found near here?' She asks, her eyes automatically focusing on the vista outside of the window where the body was found.

Morgan nods. 'It is, but I can't tell you anything else at the moment.'

'Sure, I understand. I'll let you know as soon as I've checked the stock,' Sally responds, seemingly feeling a little more cooperative than she had been earlier.

Morgan uncharacteristically smiles warmly at Sally Stockbridge then indicates for her to sit back down at the desk so she can return to her work. He makes his way back out of the club house, shutting the door firmly behind him.

The low winter sun is starting to set behind the ancient oak trees that line the grassy bank on the opposite side of the river. Morgan drinks in the exquisite view, noting the pale orange and pink streaks that replace what was blue sky only moments before. He could never tire of this view, Morgan muses, especially at sunset. The detective allows himself a moment longer to enjoy the view, his gaze roaming across the river, listening to the sounds of ropes clanging against masts and seagulls cawing as they circle the small sailing boats anchored offshore, enjoying the last of the suns' rays. Morgan could not imagine a more beautiful place and as always, feels very lucky to live here.

As Morgan opens the door to the teams' office, he is immediately halted by Cook, who is walking around the room to check up everyone's progress.

'Morgan, I've just had a call from the mortuary - they're ready to do the postmortem. I think we should go and take a look,' Cook says.

'Sure,' Morgan replies, turning around again and heading back across the threshold, his hopes of a quiet afternoon in the warm office dashed.

Morgan is feeling more than a little pensive as he walks towards the car. Watching postmortems are one of his least favourite parts of the job. He has quite a queasy stomach when it comes to blood, let alone the vile smell from the mortuary suite that seems to linger long after you have showered. Despite numerous people telling him otherwise, it is not a sight he has ever become used to and vows that he never will. The day he becomes immune to the sight of a dead body is the day he should retire. It is not enough to just do this job half-heartedly, he concludes, as he climbs into the driver's side of the car - it is a job that requires passion and commitment. Many of his fellow officers are married to the job and he can see why. It is hard to juggle the two and he knows that he has let Celia down far too many times, a feeling of guilt that is always with him.

The short journey gives both men time to reflect on recent events. 'What do you think then?' Cook asks, turning to look at Morgan, who is busy concentrating on pulling out of a T junction. 'It seems to me to be a clear-cut accident, what with the discovery of the canoe?'

'I don't know,' Morgan replies truthfully. 'My gut feeling tells me there's something wrong, especially after the fire at the tearoom.'

'You could be right, let's see what Lens discovered,' Cook concludes, always eager to take on the role of diplomat.

Morgan indicates left and pulls into the hospital grounds. They pass by an over-sized sign for 'Hemley Hospital', with a smaller sign underneath that states 'No smoking on hospital grounds', which always makes Morgan chuckle. Although he has never smoked, he understands that the one time you really need to light up is at a hospital, where life and death occurs with such apparent ease. He wonders how it helps patients and visitors to be forced to walk across a busy car park and out onto the street in order to satisfy their craving for nicotine. Perhaps it would be more ethical to offer them nicotine replacement therapies, but he guesses that would cost too much money from an already stretched budget.

He often wonders how long it will be before the NHS will need to be privatised.

Morgan locates a space in the visitor bay outside the mortuary, which is situated at the far end of the hospital grounds, hidden away from those that might be offended by the sight of a dead body. Locking the car behind him, he walks alongside Cook in an uneasy silence. Morgan wonders if his friend detests this part of the job as much as he does. Neither of them would ever admit to it though, at the risk of being called a sissy.

Cook reaches the mortuary entrance first and pulls open the heavy outer door. He strides purposely into the small reception area, which comprises of three grey plastic chairs and a small melamine table laden that has a selection of out-of-date women's magazines strewn across it. Morgan glances down at the pitiful offering, which he assumes is so pathetic as the larger share of the mortuary budget gets spent on the dead, rather than the living.

Most of the mortuary staff know the two men from previous visits. The receptionist even seems pleased to see them, greeting both Cook and Morgan as if they are long lost friends. After making some small talk with Maggie who is perched as usual behind the reception desk, the two men make their way through the familiar dark corridors towards the glamorously named 'viewing room'; a small dark room with a large window across one side to enable visitors such as students to see what is happening in the mortuary suite, without having to endure the erroneous odours associated with both the deceased and the post mortem process. It is definitely Morgans favoured location for observing such proceedings.

Cook removes his heavy over-coat and takes up residence in one of the unoccupied chairs. Morgan settles into one of the other chairs then reluctantly peers through the viewing window, where he can see that a body has already been laid out on a mortuary slab. Harry Turner is standing at the far end of the room, a digital camera in his hand, ready to record every stage of the examination for evidence.

Dr Bootle and Harry have spent most of the morning tying up loose ends, so that they can turn their full attention to the unidentified cadaver as soon as the police officers arrive. With the two detectives now in situ, the postmortem can finally begin. Harry begins by taking images of the woman's unclothed body before obtaining hair samples, which he carefully deposits into small tubes that are immediately sealed and labelled, ready to be sent off to the forensics laboratory for DNA analysis; if they are really lucky, her DNA will already be in the police database.

Dr Bootle speaks out aloud into his Dictaphone, which he still insists on using, having no faith in more modern technology. He begins by describing the woman as approximately 5 foot 3, slightly built, with platinum blond hair whose roots were beginning to show, yielding a soft chestnut colour underneath the harsh tones of the paler dye. She appeared to be in her early twenties and the presence of fully formed wisdom teeth confirmed that she was over the age of eighteen. Samples of the long bones in her legs and arms could help narrow down the age if needed, as the growth plates would no longer be open if she were over the age of twenty-five, but this type of expensive analysis was normally only required if the cadaver could not be identified by other means. Dr Bootle is always considerate of his limited budget when he orders any additional tests.

Dr Bootle walks around the cadaver, verbally noting that she was found wearing dark blue jeans and a pale pink t-shirt, both of which had originated from a national high street shop that sold thousands of them every year. Her clothes, which were removed prior to the postmortem, will be retained for further analysis should they be required.

The pathologist continues to talk out aloud, pointing out the fine cuts to her face and the small head wound to the back of the skull. He takes a closer look at the wound under the microscope, verbalising for his audience that there are few signs of bleeding from the tissues, suggesting that the wound occurred around the time of, or shortly after death.

Dr Bootle stands back a little to scour the remainder of the body, placing his gloved hands on his hips as he wanders up and down. 'Well, that seems to be about it. Nothing else of significance other than some well-developed bruising to the knuckles on her right hand, which would have occurred whilst she was alive.' Dr Bootle turns to look at his audience to ensure they are still listening. 'There are no signs of sexual assault, although there is a slight swelling of the lower abdomen, which could indicate early pregnancy.'

Morgan looks at the cadaver, whose grey skin has now tightened, giving her face a sallow, pinched look. He is, as ever, grateful that they can observe from a safe distance. He stretches forward and reaches out for the microphone, which connects the viewing room to the mortuary suite. 'Dr Bootle?' Morgan interrupts, 'How come the body hasn't decomposed more given she died several days ago?'

'The cold temperatures we had over the weekend would have delayed decomposition. Can you see there's some puffiness around the hands and face?' Dr Bootle asks, turning to look at Morgan.

Morgan nods automatically, even though he is not certain if the pathologist can see him through the glass.

'Well, that indicates she was in the water for some time, even if the cold weather did slow down the decomposition process. Rigour mortis has also begun to diminish, suggesting she may have been dead for up to thirty-six hours. At this stage I would estimate time of death to be Friday evening.' Dr Bootle returns his focus to the cadaver and begins to open-up the thoracic cavity ready for internal examination. Harry is standing beside the pathologist, ready to assist with the removal of the heart and lungs, which he will weigh before putting them to one side for further examination.

Dr Bootle continues to verbalise his thoughts for his audience. 'The lungs are filled with fluid, which could be consistent in the case of a drowning, but there are other possibilities to consider, such as pulmonary oedema caused by passive inhalation if the body was submerged after death.' Bootle pauses for a moment to instruct Harry to take some blood samples to look for alcohol or drugs. 'Blood gas levels will also need to be checked to establish if the woman was starved of oxygen before death as this will help to determine if she drowned. A sample of the bone marrow will allow us to look for the existence of diatoms, which could be present if she was alive when she entered the water.'

The pathologist moves further down the body, whilst continuing to talk aloud. 'The stomach is full, so she had eaten within two hours of death. We will take samples of both the undigested food and stomach acids for analysis, to look for any drugs she may have ingested.' Dr Bootle then moves down to examine the lower abdomen. 'As you can see, she was indeed pregnant, I would estimate four months by the size of the foetus.' Dr Bootle turns to the viewing window to ensure Morgan and Cook are still listening.

Leaving Harry to wash and clean the mortuary slab, Dr Bootle meticulously notes the findings for his postmortem report, then relocates to the viewing room, to recount his findings to the two detectives.

'Well, it's probable that she drowned, but I'll send you a more definite report in the next few days when the other test results come in. There's less bloating and decomposition then I would normally expect to find, but it isn't improbable given the cold weather.'

'Thank you, Dr Bootle. Please let us know as soon as you have any further results, especially the DNA test results,' Cook says, rapidly pumping the elderly pathologists hand up and down.

Dr Bootle grunts his assent then heads back to the mortuary suite. Cook, suddenly finding himself alone, runs to catch up with Morgan, who is already striding off towards the exit.

Morgan allows the heavy outer door to slam shut behind him without waiting for Cook to catch up. He leans against the red brick wall, just outside the mortuary and inhales deep lungsful of the fresh, cold air. He does not know what it is about hospitals, but he has always hated them. They make him feel so tense, yet he has no idea why. Maybe everyone feels that way he wonders as he shifts to one side to allow Cook to exit the building. Morgan is grateful for the short respite - he is acutely aware that his working day is not yet over, however much he wishes it could be.

Chapter 7

With rush hour dissipating, it takes little time for the two officers to return to the station. Cook immediately checks up on the teams' progress - it is imperative at this early stage to keep up the pressure. To his delight, Cook learns that whilst he and Morgan were at the mortuary, Fallow has located the whereabouts of Luke Fields who is living in Marham, some ninety miles from Deben Quay. That however is the extent of Fallows good fortune, as the phone the number listed in the directory has so far continually rung out unanswered, leaving the team no choice but to visit Luke Fields in person.

'Morgan, I have an urgent job for you,' Cook says as he approaches the detective, who is as ever standing next to the coffee machine.

Morgan shoves a stained mug underneath the percolator then flicks on the switch, watching as the empty vessel fills up with the remnants of the sludgy stewed coffee that someone else made earlier. Morgan winces as he swigs down the lukewarm liquid, however unpalatable it is though it does at least still contain caffeine concludes Morgan, who perseveres with drinking it. 'Yes boss,' Morgan says cheekily. He knows that one day he will push his friend too far, but the temptation at present is far too great to worry about it.

'I hope you didn't have plans for this evening,' Cook says sternly, becoming quite vexed with Morgans ongoing attitude towards him.

Morgan groans, slamming the empty mug down theatrically onto the stained table. 'Does it matter if I did?'

'C'mon, you know this goes with the job.'

'Yeah, I know, but that doesn't mean I have to like it and nor does my wife.'

'Well, you can always find another job, can't you,' Cook says evenly.

For once, Morgan cannot tell if his friend is joking or not, though he suspects it is the latter. Perhaps he has pushed him too far already.

'What do you need me to do?' Morgan asks jovially, trying to smooth over the tension.

'Go to Marham and speak to Luke Fields.'

'Yes boss,' Morgan replies in a tone that is difficult to interpret.

'Oh, and take Fallow with you, he needs the experience.' Cook says, grimacing, knowing full well what Morgan will be thinking at this precise moment.

Morgan is still trying to stop himself from seething at the news that he is going to have to spend the evening with Bennetts nephew rather than his wife, when he spots Fallow still diligently working at his desk. He watches as the rookie officer pedantically sorts through Mrs Fields paperwork, searching for any other potential lead that could help them to locate the elderly widow. For a moment Morgan almost feels sorry for Fallow, it is a hard slog going through reams of paperwork and often with no tangible results. On the other hand, perhaps it will do him some good to learn that police work is mostly about tedious leg work with very little excitement in between.

'Ready for a trip to Marham?' Morgan asks as he pulls on the coat he removed only a short time earlier.

Fallow nods then carefully pack's away the paperwork that he has been sifting through into evidence boxes. He stacks them in the lockable walk-in cupboard at the far end of the room, taking care to lock it again afterwards. With the task complete, he pulls his jacket off from the back of his chair and hurries to catch up with Morgan, who has already left.

Morgan is looking forward to the journey even less now that Fallow has offered to drive. Fallow is known to be the most careful of drivers, to the point of being excruciatingly slow, infuriating many of his unfortunate passengers let alone other drivers who have the misfortune to be behind him on a single carriageway. On the plus side, Morgan is shattered and welcomes the chance to relax and listen to the radio, which also has the plus point of successfully tuning out Fallows occasional interjection that serves to represent polite conversation.

The roads are already beginning to freeze. The hazardous conditions prompt Fallow to be even more careful than usual and it takes over two hours for them to reach Marham. As they drive through the outskirts of the large town, the snow, which has continued to float down from the sky the entire afternoon, is beginning to build up along the roadside, promising to make their return journey even more dangerous, especially as the roads will begin to freeze as soon as the sun dips below the horizon.

Luke Fields is listed on the electoral roll as residing at an address in Church Lane - a quiet road at the edge of the town, which mainly consists of narrow Victorian terraces. Fallow quickly finds the house located at the end of the lane next to a railway bridge, whose electrified line carries the express trains between Peterborough and London. The narrow, end of terrace house is in-keeping with the remaining properties in the road; with a stubby front garden enclosed by iron railings; sash windows and a stained-glass front door. The modest dwellings were originally built for the workers of a nearby corn mill, which was demolished many decades before, leaving only the red-brick houses as a reminder of the towns once prosperous industrial past.

Fallow manages to find a space in the crowded street, not too far from Luke Fields house. He parks as close to the snow-covered pavement as he dares without scraping the hub caps, squeezing his Fiesta in between a dark green Land Rover and a battered maroon MPV. Before Fallow has even switched the engine off, Morgan has flung open the door and is swinging his long legs out of the cramped vehicle then thrusting them onto the pavement; sitting for long periods of time always makes Morgans legs ache, leaving him wondering if he is starting to develop osteoarthritis.

As Morgan stands on the icy pavement waiting for the numbness in his legs to subside, he watches with envy as Fallow leaps out of the car with such apparent ease. Suppressing his unjustified irritation towards Fallow once again, Morgan takes the lead as they make their way up the concrete path that is littered with autumnal leaves amongst a fresh dusting of snowflakes. He raps loudly on the door, then takes a step back as the door immediately opens, revealing a tall man wearing a blue cashmere jumper. Behind him a radio is on, classical music softly filling the small building.

'Can I help you?' The man looks at the two men in puzzlement and perhaps with a little resentment at the intrusion to his quiet evening.

'Sorry to disturb you Sir, but my name is Detective Inspector Morgan and this is Detective Constable Fallow, we're from Deben Quay Police Force,' Morgan introduces. 'I'm not sure if you're aware, but your mothers' tearoom was badly damaged in a fire in the early hours of this morning. We're trying to locate the whereabouts of your mother who hasn't been seen since yesterday afternoon.'

'I see. You'd better come in.' Luke Fields pulls the front door open a little wider to allow the two men to enter into the narrow building, bringing with them a strong gust of wind and with it a flurry of snowflakes that blow straight through the tiny, but well-proportioned living room. 'I'm not really in contact with my mother, so I'm not sure why you're here?'

'Well, obviously we're concerned as to your mother's whereabouts and wondered if you'd heard from her or seen her in the last few days?' Morgan says bluntly, slightly taken aback by Luke Fields flippant attitude.

'No, I haven't seen her for a couple of years now. Do you think she's gone missing then?'

'It's starting to look that way. We're still waiting for the official fire investigators report, but from the ferocity of the fire, we suspect it was arson. Do you know if your mother had any financial concerns?'

'I have no idea. I didn't even know she still had the tearoom. I thought she would've retired long ago. I suppose she enjoys the company, she's been on her own since my father died.'

'How long ago was that?' Morgan asks, his eyes searching around the perfectly symmetrical room, noting the neatly stacked oak bookshelves either side of the chimney breast, which houses a wood-burner. Close to the fire is a dark brown cosy leather sofa that is positioned opposite a wall-mounted LED TV.

'Oh, about fifteen years ago. He had a boating accident with my sister Charlotte. They never found Charlotte, but my father's body washed up several days later up near Kirton Creek.'

'I'm sorry to hear that Sir. Do you have any other relatives?' Fallow interjects.

'No one she'd still be in contact with.' Luke Fields shakes his head.

'I'll leave you my card just in case you hear anything from your mother,' Morgan says as he reaches into his pocket and retrieves the leather card holder that Celia had bought him for their wedding anniversary the previous year.

'Thanks.' Luke Fields stretches out a muscular arm to take hold of the object. 'Let me know if you hear of anything.'

'We will Sir,' Fallow replies, striding across the varnished floorboards towards the front door, his lanky legs stretching across the minute room in seconds.

Morgan quickly follows and exits through the stained-glass wooden door that Fallow is politely holding open for him. The air has cooled considerably since they arrived in Marham and Morgan can see his breath dissipate into the night air as he exhales. At least it has stopped snowing though Morgan thinks as he gingerly retraces his steps down the slippery path again, trying not to shiver at the sharp contrast in temperature compared to the warmth of Luke Fields front living room.

'Well, that was a waste of time,' Morgan grumbles as soon as they are out of ear shot of Luke Fields.

'I don't know Sir, at least we know she's not here,' Fallow states cheerfully. 'It must have been a shock to Mrs Fields finding that body, especially given she lost her daughter in a similar way. Perhaps she just needs a few days to herself?

Morgan grunts, unwilling to concede that the young detective might have a valid point.

'I can drive back Sir,' Fallow eagerly volunteers.

Morgan is for once too exhausted to argue and nods in agreement. Perhaps he is getting too old for this job, he wonders as they skid their way back up the road. He wonders how he will manage to continue in his current role until retirement if he feels this exhausted now. Perhaps in a few years he will have to find something easier to do he muses.

Morgan stares out of the Fiestas side window as the lights of the houses disappear, giving way first to pitch-black fields, then to the brightly lit dual carriageway, which will take them all the way back to Deben Quay.

There is little conversation between the two men on their return journey; Fallow is busy concentrating on the icy, snow-laden roads; Morgan is in a pensive mood, trying to piece together the day's events and wondering what they should do next. Eventually Fallow turns on the radio, just loud enough to be audible, without causing annoyance to the senior officer. The gentle sounds of 'love hour' soothes Morgans tired mind and by the time they reach the outskirts of the Deben Quay, he is almost asleep.

It is close to nine pm by the time they return, still early enough for Morgan to visit the Eels Foot for a pint. He gets Fallow to drop him off near the pub, then carefully makes his way across the icy path to the pub. There are only a few customers, which is not surprising given the adverse weather. The cold weather and ongoing threat of an impending recession are badly affecting an already dwindling pub trade that was critically damaged by the enforced smoking ban; disallowing the British public to satisfy their cravings for alcohol and nicotine at the same time resulted in many customers staying at home, where they could smother their lungs in carcinogenic substances and calcify their liver at the same time.

Morgan immediately spots Cook, who is perched on a tall wooden stool at the bar, talking to Phil Wattle. It seems that Cook has also managed to sneak out for a couple of pints, a relative rarity since he became a parent.

'I was just telling Phil that we think the fire at the tearoom might've been arson,' Cook explains to Morgan who is removing his coat and flinging it over the bar. 'Any luck with finding Mrs Fields?'

'Not yet. Turns out that her son hasn't been in contact with her for a few years. He seems a bit strange though, not too concerned about his mother going missing. We might have to go back for another chat if we don't find her soon.' Morgan pulls across another bar stool and sits down next to Cook. He orders a pint of bitter from the bartender who is waiting politely then offers his companions a refill at the same time.

'Well, that's me done for the day,' Phil Wattle says, draining the rest of his pint. He replaces the empty vessel onto the polished surface then picks up his long grey overcoat from the coat stand next to the main door.

'Phil's going to run an article on the fire, try to entice more witnesses to come forward. They're going to keep the body story prominent as well. You know what people are like 'round here, they'd rather talk to the press then the police.' Cook pauses to drink deeply from his half-empty glass.

'I suppose so,' Morgan says unconvinced. He drains every last drop he can glean from the glass, then gently sets it down onto the bar. He looks at the glass for a moment as if trying to decide whether or not to order a refill. 'I'd better get going, Celia will be worrying about where I've got to, especially with this foul weather. What time's our briefing tomorrow?'

'Nine, but I'll be in from seven thirty, if you fancy keeping me company?'

Morgan rolls his eyes at his friends unconcealed attempt to get him to work extra hours. 'Ok, I'll see you tomorrow.' Morgan replies, ignoring the smirk spreading across Cooks face at the easy victory. He pulls on his thick grey coat in readiness of heading back out into the cold night then bids Cook a good evening and leaves before he can change his mind about having another drink.

Now that night has fully descended, the air has become even cooler and the pavements sparkle with icy particles. It is only a five-minute walk to Morgans home, but even so, he is frozen to the core by the time he has shut the front door behind him. The house is shrouded in darkness, indicating that Celia has not yet returned from her yoga class. Morgan wanders into the kitchen and flicks on the light switch. He blinks for a few moments as his eyes adjust to the harsh brightness of the spotlights that Celia insisted they had fitted a couple of years ago, then heads straight for the fridge, where Celia has left a covered plate for him to reheat. The beef stew has congealed into a glutinous mass on the plate, but it is food none-the-less and Morgan is far too hungry not to eat every scrap of it.

After the meal has been eaten, Morgan decides to risk his wife's ire and leave the washing-up for the morning, instead opting to go to bed early without waiting for Celia to return. Tomorrow will be yet another busy day.

Chapter 8

The morning starts out bright and sunny, with what would have been a hint of spring had it not been for the bitter chill in the air. Crocuses and snowdrops are starting to push through the sparse grass in front of the police station, a sure sign that spring is on its way at long last. It cannot come soon enough thinks Morgan, as he hurries up the stone steps and pulls open the front door to the station, allowing it to slam against the red-brick wall.

The wintry weather has been causing endless problems for the towns small police force, with vehicular accidents, flat car batteries and dangerous road conditions resulting in officers being unable to make it into work on the days they are needed the most. Already stretched resources are now at their limit, especially with the current investigations commanding so much of their time and funds. Cook has been dutifully voicing his concerns about the need for additional staff for some time now, a need made even more apparent by recent events, but expectedly, his pleas seemed to have gone unnoticed by Chief Superintendent Bennett, or perhaps even ignored given the impossibility of finding any additional resources from the ever-dwindling budget. Although he knows that it is an impossible task, Morgan cannot help but feel that perhaps he might have done a better job at it than his friend, had he been given the chance to do so. Morgan wonders if he can continue to work under Cook given how much he had wanted that job, or whether he can somehow reconcile the fact that his best friend has been promoted above him to a job that he felt certain that he should have had. At least though he was given a promotion to DI, Morgan concludes, if he hadn't then he would certainly have found another job by now.

The morning edition of the local paper 'The Suffolk Times' has already arrived, along with some of the national newspapers that are regularly delivered to the reception desk at Deben Quay police station. Morgan picks up the local rag and shoves it under the crook of his arm as he wanders past the front desk. The inner corridors, where the public rarely visit, are dim and unwelcoming, a depressing reminder of the dire financially difficulties that they are all facing and the need not to spend money unless it was absolutely necessary. Minutes later, Morgan arrives at the teams' office, which has now been set up as an incident room, with a large whiteboard and notice board having arrived unseen during the night, awaiting ideas and facts to be added to them.

Morgan trots over to the coffee machine and switches it on. As he perches on the edge of a radiator to warm his legs a little, the detective flicks through the paper. As he had expected, the fire at the tearoom is on the front page.

THE SUFFOLK TIMES

Tuesday 24 February 2006

Body Confirmed as a Woman
by Caroline Woods

A body found in the River Deben at the weekend has been confirmed as being that of a young female. A postmortem has been carried out to establish cause of death but details have not yet been released. The area where the body was found is still cordoned off while police continue with the search of the area. The police have asked for anyone who was in the area at the weekend to get in contact with them, in particular anyone who was on the river at the weekend and may have seen the woman. The woman is described as being in her early to mid twenties, with shoulder-length blond hair, slim, about 5 foot 3. Anyone who may know who the woman was should also contact DCI Cook at Deben Quay Police.

Dog Show Success
by Leah Hart

The Annual Deben Quay dog show took place on Saturday with great success. Over 50 dogs were entered and the best dog was won by Snuggles, a Parsons Jack Russell terrier.

More Snow Causes Mayhem
by Russell Carter

Yesterday's snow flurries caused mayhem on un-gritted roads according to residents living in the Deben Quay area. Council workers blamed the lack of foresight in gritting the roads on the recent strike which has disrupted normal gritting procedures.

Arson Suspected at Tea Room
by Phil Wattle

A fire at Mrs Fields tearoom on Monday is thought to have been started deliberately. The fire almost completely destroyed the tearoom, which is located on the quay side near to where a body was found at the weekend. The owner, Mrs Fields, was not available for comment. Any information about the fire should be given to DCI Cook, Deben Quay Police.

Vickers Fruit and Veg
Locally grown fruit and vegetables at yesterday's prices
Sold every Thursday at Deben Quay market

DCI Cook begins the morning briefing a little after nine o'clock, just as the last of the team are arriving to an accompaniment of light-hearted heckling from their more-timely team colleagues.

'As I was saying, for those who haven't already heard, a postmortem has been carried out on the young woman found at the quayside. It appears from the preliminary findings that she drowned, but we haven't had the toxicology reports back yet. Even if the final report does confirm drowning is the cause of death, we still have some unanswered questions; why didn't she have any ID on her or any warm clothing? Where did she eat her last meal, approximately two hours before she died? So far, the searches along the river path and the nearby woods haven't revealed any further items that might have belonged to her.' Cook pauses as the newest member of the squad strikes up his hand. 'Fallow, do you have something to say?'

'Yes Sir, I wondered if time of death has been established yet?' Fallow asks, ignoring the officer sitting next to him who is rolling his eyes.

'Dr Bootle has estimated time of death to be Friday evening.' Cook shoves his hands into his trouser pockets and begins to pace up and down the front of the room.

'We have however received information about the disappearance of a young woman named Lucy Mortimer, so we have a possible ID. The name also appears in our missing person files, but if it is her, she has dyed her hair blond since she was reported missing last September. And if it is Lucy, we need to know where she's been living during the last few months. Morgan, do you want to recap on your conversation with Mrs Fields son?' Cook motions for Morgan to join him at the front of the room.

'Luke Fields doesn't seem to have been in contact with his mother recently, so I don't think he'll be much help in finding her,' Morgan begins, taking Cooks place at the front of the room. 'Mrs Fields husband and daughter died in a boating accident fifteen years ago and he doesn't know of any other close relatives that she might be staying with. I don't think he would have any idea of who her friends are either as he clearly doesn't speak to her very often - he didn't even know she was still running the tearoom.'

Morgan perches on the lip of the desk nearest to him, both feet planted flatly onto the industrial grey carpet. 'I didn't have much luck at the sailing club either, but I have got a list of the names of everyone who has hired out kayaks and canoes during the last couple of weeks. All the ones hired out were booked back in, so they're going to do a stock check to see if any have been stolen. Sally Stockbridge did tentatively identify the kayak as being one of theirs from a photo. Once we get the serial number from forensics, we can cross match and confirm.'

"Thanks, we need to keep up the pace to identify the body and of course locate Mrs Fields,' Cook says, moving back to his previous location in front of the whiteboard. 'We also need to start interviewing neighbouring properties, find out if they saw or heard anything. Morgan, can you go down to the boatyard and see if they have any CCTV?'

Morgan nods then shuffles off the desk where he is still perched; his temporary seat is becoming uncomfortable and he can tell that the meeting is drawing to a close.

Cook gives the rest of the team instructions then closes the meeting. As soon as the team has dispersed, he takes Morgan to one side. 'I'll come with you to the boatyard, I want to take another look at the tearoom and see if any more progress has been made.'

'Sure,' Morgan replies, grabbing his coat from his desk and pulling it on. 'It'll be like old times.'

Cook stares at his friend for a moment, trying to deduce whether the last comment was meant in jest or not. He decides its safest to just ignore it, Morgans displeasure at his promotion is a well-known item of gossip at the station and Cook is mindful not to feed that particular issue. Instead, he strides into his small adjoining office and collects his coat up from the back of the chair. When he returns, Morgan is already striding across the room and heading towards the door. Cook runs to catch up with him and has almost reached him when he hears Fallow behind him.

'Sir, the fire investigator is on the phone. The fire at the tearoom has been fully extinguished so you can go in.'

Cook grins - progress with an investigation always cheers him up.

'There's one more thing, Sir. The fire investigators found the remains of a body amongst the wreckage,' Fallow blurts out.

'Well, well, well. I don't suppose the body is female?' Cook asks.

Fallow nods eagerly. 'The charred remains appear to be that of a woman. I guess Mrs Fields has been found then.'

'Let's head to the tearoom first,' Cook says to Morgan who has come back into the room after overhearing the conversation.

The two men hurry down the stairs and through the narrow beige corridor towards the back door, which leads onto the meagre station car park.

'I'll drive boss,' Morgan says cheekily as he opens the door on the driver's side.

Cook narrows his eyes and glares at his friend. They have known each other for far too long to take offence at a little ribbing, however, he would have been less amused however if they had had an audience - he is after all still a senior officer as well as being Morgans line manager. His patience with Morgans attitude towards him is wearing thin. If it carries on much longer, he will be forced to have a word with him.

The traffic is light and it takes little time for the detectives to reach Ferry Lane. Morgan pulls the car up onto the grass verge, which is visible now that the layer of snow has almost disappeared. Morgan swings his legs out of the car, his heavy boots crunching onto the lightly frozen fronds of grass. He shivers as he walks around the car and unlocks the boot, revealing a heap of jumbled up equipment and clothing.

Cook smirks when he sees the mess in the car boot. 'Well, married life hasn't made you any tidier, has it?' Cook teases.

Morgan sighs theatrically then hands Cook a pair of protective shoe covers. He takes out another set out for himself and pulls them on as best he can over his boots, then the two men make their way across the long grass towards the remains of the tearoom.

The fire investigator, Steven Farley is pacing up and down outside the building, trying to keep warm as he waits for Morgan and Cook. 'It's just over there,' Steven Farley says, pointing towards the location of the burnt remains that is still lying *in situ*.

Dr Bootle is already inside the tearoom, carefully stepping around the deceased whilst verbalising aloud his observations for his assistant Harry to diligently note. Next to Harry is a photographer who is also treading cautiously around the body, taking pictures of both the corpse and the tearoom from a variety of different angles.

'What do you think we're looking at then?' Cook asks Dr Bootle as the pathologist picks his way back out of the tearoom.

'Well, the cadaver is female judging from the shape of the pelvis and overall size. It's difficult to tell how she died as the remains are rather burnt. I can say however that she must have been around the source of the fire to be so well cremated,' Dr Bootle responds with his usual directness.

'Thanks Len, I'll come and watch the postmortem, if that's ok with you?' Cook asks.

'Of course! I'm always glad of some decent company,' Dr Bootle says, ignoring the fact that Harry is standing next to him. 'Give me an hour or so to get back to the morgue and we can make a start.'

'Can you go to Charlies boatyard by yourself?' Cook asks Morgan, who is standing behind him, as far away from the body as possible. 'Once we've got a definite ID, we'll need to send someone to inform Mr Fields that we've found his mother. In the meantime, I'll ask SOCO to take another look at Mrs Fields cottage.'

'Let's hope the news doesn't reach the press too quickly then, we wouldn't want Luke Fields to hear about it in the papers first. I can't imagine him taking second-hand news too well,' says Morgan, before turning around and heading down the path towards the boatyard.

Chapter 9

Simpsons boatyard is located in the middle of the old quayside, a few hundred yards from the tearoom. Despite its central location, it is peaceful, with the quietness only being disturbed by the rhythmic clanging of ropes against metal masts and the distant sound of hammering.

Morgans boots crunch over the gravel yard as he makes his way towards an imposing building that is nestled at the back of the plot. Somewhere from inside the enormous warehouse, Morgan can just about make out a faint humming that is almost drowned out by the elevated sound of a radio emitting country and western music. Stopping to enter through a small access door on the right-hand side of the building, Morgan follows the humming sound, which leads him to the rear of the building where a short stocky man with thinning grey hair protruding from his cap is sanding down the hull of a schooner.

'Hallo, what can I do for you?' The man asks cheerfully.

'Hello, I'm DI Morgan. I'm looking for the owner of the boatyard. Would that be you by any chance?'

'It certainly is, I'm Charlie Simpson.' The boat yard owner replies, reaching forward to shake Morgan's outstretched hand. 'What can I do for you?'

'We're investigating the death of a young woman who was found further up the river on Sunday morning. I see you have CCTV cameras up around the perimeter of the yard. Do you by any chance have any footage from last weekend?'

'Yup sure do, but I'm not sure if it will help much being up this end of the quay. You're welcome to come and take a look though.'

Morgan ducks underneath the boat Mr Simpson is working on and follows him to the other side of the building where there is a small office, crammed full of paperwork that has been left strewn across every available surface. On the desk is a dust-covered TV, which has clearly not been utilised by the current occupant. Morgan allows his eyes to continue to comb through the dimly lit room, wondering how anyone can bear to work in such a disorganised, chaotic environment.

Morgan politely declines the offer of a coffee as he spies the lime-scale covered kettle, a carton of out-of-date milk and two stained mugs on the top of a nearby filing cabinet. He watches as the boatyard owner rummages through the bottom drawer of his desk and pull out two unlabelled video tapes. Clearly modern technology has not yet graced its presence in Charlie Simpsons boatyard.

'You're in luck. We normally only keep these for a couple of days, just long enough to check them over. Do you want to see them now or do you want to take them with you?'

'Now, if you don't mind,' Morgan says, uncertain if Deben Quay police station still possesses a video player. 'We're particularly interested in Friday evening and early Saturday morning.'

Morgan peers over Charlie Simpsons shoulder at the undersized TV screen. The images are grainy, made even worse by the snowy conditions at the start of the weekend. The two men flick through several hours of the tape from Friday evening before the first images of people appear on the screen; a couple can be seen walking past the yard at 11.45 pm, dragging what looks like two bags with them.

'They're the two tramps who've been staying on the quayside. They quite often sleep in the bandstand near the tearoom. Funny thing is I haven't seen them the last few days, I reckon all the police presence has scared them off,' Charlie Simpson explains to Morgan.

'Most probably. Is it ok if I take these tapes with me? We might be able to zoom in and get a closer look,' Morgan asks, hoping that someone in his team has enough technical know-how to examine the old-fashioned technology.

'Sure, the ones from Thursday and Sunday are here as well, if you want them?'

'Thanks,' Morgan replies, taking the tapes from Charlies outstretched hand.

Morgan thanks Mr Simpson for his time then makes his way back out of the building the same way that he came in, albeit with some reluctance at having to leave the relative warmth of the warehouse and head back out into the cold. As Cook has taken the car to the mortuary, Morgan will have to walk back to the police station. Stoically, he pulls on his hat and gloves and strides off at pace, taking the shortest possible route through the town centre. It is quiet, with few residents seemingly feeling a strong enough desire to frequent the small independent retail units and copious numbers of charity and coffee shops, given the bitterness of the weather.

Twenty glacial minutes later, Morgan arrives back at the station. He pulls open the heavy outer front door, noticing that the blue paint is starting to peel. He wonders if there is enough money in the budget for repairs to the aging woodwork or even if they will eventually be forced to relocate to a new building closer to the Hemley estate and the hospital. Talk of constructing a more economically viable building has been going on for as long as Morgan can remember. A site was even allocated, but the ever-dwindling budget has never allowed for the proposal to come into fruition. Morgan has a niggling doubt whether the move will ever happen. It is far more likely that their small police force will be amalgamated with that of the adjacent town, which is far larger with a bigger budget and much newer facilities. That is not something to look forward to decides Morgan, as he enters the station.

Morgan stamps his feet onto the tiled floor, trying to revive them a little, then makes the climb up the four flights of stairs to the team office. The room is deserted apart from Fallow, who is ambling around the room, seemingly lost for something to do.

'Fallow, I've got something for you' Morgan says, waving the tapes in the air.

'Yes Sir!' Fallow answers gratefully, a large grin erupting across his face.

'These tapes need to be checked and documented - they're CCTV recordings from Charlie Simpsons boatyard. See if there was anyone about on both Saturday and Sunday night.'

'Yes Sir,' Fallow responds, eagerly taking the tapes from Morgan, who is equally as pleased to be rid of them.

'Before you get settled though, can you go to Betty's sandwich shop and collect the lunch order,' Morgan instructs, ignoring the look of displeasure on the young man's face. It is an unsaid rule that the newbies get all the worst jobs and being the Supers nephew does not excuse Fallow from it.

Cook is in no mood for lunch after spending most of the morning at the morgue, witnessing the initial examination of the charred remains from the tearoom. He made the mistake of going into the mortuary room itself and can still smell the stench of disinfectant mixed with the aroma of burnt flesh, leaving him doubtful will ever stomach eating barbecued meat again.

During the postmortem, Dr Bootle confirmed that the body is female and over the age of eighteen. The presence of some damage to the hip and knee joints, as well as pitting to the ribs, suggests she was 50-65 years old. Her teeth are also missing and Cook makes a note to check both the tearoom and Mrs Fields house for any dentures.

A full report of the postmortem will be emailed over to them later in the week, but it is clear that the body was at the epicentre of the fire. Tissue samples taken for further analysis will establish if an accelerant was poured over the victim before she was set alight. It seems likely given that a chemical aroma could be smelt on the body, as Cook experienced for himself during the post-mortem. He just hoped she was already dead when the fire started.

'Looks like we've got another relative to contact,' Cook says to Morgan, once back in the incident room. 'I think we should visit Lucy Mortimers parents first though and ask them to come and identify her body. It might be an idea to get some DNA samples as well. Once her identity has been confirmed we'd better do another press release.'

Morgan holds up a bacon sandwich and offers it to Cook, who promptly grimaces and shakes his head. A second offering of a cheese and pickle baguette is however gratefully received. The two men eat their food in silence, each contemplating the task ahead with heavy hearts. This is by far the worst part of their job and one that does not get any easier with practice.

The Mortimers live in a newly built detached house close to the edge of town, as far away from the less amenable parts of Deben Quay as possible. Morgan drives straight down to the bottom of the sweeping cul-de-sac, swiftly executes a three-point turn and returns half-way up the road again, where he pulls up alongside the footpath, inadvertently parking across a dropped-kerb in the process.

Morgan gets out of the car and looks around the quiet neighbourhood then returns his focus to the property in front of him, with its small but carefully manicured rectangular lawn surrounded by a neat border of daffodils and bluebells. The immaculate lawn is separated from the neat block-paved driveway by a low, red-brick wall that stops a metre or so before it reaches the front door. In front of the small integral garage, which is probably not fit for purpose given the size of the owner's car, is a brand-new Mercedes C class. It seems that the residents of the house are at home.

Hearing the car door slam behind him, which heralds the imminent arrival of Cook, Morgan reaches out to press the doorbell. The chimes reverberate around the dwelling and from somewhere inside.

A few moments later a short, stout woman tentatively pulls back the door, holding tightly onto the white plastic-frame. 'Hello, can I help you?'

'Hello, my name is DCI Cook and this is DI Morgan.' Cook holds out his ID card, pushing past Morgan in the process. 'I'm sorry to disturb you, but your daughter Lucy was reported missing in September last year, wasn't she?'

'Yes, that's right. Have you got some news?' Mrs Mortimer asks hesitantly, the hand that is still holding onto the door now visibly trembling.

'Perhaps we could please come in?' Cook says gently.

Before Mrs Mortimer can respond, her husband appears from behind her and places a hand onto her right shoulder. 'Of course, please come in,' Mr Mortimer says, gently moving his wife out of the way then opening the door wider to accommodate the two men.

The two detectives follow the couple through the wide hallway and into the first door on the right. The immaculately decorated sitting room is adorned with matching oak furniture, a white leather recliner sofa and a very large flat screen LCD TV that dominates the far wall. Mr Mortimer swiftly traverses the room to switch it off, plunging the room into an uncomfortable silence.

Cook coughs gently then motions for Mrs Mortimer to take a seat on the cosy armchair closest to the electric fire. Her husband stands beside her, one hand on her back, gently squeezing her shoulder, leaving Cook and Morgan standing awkwardly in the centre of the room, awaiting the invitation to sit down that never comes.

'Mr and Mrs Mortimer, you may have seen in the news that the body of a young woman was found in the river Deben at the weekend. I'm sorry to inform you that from the description you gave to the police, we believe that the deceased may be your daughter,' Cook says quickly, as if trying to lessen the blow.

Mrs Mortimer slumps back into the armchair, her shoulders sagging in defeat. She closes her eyes for a moment, as if a wave of pain is traversing through her. 'I thought you'd come to say that you'd found her alive. We thought she'd gone off with an older man you see. It caused quite a scandal in our community. We thought maybe Lucy had felt unable to come home again because of it.'

'Can we see her?' Mr Mortimer asks in a small, shocked voice.

'Yes of course,' Morgan replies. 'We'll need you to formally identify her in any case. Whenever you're ready we can take you to see her.'

'Thank you,' Mr Mortimer says quietly, his voice barely audible. 'Shall we go now? There's no point putting it off any longer. We've been in limbo for so long you see, not knowing what has happened to her. At least now we might have some closure.'

'If that's what you want to do. I will ask my colleague here to phone the mortuary to make the arrangements,' Cook replies, glancing sideways at Morgan.

Mr Mortimer nods, his attention drawn to his wife who is staring at the mantelpiece where a large photograph of Lucy stands in prime position. Morgan follows her gaze to the photo. There was no doubt in his mind that the body is Lucy.

Chapter 10

Hemley Hospital is in desperate need of refurbishment, deduces Morgan as he once again drives down to the end of the car park to find a parking space close to the mortuary entrance. The entire hospital is in need of a drastic upgrade, having been constructed in the early 1960's, which produced a short, squat building with a drab but functional exterior that is typical of the era. It fares little better inside, considers Morgan as he pulls open the main door and is immediately affronted with yellowing walls and peeling posters on the notice boards that line the dark corridors. The clinical aroma that assaults their nostrils as soon as they step inside the reception area, prompts Morgan to wrinkle up his nose. The crude attempt to mask the smell of death with artificial air fresheners only serves to make any visit to this part of the building even more distasteful.

    The Mortimers follow the two detectives into the small waiting area, where they check in with the receptionist. A short while later, Harry arrives to show the couple through to the viewing room, with Cook and Morgan following behind at a respectful distance.

    Morgan thinks that the Mortimers seems remarkably calm as the curtain is drawn back to reveal their daughter's body. Mrs Mortimer does not visibly react, frozen in shock, her husband's shoulders sag, his face relaxing in acceptance that at the very least, their search for their only child is now over. Morgan can only suppose that the knowledge that their daughter has been found after all this time, must almost be a relief to the Mortimers, even though of course it is not the outcome they have been desperately hoping for. It will take some time for the shock to wear off and for the couple to then experience the intense pain of knowing they will never see their daughter alive again.

With the formal identification done, Cook and Morgan leave the couple to say their goodbyes. They walk slowly back through the corridor in search of Dr Bootle, who is working in another part of the building. They locate the pathologist with ease - he is busy examining the remains found in the tearoom. This time though he is accompanied by some of the forensics team who, having stopped by to collect some samples, have now been way-laid by Dr Bootle's dogged enthusiasm for teaching. The two detectives stay for a while, catching up on news of the two cases. When they return to the waiting room, they find that the Mortimers are already there.

Mr Mortimer sees Cook and Morgan approach and immediately rises up from his seat to ask how his daughter died. 'We read in the paper that it was some kind of boating accident. It seems strange that she would come back here and take a trip out on the river?' Mr Mortimer rambles.

'We haven't had a final report from the pathologist yet, but it looks as if your daughter drowned,' Cook replies. 'We're still doing tests though so can't say for definite yet what happened to Lucy.'

A stunned silence descends as the couple try to absorb the news.

'I also need to inform you that your daughter was pregnant at the time of her death,' Cook continues.

Mrs Mortimer groans and sits back down into a hard-back plastic chair. 'Please can we go home now, I want to be alone,' she says softly.

'Yes, of course,' Cook responds. 'We may need to talk to you again though and we will of course keep you informed of our progress with the investigation.'

After dropping the Mortimers back home, Cook and Morgan return to the station to prepare for another press release; they need more information as to the whereabouts of the young woman during the last few months and it is time to get some help with it.

The editor of the Suffolk Times, Phil Wattle, who has already heard about the discovery of a body in the tearoom, is ferreting about in the reception area of the police station, hoping to get the first scoop on the story. 'Hallo Tom, any news for me?' Wattle asks optimistically as Cook walks in through the front door of the station.

'I'm about to do a press release,' Cook responds. 'Fancy a quick drink in my office first?'

Wattle gleefully accepts the offer and follows Cook through the inner security door and up the stairs to his office. With the door firmly shut behind him, Cook retrieves a bottle of whisky from the top drawer of his filing cabinet and takes out two glasses from a nearby shelf.

The two men sit in silence for a moment, sipping the fiery liquid, which spreads a glowing warmth through their bones. Eventually Cook breaks the silence, 'We've identified the body found in the river.'

'Do the family know?' Wattle leans forward in his chair, balancing his half-empty glass in the palm of one hand.

'We've just come back from the mortuary. The parents identified the body - it's definitely Lucy Mortimer. We're going to release her name officially, but no details about how she died yet as we haven't had all the test results back.' Cook takes another sip of his whisky, feeling it burn a tract down to the pit of his stomach.

'A body has also been found in Mrs Fields tearoom. We're not sure of the cause of death yet and identifying it is going to be a problem, although at this time, the assumption is that it's Mrs Fields. We'll give you first scoop on that story, but could you give us a day or so before releasing it? You know what it's like, people come out of the woodwork trying to help and more often than not it makes it all much harder. We also need to speak to Mrs Fields son as yet.'

'Sure, no problem.' Wattle has known Cook long enough to know when to keep his mouth shut. 'I'll have a dig around as well, sometimes people talk more to the press. A cash incentive often helps. What time's the press release? I'll send our new lass, Caroline Woods. She's very keen, rather like a terrier, ferreting out rabbits.'

'What's the time now?' Cook asks.

'Four thirty,' Phil Wattle replies, looking at the gold-plated watch he received for his sixtieth birthday. 'If we said five thirty, that would give you time to draft a statement and give us time to get the news out for tomorrow morning?'

'Sounds good. I'll get our press officer to make the calls.'

Wattle drains the remainder of his glass, then gingerly stands up.

Cook watches, smiling at the aging reporter. Neither of them is getting any younger and it is starting to show.

Wattle stretches out an arm to shake Cooks hand. 'Thanks Tom, I'll head back to headquarters now and let you get on.'

Cook fixes a smile on his face as Wattle leaves. He waits for the door to bang shut, then pours himself another large measure of whisky.

Upstairs in the larger of the two offices occupied by the Suffolk Times, the team are beginning to pack up for the day, ready to head off to a local pub, the Cherry Tree, for a few drinks before heading home.

'Listen up everyone,' Wattle shouts above the din, motioning for the team to quieten down. 'There's going to be another press release from the police about the dead body. Caroline, can you go to the police station in a bit, I'm going to look into the fire at Mrs Fields tearoom a bit more closely. We've been promised first dabs at it, so we need to keep them sweet over the body in the river story, so no releasing anything until its official.' Wattle waggles his finger at the team. 'Russ, I want you to look into the latest car break-ins tomorrow and find out if the police have any updates.'

Russ groans theatrically, quickly followed by a peel of laughter that ripples through the room. 'Ok, ok, settle down,' Wattle jests. 'Go on then, get on with it Caroline, the rest of you can bugger off to the pub.'

The team immediately dissembles, accompanied by a few murmurings and a little ribbing about the new girl being given the best job. Though the comments are made lightly, in truth the rest of the team are more than a little put out by the blatant favouritism being shown to the new member of staff. The rest of the team are still gossiping as they make their way out of the building, eager to get to the pub before the roads freeze again.

Caroline follows behind them for a while, then stops to watch as her work colleagues meander off down the road. She waits until they disappear from view and she can no longer hear their laughter, then turns around to walk to the police station alone. She refuses to allow the harsh words of her colleagues to bother her, she tells herself, as she ambles along the narrow, cobbled street towards the police station, her kitten heels clacking on the slippery stones. She is used to banter in her profession, however misplaced it might seem to an outsider, but still, she is not daft enough to think there is no substance to the teasing. She is also acutely aware that she will be liked even less if she complains about it.

Caroline pulls her navy wool coat around her more tightly to keep out the biting wind and quickens her pace as the town police station comes into view. She arrives to a hum of activity and quickly meanders her way through the narrow corridors towards the room that has been allocated for the press release, letting the sounds of raised voices and laughter guide her through the building. Opening the partially glazed door reveals a throng of journalists, both local and national, crammed into the tiny room, all jostling for the best position. Caroline picks her way through the lines of plastic chairs and settles down in the third row from the front. As they wait for the press release to begin, Caroline observes the unfamiliar journalists who are sitting either side of her and who make no attempt at polite conversation.

A hush rapidly descends across the room as Cook opens the door then makes his way to the front. Cook pulls out a piece of paper from his trouser pocket and unfolds it, automatically smoothing out the creases as he positions himself in front of the microphone.

Deben Quay Police Force Press Release - 24 February, 2006

The body of a young woman found in the River Deben on Sunday morning has been identified as Lucy Mortimer. Lucy, who was 23 and originally from the Deben Quay area, was reported missing by her parents in September last year. It is believed that she left Deben Quay voluntarily with an unknown male.

Anyone who may have been in the quayside area during the last few days, or knew Lucy during the months she was missing, should contact DCI Cook at Deben Quay Police Force.

Morgan turns up just as Cook finishes delivering the statement and the onslaught of questions begins. As promised, Wattles' keenest member of staff is living up to her reputation, asking question after question, all of which they decline to answer. Morgan barely manages to conceal his irritation at Caroline Woods' blatant attempts to elicit further information, even after it has been made clear that no more details can be given out at this stage. He watches the journalist with interest, it seems that her reputation for dogged determination is well-founded.

The press release is neatly brought to a close and Fallow ushers the journalists out of the room towards the reception desk and main door. As soon as the room empties, Cook and Morgan retreat to the incident room.

'We haven't been able to contact Luke Fields yet, so I'll need you to go up there again tomorrow and find him.' Cook says, pouring some stewed coffee from the machine into two mugs. 'If he's disappeared, then we could have a suspect.'

'Sure, I'll ask around the area as well, see if I can find anything else out about him,' Morgan replies. He empties the contents of two sachets of brown sugar into his mug and stirs it vigorously with the stained teaspoon that is lying prone next to a carton of milk on the table.

'Can you go to the Lambs Inn this evening and see where Lucy Mortimer worked - talk to her boss Tom Baxter?' Cook says, before taking a sip of the scalding liquid, then immediately wincing as it burns the tip of his tongue. "See if he knows anything about why she disappeared and who she left the town with.'

'Will do, Tom. I'd better go home and change first though, I think I could do with a shower and something to eat.'

Cook looks at his friend and laughs, 'Yes I think you should.'

Morgan glares at him. He does of course realise his friend is teasing him, but he is more than a little sensitive about his appearance and Tom knows it.

Cook slaps Morgan on the back to reaffirm that his comment should be taken light heartedly, and the action manages to elicit a slight smile from Morgan.

'I'll let you know if I find anything of interest,' Morgan says, playfully shoving his friend as he leaves.

Chapter 11

So far, Celia Morgan is having a very productive afternoon that has culminated in a pile of shortbread and fruit scones, ready for her husband's return. Now that she has no job to go to the days seem even longer than ever, especially during such a harsh winter where the endless hours of darkness do not yet seem to be receding. Celia supposes she will have to find some other way of passing her time. Perhaps she should start looking for another job? Having too much time to think is not helping either her state of mind or her marriage. The lack of distraction is allowing the opportunity for her long-buried fears to arise again - that her husband is disappointed with both her and their childless marriage.

She is also starting to age. Deep lines have already begun to appear in the delicate tissue around her eyes, her jowls are beginning to thicken along with her once slim waistline. She knows from her friend's failed marriages, that this could be a dangerous time for a woman, it seems that often a marriage can fade with the looks and energy of the wife. Not for the first time that week, Celia wishes that they had been blessed with children to fill the chasm that seems to be deepening between herself and her husband. She is not daft enough to really believe that the addition of children would improve their marriage but at least she would not feel quite so alone.

By the time Morgan arrives home, Celia has cleaned the entire house, cleared the garden of yet more debris from the previous year and slow-cooked a lamb shank in red wine - one of her husband's favourites. The comforting food is well received by the weary detective, who speaks little during the meal and avoids talking about the case altogether, a usual pattern when her husband is wrapped up in an investigation.

Morgan seems to be barely listening to Celias constant chattering and futile attempts to engage him in conversation. Instead, he quickly eats, showers, then changes into clean clothes, before going back out into the cold again. Celia stares at the pile of washing up in the kitchen sink, sits down at the kitchen table and cries.

The Lamb Inn is located at the centre of town, on a corner of the pedestrianised high street - a narrow, cobbled street, which comprises the original part of the settlement. It is a large Georgian building that has been a pub for as long as Morgan can remember. It used to be considered a quiet establishment, with a restaurant located in the annex that is connected to a large central room via a dimly lit narrow corridor. Now it is filled with youths who enjoy loud music and cheap drinks, playing pool until the early hours of the morning. At this time of the evening though, there are expectedly only a handful of customers in the pub, resulting to an almost one-to-one ratio to the despondent bar staff.

Morgan walks through the main bar to the annex where a group of men are playing pool. Two young women are gossiping at a nearby table, taking sneaky glances at the man who is lining up to take a shot. Morgan watches as the young man takes his turn, missing the corner pocket by millimetres. The two girls snigger at his discomfiture before returning to their conversation, which clearly includes the pool players as they continue to sneak glances at them in between fits of giggles.

Morgan retreats back through the corridor to the main bar, where the landlord Tom Baxter has appeared and is helping himself to a shot of whisky. Lucy only worked at the pub for a few months before she left Deben Quay, but she clearly made an impression on her boss Morgan discovers when he questions him.

'She was a lovely girl, a very good worker, always happy and smiling,' Tom Baxter reminisces. 'I enjoyed her company, as did most of the people who drink in here.'

'Do you know why she disappeared?' Morgan asks as he settles onto a bar stool. He watches as the landlord pours himself another generous measure.

'I think she went off with a man that she met in here as it happens. He wasn't a regular like, I couldn't place him, but he did seem a bit familiar.'

'Can you remember what he looks like?' Morgan shuffles forward on his stool, his interest in the conversation deepening.

'Tall, dark hair, slim build. A bit surly looking, but Lucy seemed to get on with him. Not my type, but then I'm not a woman thankfully,' Tom Baxter says, laughing at his own joke, which Morgan does not find in the least amusing. Morgan wonders if perhaps Tom Baxter is more than a little jealous of the man Lucy had shown interest in.

The landlord excuses himself as he spots a new customer come in through the main door of the pub. Morgan immediately recognises the woman as the Suffolk Times journalist who attended the press release earlier. She looks vastly more attractive sat at the bar then earlier thinks Morgan, as he takes in her tight-fitting knee length skirt and black boat-neck cashmere jumper, her hair tied back into a neat ponytail that caresses the nape of her neck.

'Hi, you were at the press release, weren't you?' The journalist asks as she walks towards Morgan.

'That's right, I'm DI Morgan,' he says formally, reaching out to shake her outstretched hand.

'Well, hello DI Morgan, I'm Caroline,' she laughs at his formality.

'James. Sorry, it's been a long day.'

'It certainly has. Are you here for work or pleasure, or shouldn't I ask?'

'I could ask you the same question,' Morgan says, deftly avoiding answering.

'A bit of both really. I heard that Lucy Mortimer had worked in here, so I thought I'd check it out.'

'Your right, she did work here, but you didn't hear that from me,' Morgan winks. 'I don't suppose you've found out anything that you'd like to share with me?'

'I'm not sure I would tell you if I did,' Caroline says playfully, pulling up a bar stool next to Morgan. She sits down elegantly, crossing her slender legs as she perches on the stool, her petite frame barely able to reach the ground.

'Fair enough. I'd better get back to work,' Morgan snaps.

'If you want to know what I think,' Caroline says, trying to placate the detective. 'I think that Lucy may have been seeing her boss, either that or he was fantasising about it.' Caroline turns to stare at the landlord, who is standing at the far end of the bar.

'Hmm, I was wondering the same thing.' Morgan follows Carolines gaze and watches as Tom Baxter leans across the bar and whispers into a customer's ear. Morgan cannot tell from this distance if the woman is enjoying the attention or trying to extract herself from the landlords unwanted advances.

'Can I buy you a drink, or do you need to rush off?'

'I could do with a quick one. A drink I mean.' Morgan blushes, feeling like a foolish schoolboy.

'A drink it is then,' Caroline says, laughing at his obvious embarrassment.

'What can I get you?' Morgan asks.

'I'll have a pint of bitter thanks.'

Morgan orders the drinks from one of the bar staff, managing to disguise his surprise that a woman who he considered to be intelligent and attractive, would drink pints. 'So, how long have you been a journalist?' Morgan asks before drinking deeply from his glass. He replaces the partially empty glass back onto the worn mahogany bar then wipes the froth from his mouth with the back of his hand.

'Quite a few years now. I was lucky and got work experience at a newspaper in London and they kept me on. I've only been here a few months, I got tired of the pace in London.'

'I don't blame you. I've been here all my life and still love it.'

'What made you become a policeman?'

'I don't know really. I guess I thought it would be exciting. I'd hate to be stuck in an office, I get bored quickly.'

'I'm sure you do,' Caroline teases. 'I guess I'd better go, I've got another early start tomorrow.'

'Was that you I saw outside Mrs Fields tearoom on the night of the fire?' Morgan asks clumsily, trying to prolong the conversation.

'It was, we're like you, you know - always on call.'

'You certainly got there quickly,' Morgan says.

'You know how it is, we can't reveal our sources,' Caroline teases then slides gracefully off her stool. She pulls her long red wool coat around her and fastens the buttons, then fishes out a packet of cigarettes and a box of matches from the pocket. 'Well, I hope you get somewhere with our friend the landlord. He doesn't look too forthcoming.'

Morgan smiles, watching as Caroline gracefully glides across the sticky carpet. Just as she reaches the door, Caroline turns around to look at Morgan again, raising one hand to say goodbye. She stares a little longer then could be considered polite before shoving open the heavy outer door, letting a cold blast of air into the pub.

Morgan waits until the door fully shuts behind the journalist, then returns his attention to what is left of his pint. When the glass is empty of its contents, Morgan decides that he too should head for home and get a good night's sleep. It will be another long day again tomorrow.

Chapter 12

The sun is just beginning to push away the heavy darkness when Morgan awakes. Carefully he pulls back the duvet, trying not to wake Celia, then gingerly creeps across the room, deftly avoiding the creaky floorboard near the foot of the bed.

Having safely traversed the room without awakening his wife, Morgan pulls back a corner of the curtain to observe the weak winter light that is starting to rise above the rooftops of the houses on the opposite side of the road. He watches for a few moments as streaks of pink and orange bleed across the sky, then tiptoes back across the room. Kneeling down next to his side of the bed, Morgan stretches out a hand and feels about on the floor for the clothes he dumped on the carpet the previous night. It is far too early to put the light on and risk waking Celia, so Morgan just has to hope that the clothes he chooses from the pile are at least clean.

Even though the days are starting to lengthen, the darkness has not yet fully receded by the time Morgan lets himself out of the house. He waits impatiently for the car to defrost, then swiftly makes his way through the quiet streets of Deben Quay towards the police station. There are few other residents awake at such a time and Morgan only sees a couple of newspaper delivery boys and the occasional dog walker, who perhaps prefer the quietness of the early hour despite the biting chill in the air. Even the station car park is empty - a rare occurrence given the current shortage of spaces. Morgan easily finds an empty parking bay close to the rear entrance of the building then sprints to the door, shivering involuntarily despite his heavy coat, hat and thick gloves.

Morgan is just beginning to thaw out, sitting as close to the radiator as he can whilst working his way through a scalding mug of coffee, when Cook flings open the office door, bringing a gust of cold air with him.

Cook grunts in greeting as he continues to demolish the bacon sandwich his wife has made for him. Morgan wrinkles his nose in disgust. All he can stomach at this hour is a strong black coffee. How can anyone eat such a greasy meal when they have only just woken up?

While Cook continues to eat, Morgan summarises the conversation he had with Tom Baxter the previous evening, whilst slurping his way through his second mug of coffee. By the time Cook has finished his breakfast, the rest of the team have begun to appear in dribs and drabs, moaning about the foul weather whilst they wait for Cook to finish eating and get ready their usual morning briefing.

'Good morning, everyone,' Cook begins as he meanders through the uniform row of desks towards the front of the room. 'I hope you've all had a good breakfast as this could be another long day. To recap on the latest, the body of the young woman found on Sunday morning has now been formally identified as Lucy Mortimer. Lucy disappeared in September last year, possibly with an older male that she met at the pub where she worked. We've just had the toxicology report in, which showed traces of a sedative in her blood, but no alcohol or any other drugs,' Cook explains. 'Tests on the fluid found in her lungs indicates that she was alive when she went into the river. She was also fourteen weeks pregnant. Given the test results we now need to treat this as an unexplained death. And before anyone asks, yes, we've requested DNA analysis of the foetus.'

Fallow thrusts his hand up in the air. 'Yes Fallow, you have a question?' Cook says, trying not to show his irritancy at the interruption.

'Yes Sir. Is it possible then that the bruises and cuts to her hand were defence wounds?'

'Yes, that could be the case,' Cook replies. 'The other questions we need to be asking ourselves are whether or not Lucy entered the water from the river path and whether the kayak we found is in any way connected to her death. We also need to know how she got to the quayside, as well as of course why she ended up in the river.'

Cook perches on the edge of the nearest desk, pushing aside a keyboard and mouse to allow his plump frame to fit comfortably onto the structure. 'Let's start by talking to Lucys family. We need to know what made Lucy leave home so suddenly last September and where she's been all this time. Let's search her old bedroom at the family home, find out who her friends were, what hobbies she had. We also need to check CCTV footage from the town centre and the quayside on Friday night. There are quite a few shops, pubs and businesses in that area that also might have their own CCTV.'

An audible groan erupts from the back of the room - checking through all the CCTV footage could constitute weeks of work.

'Morgan, can you give us your input into the second investigation we're dealing with?' Cook motions for Morgan to take over from him at the front of the room.

Morgan clears his throat as he leans against the edge of the desk beside Cook, who's portly behind is spreading out across the surface. 'We now have a second suspicious death to investigate as a body has been found in Mrs Fields tearoom. SOCO think that an accelerant was used to start the fire and from the condition of the body and the soot patterns found above it, it seems very likely that the body was the point of origin of the fire. Tests are being carried out to identify the accelerant but paint thinner left over from the winter refurbishment of the building was found at the scene, so this could be the culprit. We've also found a set of footprints outside the back door of the tearoom.'

'Do you have any idea of the identity of the body?' Fallow asks, eager as ever to impress his colleagues.

'The assumption at this stage is that it's Mrs Fields, but the condition of the body is going to make identification difficult. Her fingers were badly burnt and Dr Bootle can't get any decent prints from them. Oddly there were no teeth found on the body either so we need to look out for dentures - check Mrs Fields house again as well as the area between the house and tearoom.'

'Thank you, Morgan,' Cook says, taking back control of the meeting. 'I need you to go back to Marham and look for Luke Fields again as we haven't been able to contact him. Once we find him, we can check his DNA against the body and see if we have a match. We also need to go through Mrs Fields finances with a fine-tooth comb. Was her business insured? Did she have life insurance? Who would benefit from her death or from the tearoom being destroyed?'

'Is it possible that Mrs Fields saw something she shouldn't have?' Morgan asks, directing the rhetorical question to the team. 'Or is it just coincidence that she was the one who found Lucy Mortimers body and then her business was set alight the same day?'

'It's possible the two deaths are connected,' Cook continues, observing several team members who are nodding their heads in agreement. 'We need to explore all possible avenues though and not make any solid assumptions at this early stage.'

Cook turns to address Fallow. 'How did you get on with the CCTV footage from the boatyard?'

Fallow pushes his chair back to stand up, then coughs discretely to clear his throat. 'A lot of people went past the boatyard during the daytime as you would expect, but Friday night was much quieter. A group of kids were captured at 7.15 pm and at 11.45 two people walked past - they've already been identified by Charlie Simpson, the owner of the boatyard as a homeless couple who have been sleeping in the bandstand. That's it for the Friday. There were surprisingly few people about on Saturday. A few families walked past the boatyard and some dog walkers but nobody in the early hours of the morning. I'll make a start this afternoon on the footage from Sunday. One suggestion brought up by the tech people, is to check if the sailing club have CCTV up at their lock-up where they keep their equipment.'

'Good point. Any other updates?' Cook says, addressing the rest of the team.

'Not yet,' Morgan responds. 'I'll go back to the sailing club this afternoon after I've been to Marham.'

'Ok, well we all know what we all have to do, so let's get on with it,' Cook says, dismissing the team.

At the offices of the Suffolk Times, the small news team are also gathering for their morning briefing.

Phil Wattle is standing at the front of the room, a mug of coffee in one hand, a Danish pastry in the other. He waits for the whole team to assemble before starting the meeting.

'Well team, it seems that the young woman found in the river Deben may not have been an accidental death after all,' Wattle begins. 'On top of that, another body has been found in the tearoom that burnt down on Sunday night. So, a possible murder, or at the very least, an arsonist is on the loose. Caroline and Russell, I want you to go down to the quayside and start talking to people, see what you can find out. You might want to try the boat yards and the sailing club as well. The rest of the team already know what you're doing today, so get on with it.'

Caroline smiles warmly at Wattle as she walks past him on her way to the door. Wattle suspects that Caroline is fully aware that Russell, who is following closely behind, is making faces at her expense. He knows that giving the new member of staff is going to make her unpopular with the rest of the team, but Caroline has a reputation for being a first-class journalist and Wattle is certain that she will prove her worth. He's also certain that she will prove to the rest of the team that he has made the right choice of who to assign to which job, something that his team have questioned in the past. Wattle suppresses a smirk as he spies Caroline hesitate at the doorway, trying to decide whether or not to allow the door to slam shut in Russell's face.

Clearly, she is aware of the feelings that her colleagues harbour for her. Instead though, she holds the door open so that Russell can catch up with her, and Wattle feels a pang of pride that his new protégé has decided to rise above the jealous gossips.

Wattle waits for his team to dissipate before retiring to the far end of the room, where a tiny office has been carved out at the back of the old building. He pushes the door shut with his foot, leaving one hand free to open the top drawer of his filing cabinet and retrieve a half-empty bottle that is nestled amongst some of the old green suspension files. The other hand deftly unscrews the lid and tips up the bottle to pour a large glug of whisky into his coffee. He sits down heavily into the old armchair that takes up one corner of the room and surveys his life, which is plastered in print across the walls; infamous headlines; photos of his most poignant moments and his degree certificate in prime position behind his desk. Wattle takes a sip of whisky and allows his eyes to settle over one object at a time, allowing himself to feel a small sense of pride for all that he has achieved. At school he was always considered to be the dunce of the class, teased by his classmates for his Suffolk accent and rural ways. His teachers were adamant that he would never make anything of his life. Wattle swigs back the remainder of the liquid then pours himself another shot. He nestles back into the sagging green scatter cushions and looks again at the walls that surround him; the extent of his achievements, his life displayed before him. This is it he thinks. This is all I have done with my life. Wattle closes his eyes, refusing to allow the tears to flow.

The traffic is unsurprisingly light given the early hour of the day. It takes Morgan and Fallow just over an hour to reach Marham, where they meander through the now familiar narrow residential roads. They park outside the front of the Victorian property once more, which is encased in darkness, appearing to be unoccupied.

Despite the low temperature and early hour, an elderly neighbour is busily pruning the Hebe's and Rhododendrons that almost entirely consume his front garden. The two men clamber out of the car and make their way towards the neighbour.

'Can I help you?' The neighbour asks as the two men approach.

'We're police detectives from Suffolk,' Morgan explains, extracting his ID card from the front pocket of his coat. 'We're looking for Mr Fields who lives next door to you. Have you seen him recently?'

'Stan Smith,' the man replies, removing one of his gardening gloves then reaching across the fence to shake Morgans outstretched hand. 'No sorry, I haven't seen him. Come to think of it, I haven't seen his girlfriend either for a while.'

'His girlfriend?' Morgan asks.

'Pretty young thing, slim with blond hair. She's been living here for a few months now.'

'I don't suppose you know her name?' Fallow says, trying to catch Morgans attention in case he has not realised the significance of what the old man has just said.

'I think it's Lucy, but I'm not a hundred percent sure.' The elderly man wrinkles his brow in concentration. 'I do know that she's got a black Honda Civic though. It's a lovely car. Mr Fields bought it for her as a Christmas present. Very generous of him, especially given the current economic situation. I'm surprised he could spare the cash. Or maybe it was on finance, they all seem to do that these days. Come to think of it I haven't seen the car for a few days either. Maybe she's left him. I wouldn't be surprised as they argue a lot. That's the problem with these old houses, very thin walls.'

Morgan looks at the old man, his heart thumping. 'Do you know where Mr Fields might be now? We really need to find him.'

'Well, he could be at work, I suppose. I think he works on the industrial estate. He's got an IT business - only a small one but he seems to have been doing pretty well.'

'Thank you, Mr Smith, you've been a great help. Can I give you my mobile number so you can let me know if Mr Fields returns?' Morgan passes a card over the fence.

Stan Smith grabs the card with his gnarly fingers then carefully pushes it into a trouser pocket. The elderly neighbour rubs the back of his hand to warm it a little, then replaces the glove and directs his attention back to his pruning, seemingly forgetting the presence of the two police officers.

Following the directions given to them by Stan Smith, the two men race to the nearby industrial estate to locate Luke Fields office. They drive around the seemingly never-ending winding roads, without once passing any signs to indicate the locations of the businesses housed on the estate. Eventually they find the office towards the end of the industrial estate, a small sign above the door announces 'Fields Futures'.

The car park in front of the unit is empty. It looks as if only one of the neighbouring buildings is currently in use; a car repair centre with a number of cars crammed inside a tiny fenced off area. Morgan immediately spots a CCTV camera at the front of the building, but notices that it is fixed and pointing in the direction of the car lot, away from Luke Fields office. A more detailed glance of the area does not reveal any other CCTV, or by the looks of it, any other neighbours.

Fallow follows closely behind Morgan, who is already striding across the concrete car park towards 'Fields Futures'. Despite being much shorter with a smaller stride, Morgan reaches the partially glazed door first and raps loudly on the door. He waits for a few moments, then tries the door handle. As expected, the door is locked.

Peering through the letterbox reveals a large pile of post on the other side of the frosted glass.

'There's not much more we can do here, we'd better head back to the station,' Morgan says with a heavy sigh, frustrated at their lack of progress. 'We'll ask the local police to search his office and house if we don't hear from him soon.'

'Yes boss,' Fallow responds playfully, trying to lighten the heavy atmosphere that has descended across the industrial estate.

Morgan rolls his eyes. He is not in the mood for Fallows crass attempts to bond with him. 'I'll drive,' he announces, walking back around the car to the driver's side before Fallow has the chance to protest. He cannot work out whether the sense of despair he is feeling is from his low mood or from the tense atmosphere across the unnaturally quiet estate - there is an anticipatory eeriness to the place which is making Morgan feel quite uneasy. The only thing he wants to do right now is to get their journey over and done with as quickly as possible, especially given that his patience with Fallow is beginning to wane already.

The two men travel back to Deben Quay in silence, each lost in their own thoughts. The traffic is still quite light and there are no accidents holding up traffic for once - an ever-increasing source of annoyance for Morgan. Luck is on their side though this time and they reach the riverside town in a little under two hours. Morgan barely acknowledges Fallows cheery goodbye when he stops outside the front of the station building to drop him off, with firm instructions for him to contact Marham police station and distribute a description of Luke Fields.

As soon as the passenger door clicks shut, Morgan reaches over and turns up the radio, then indicates to pull back out into the traffic flow so that he can continue onwards towards the sailing club. Still feeling irritated with Fallow, though without knowing why, Morgan tries instead to concentrate on the song that is being played on the radio but his mind refuses to let go of its thoughts. For some reason the young man really irked him. Perhaps it is his ever-eager attitude to please everybody; a trait Morgan would never deign to do, and which of course is the sole reason why he has not been promoted higher than his current rank.

By the time Morgan reaches the other side of town, his irritancy has somewhat dissipated. As usual, he leaves the car in Ferry Lane and walks the remainder of the journey along the unmade road to the quayside, sidestepping the usual detritus that litters the path and unkept verges. The sailing clubhouse is only a few metres further up but even so, Morgan is cold by the time he reaches the building.

There are few signs of activity at the club house; the front door is shut and the place is shrouded in darkness. With only a feint flicker of hope that his journey has not been in vain,

Morgan rings the buzzer. He paces up and down impatiently and is about to give up when a figure appears at the door.

'I'm so sorry for keeping you,' Sally Stockbridge says, looking slightly dishevelled.

'Sorry to bother you again, but I wondered if you'd had any updates on the kayak?' Morgan stops pacing for a moment, which he instantly regrets as a damp chill immediately begins to seep into his legs.

Sally runs her fingers through her long hair, trying to detangle the curls. 'Oh dear, I completely forgot about it. Have you got time to come with me to the lock-up now?'

'Ok,' Morgan says tersely, pushing up the sleeve of his coat to look at the stainless-steel watch on his left wrist. 'While we're there, do you have CCTV at the lock-up?'

'We do, but to be honest I don't know when the tape was last changed. We tend to just record over the one that's in there. I know it's bad practice, but at this time of year little happens around here. We can take a look though, if you like?'

The lock-up is only a short distance from the sailing club, slightly further along the quayside path in the direction of the town, nestled between two boat yards.

'It's used to store wetsuits, kayaks and other equipment that's hired out to members of the sailing club,' Sally informs Morgan as they walk along the path.

As they approach the building, Morgan immediately spots that the main door has been forced open, the broken padlock having been hastily discarded onto the ground.

'When was the last time you came here?' Morgan asks as he carefully opens the door to look inside, taking care not to touch anything.

'I'm not sure. It certainly wouldn't have been since Sunday, as you lot have stopped anyone from coming down here.'

'So, this could have happened on Saturday night then?'

'I guess so, or it could've been before then. Some of the canoes are kept at the club house in the winter. We have so few clients that we just keep a couple to hand just in case. We would've used those ones on Friday and Saturday. I'll have to look through our records to see the last time a large number of people hired out any equipment. I'm not even sure if I've been down here since I did a stock take at the end of October,' Sally rambles, her cheeks reddening.

To add to Morgans annoyance, the singular CCTV camera inside the lock-up has been smashed and the tape inside destroyed. 'I'll get someone to secure the lock-up for you,' Morgan says reassuringly. 'In the meantime, let's go back to the club house and go through those records.'

'Sure,' Sally replies, visibly upset that someone would target a small business that relies heavily on its limited stock.

As they arrive back at the clubhouse, Morgan and Sally both notice a woman waiting outside, accompanied by a short, dark-haired man.

'Hi, I was hoping to talk to someone from the sailing club,' Caroline Woods says in an over-friendly manner.

'Oh no, not more interruptions,' Sally responds curtly. 'There's nothing I can tell you.'

'We just wondered if the kayak found near Lucys body was from here?' Caroline persists.

'Sorry, but we can't say anything at the moment. Any information regarding the case is confidential,' Morgan interjects. He ushers Sally back into the sailing club then follows suit, shutting the door behind him. Morgan watches pointedly until the journalists retreat back down the gangplank.

'Do you have a list of the serial numbers for the equipment in the lock-up?' Morgan asks, once he is certain that they are alone.

'Of course, I've got the paperwork here, I'm not that inept you know,' Sally snaps, striding off into the small office.

Morgan holds back a retort as he pulls out his notebook, which contains the serial number of the kayak that was found in the river close to Lucy Mortimers body. He watches as Sally retrieves the stock list from a tall filing cabinet, momentarily wondering why it is that the club have not yet computerised their records, but, he supposes, it seems likely that those employed at a sailing club are more interested in boats then computers.

Sally returns with a book and opens it to the required page, then offers it to Morgan so that he can take a look for himself.

Morgan traces down the list with his finger. Less than half-way down, he finds what he is looking for; a serial number that matches the kayak that is currently stored in the forensics warehouse. Morgan places the book into an evidence bag and then opens the outer door ready to step back out onto the gangplank.

'I'll need to keep this as evidence. Perhaps in the meantime you could look into investing in a burglar alarm?'

'Sure, thanks,' Sally mutters under her breath.

'Well, thanks again for your time,' Morgan says as he passes through the door and shuts it firmly behind him. He feels a slight jolt of excitement that at long last progress is being made.

Chapter 13

Cook is decidedly feeling that he has drawn the short straw, having been primed with the unenviable task of visiting the Mortimers house to inform them that their daughter's death may not have been an accident after all. To make things even more awkward, several scenes of crime officers will be accompanying him to search Lucys room. However uncomfortable it makes him feel to carry out such an odious task, Cook understands that it is a necessary part of the investigation; sometimes it is the family members know the least about what actually went on in their loved one's lives and bedrooms often hid their darkest secrets.

Lucys room looks as if it has not been decorated since the nineteen eighties; with its' pale pink walls adorned with a floral border that horizontally divides the room. Pink venetian blinds stretch across the narrow PVC window that overlooks the neat front garden. The shelves above the bed and desk are filled with books, teddy bears and other childhood souvenirs. The bed looks as if it has not been touched since Lucy disappeared; the duvet is still crumpled from its occupants last slumber in the house.

For all intents and purposes, the room resembles that of a teenager, not of a grown woman deduces Cook, who is standing in the doorway to the small rectangular room. He pads softly across the deep-pile carpet towards the window and pulls open the top drawer of the knotted pine desk and begins to sift through the letters, certificates and newspapers clippings that are stuffed inside. At the back of the second drawer is a scrap book.

Cook sits down on the edge of the bed and flicks through the childish drawings and collages of pictures that Lucy arranged onto the pages, the montage giving an interesting snapshot of the young woman whose life has been cut short. By the time he finishes looking through the scrap book, Cooks calf muscle has started to seize up from an old rugby injury that sometimes flares up, especially in cold weather. Cook stretches the limb out straight and wiggles his foot a little to ease the cramp, whilst promising himself yet again that he will find time to start swimming again and strengthening up the leg.

With the pain easing, Cook stands up and walks back across the room where he replaces the book into the drawer. On the top of the desk are the usual clutter that you would expect to find in a young female's bedroom; a furry pink case full of felt-tip pens, magazine clippings from fashion pages and a large notepad containing pencil-drawn images. The only item that catches Cooks attention is a bible with Lucys name and age written on the inside of the front cover in a childish scrawl. He places the item back again, suddenly feeling ashamed of the disturbance. However necessary it is, Cook cannot help but detest this need to intrude into someone's life in this way.

With the cursory search complete, Cook retreats from the bedroom to allow the forensics team to carry out a more thorough examination. It does not take the experts long to find what Cook missed - a box of diaries underneath the bed, hidden behind a plastic storage drawer. The diaries are covered in dust and clearly not been touched for some time, but they will at the very least provide an insight into who Lucy was as a person.

Cook cannot put off the inevitable any longer. Solemnly he traipses back down the carpeted stairs to the living room. It is time for him to speak to Lucys parents. As he enters the neatly decorated living room that stretches across the length of the house, Mr Mortimer rises from the wing-backed chair he has been perching on.

'I'm sorry to put you through all of this, but it might help us with the investigation,' Cook says, trying not to show his discomfort.

Mr Mortimer nods, tight-lipped, then glances at his wife, who is gently sobbing into a tissue.

'We've spoken to Lucys employer at the pub, but wondered if there was anyone else she might have talked to regularly, perhaps a friend she might have confided in?' Cook asks.

'I'm not sure,' Mr Mortimer replies, looking at his wife. 'She didn't go out much but of course she could have made some friends at work who we didn't know about. She was only doing that job to make some money for university. She wanted to study sociology, to be a social worker. That was Lucy. She was kind and always worried about other people. Do you think she knew whoever it was who was responsible for her death?'

The directness of the question surprises Cook but perhaps the presence of a senior officer and SOCO have alerted the Mortimers to a change in focus of the investigation. 'It is possible that someone was responsible for her death, rather than it being an accident. We need to find out as much as we can about Lucys life, who she knew, where she went. We really need to find out where she was during the last few months and what made her come back to the town.'

Mrs Mortimer stops crying and instead diverts her attention to looking out of the window, as if wishing to escape from the nightmare that has enveloped her. Cook does not want to imagine the pain she must be feeling at losing her only child.

'Thank you for all you are doing,' Mr Mortimer says in a way that makes it clear that the conversation is over.

'I'm sorry again for your loss, please let me know if there's anything I can do,' Cook says awkwardly, before standing up and moving towards the front door. It is time for the couple to be left alone with their grief.

Morgan takes a large stride across the gangplank that stretches across the frothy river, almost slipping on the damp wooden surface. He grabs hold of the narrow handrail with one hand, the other still clutching tightly onto the stock list and feels more than slightly relieved when he makes contact with the concrete path. It is only then that Morgan looks up to discover that Caroline Woods is standing on the path watching him, only a short distance away from the sailing club.

'I'm sorry if I got in the way, I've a job to do as well,' Caroline breezes, running to catch up with Morgan as he squeezes past her and begins to stride off at speed.

'So have I and you're not really helping,' Morgan snaps. He stops abruptly on the path then turns around to give the young woman a withering look.

'Well, as I said I'm sorry. We want to find out what happened to Lucy as well. Our readers want to know the truth,' Caroline says, almost breathless from trying to keep up with the detective.

'I realise that,' Morgan retorts. He takes a deep breath to calm himself. The journalist is after all only trying to do her job. 'Maybe we should try working together on this instead of against each other?'

'Sounds like a good plan.' Carolines face relaxes into a smile. 'Why don't we go for a drink and talk it over?'

'Ok, I'm due for a break anyway. We could try the coffee shop in the high street?'

'I was thinking of something a little stronger,' Caroline laughs.

'I'd better not, I'm still on duty, but I could get a soft drink,' Morgan replies curtly.

They begin walking again, this time side by side. The path takes them towards several boatyards then onwards towards the towns small train station, where they then take a left turn away from the damp, misty quayside. The cobbled path merges onto Sidegate Lane, a one-way street that narrows into a pedestrianised area. On the corner of the two roads is the Rose and Crown, one of the oldest buildings in the area; with a welcoming log fire in one corner and comfy sofas hugging the walls around the cosy room.

At this time of the day and with the drizzly damp weather beginning to worsen, the pub is unsurprisingly quiet. Morgan orders their drinks at the bar whilst Caroline finds an unoccupied table close to the fire.

'So, any suspects yet?' Caroline asks as Morgan approaches clutching a glass in each hand. She pulls her chair closer to the fire, spreading her hands out towards the flames to feel the heat.

Morgan chuckles, 'You don't waste any time, do you.' He gulps down half of his orange juice then places the glass onto the small, mahogany table.

'Life's too short to worry about niceties, don't you think?' Caroline says.

'I suppose so, I hadn't really thought about it. So, have you found out anything we should know about then?' Morgan asks jovially.

Caroline laughs at the policeman's poor attempt at wit though appreciates the effort he is making. 'Nope, I was hoping to find something out from you.'

'Well, it looks like neither of us has anything to say then,' Morgan says, with a hint of a smile forming. He finishes his drink then waits politely for Caroline to finish hers. 'I'd better get back to the station. Here's my card if you think of anything you think I should know.' Morgan winks as he hands over the oblong card.

'Sure,' Caroline says. 'And here's mine, in case you think of anything.'

Morgan reaches over to take the card then pushes it into his trouser pocket. He stands up to pull on his heavy coat then picks up his gloves from the adjoining stool where he left them earlier. 'Thanks for the drink and the chat,' Morgan says before turning around and striding across the deep-pile carpet. After pulling open the weighty outer door, Morgan heads back out into the cold again, without looking back.

Morgan is just pouring himself another coffee when Cook arrives back in the office. 'How did it go at the Mortimers?' Morgan asks, grabbing another mug from the windowsill and filling it with the same bitter concoction.

'We found some diaries that might help,' Cook says unconvincingly. 'Forensics are having them tested first but will let us have them once they've finished. How about you? Did you find out anything at the sailing club?'

'The kayak matches one from their stock list, but they've had a break-in and their CCTV's been vandalised. The break-in could have happened anytime over the last few months as the kayaks they've been hiring out over the winter weren't kept in the lock-up.'

'Damn', Cook says, looking crestfallen at the thought of lost evidence. He sits down heavily into the chair closest to him then cautiously tests the temperature of his coffee, which is starting to cool. Once he is certain the liquid is at a drinkable temperature, Cook begins to sip the coffee, feeling the warmth spreading throughout his cold body.

'I think we should take a look at the CCTV from the town centre, see if Lucy was in town the night she died,' Morgan says. 'Maybe she went back to the Lamb Inn, though I would've thought the landlord would have told us if she had?'

Cook nods thoughtfully before draining the remainder of his mug of its contents that is now almost cold.

'Did the Mortimers know anything that might help?' Morgan asks.

'The parents don't seem to know much about Lucys personal life or if they do, they're unwilling to divulge anything, so no joy there. Let's hope we find Luke Fields soon, we need a break on this one. You might as well go home, hopefully we'll get some better news tomorrow.'

'Well, it can't get much worse can it. Have SOCO managed to find Mrs Fields teeth yet?' Morgan asks, trying to lighten the mood a little.

'No, they haven't, which is a bit strange. Maybe someone's trying to hide her identity?' Cook ponders, placing his empty coffee cup down onto the desk nearest to him.

'You could be right. It's a pity the tearoom doesn't have CCTV. I'll get Fallow to check the town centre cameras tomorrow, see if he can find any trace of Lucy during the weekend she died.' Morgan puts on his coat and heads out through the doorway before Cook changes his mind about letting him go home early.

Morgan cannot put off any longer the unenviable task of telling his wife that the woman who was both her friend and employer is dead. He breaks the news as gently as he can, sitting opposite Celia at the kitchen table.

Celia grimaces as she gulps down the neat whisky Morgan has already poured out for her. 'Does this have anything to do with that other girls' death?' Celia asks before taking a tiny sip of the fiery liquid.

'It might do. It's certainly a strange coincidence that Mrs Fields found Lucy Mortimers body and now she's also dead,' Morgan replies.

'Could she have seen something she shouldn't have?' Celia asks.

'It's possible, or it could just be a coincidence.' Morgan sighs then reaches forward to take hold of his wife's hand. 'At the moment we're just not sure.'

Morgan places Celias hand onto the kitchen table then pushes the chair back, ignoring his wife's automatic grimace as the wooden chair scrapes across the floor leaving a feint black mark on the surface. He walks around the table to stand behind Celia, momentarily squeezing her shoulders, then continues on with his journey to the cupboard above the kettle which he opens to pull out two glasses. A cold jug of water is always kept in the fridge and Morgan fills both glasses, adding ice cubes from the freezer.

An anticipatory silence descends on the household with both occupants lost in their own thoughts, digesting the information that they have learnt and beginning to process the plethora of feelings that are flooding through them.

The silence is eventually broken by Morgan. 'Why don't we go to bed,' he says softly, still holding the glasses of water. Morgan motions for Celia to go through the doorway first, then follows her upstairs. They must try to rest even though it is unlikely either of them will get much sleep given they are still embroiled in a whirlwind of thoughts and memories of a lady who was part of their lives and an important figure in the town, for so many years.

Chapter 14

Despite it being such an early hour that the sun has yet to rise, Cook is already at his desk. He is hoping to take advantage of the empty office to catch up on some work whilst it is still quiet. Even the diligent Fallow will not arrive for at least another hour and Cook relishes the opportunity to work without constant distractions both in the office and at home.

Cook switches on the small desk lamp that is perched precariously on the corner of his overcrowded desk. His eyes are immediately drawn to an unfamiliar object that was not there the previous night; Lucy Mortimers diaries are now stacked on top of the mound of unsorted paperwork in the centre of his desk.

The detective reaches across the ever-growing pile of reports, letters and internal communications to remove the diaries, which are still wrapped in plastic evidence bags. Carefully Cook extracts the books then begins to flick through them though cannot quite bring himself to study them in detail - the thought of reading his own daughters diary uncomfortably sitting at the forefront of his mind. Instead, Cook walks through to the team office next door and hands them over to Fallow, who has just arrived and is eagerly booting up his computer.

'Morning Fallow, can you take a look at these please.'

'Yes boss. What are they?'

'Lucy Mortimers diaries, see if there they mention anyone friends or boyfriends. We need to find out where she was living when she went missing and why she came back here.'

Fallow takes hold of the topmost book and begins to read in earnest whilst the rest of the team begin to filter into the office, their busy chatter filling the once quiet void. As usual, Morgan is one of the last to arrive, an ongoing source of irritation for Cook, who makes a mental note that he will yet again need to chastise his friend for his sloppy conduct. He understands that Morgan is still feeling bitter about being passed over for the top promotion but his childish behaviour will not have helped that particular cause.

Cook leans against the doorframe to his office and tips his head towards Morgan who waltzes past as if he has all the time in the world instead of being in the middle of two serious investigations. Cook bites back the retort he wishes he could make and instead hands to Morgan a forensics report that he is holding. 'Can you go through this please and report back anything of interest?'

'Yes boss,' Morgan says, a cheeky grin erupting across his face.

Cook glares at Morgan then turns around and marches back into his office, slamming the door behind him.

Morgan knows when he has overstepped the mark and meekly sits down behind his desk, where he begins to sift through the preliminary report on the fire at the tearoom. He is almost a quarter of the way through the document, when he is distracted by Fallow rushing past him, waving one of Lucys diaries in his hand.

Morgan watches as the young detective excitedly knocks on Cooks office door then immediately enters the room without waiting. Morgan watches Fallow disappear into the office, then pushes back is chair and follows him, eager to discover the cause of all the excitement.

'Lucy Mortimer did know Luke Fields,' Fallow exclaims, waving the diary about in the air. 'She mentions a guy called Luke who was helping out at a youth club run by the church. She goes on about fancying him and wrote an entry that Luke told her that his father and sister died in a boating accident.'

'Let's take a look,' Cook replies eagerly.

Fallow passes over the book, which now contains a number of lurid yellow post-it-notes. 'I've marked all the places where Luke has been mentioned.'

'Bloody hell, you could be right,' Cook says as he flicks through the marked sections of the book. He pushes back his chair to stand up, only then noticing that Morgan is standing at the threshold to the office. Cook motions for Morgan to come in. 'Morgan, we need to go back to the

Mortimers. It looks like we now have proof that Luke Fields knew Lucy Mortimer.'

'Well, well, well, so Luke Fields' neighbour was right. He said that the girlfriend was called Lucy,' Morgan replies, his grin widening.

Cook places a hand on Fallows shoulder, who is also grinning unashamedly. 'Fallow, can you please contact Marham police, it's time for Mr Fields properties to be searched. Let's also see if he's got a police record as well. After that, we need to go through the CCTV footage for the town centre as a matter of urgency, see if Lucy was in the town centre the night she died.'

Although a grain of suspicion had already been planted by Luke Fields elderly neighbour Stan Smith, that the two cases could be connected, proof was still needed and Lucys diaries might just provide it. It is time for Cook and Morgan to talk to the Mortimers again.

From their position outside the Mortimers house, Cook and Morgan have the perfect opportunity to observe the occupants through the lounge net curtains, which do little to hide any movements inside mainly thanks to a large central ceiling light that lights up the entire room. Mr Mortimer seems to be intensely reading the headlines of the local newspaper over and over again and the two police officers can only assume that the source of such interest is yesterday's police press release that has made the front page of the morning edition.

THE SUFFOLK TIMES
Thursday, 26 February 2006

Suspicious Death at Deben Quay
by Caroline Woods

The death of Lucy Mortimer, whose body was found in the river at Deben Quay on Sunday, is being treated by local police as an unexplained death. A post-mortem revealed that Ms Mortimer drowned sometime either on Friday night or in the early hours of Saturday morning.

Lucy Mortimer was reported missing by her parents several few months prior to her death and police are appealing for any information as to her whereabouts between September 2005 and 22 February 2006. Local police would also like to hear from anyone who was in the quayside area last weekend and may have seen Lucy in the area.

Two Hurt in Car Crash
by Russell Carter

A car skidded off the road on the Thoroughfare yesterday evening. Two of the occupants, who are both residents of Deben Quay, were taken to hospital but are not thought to be seriously hurt. Icy road conditions were probably to blame for the accident. A witness who stopped after the accident stated that the road conditions were very bad and that it did not seem as if the roads had been gritted. The council declined to comment on the condition of the road.

2 for 1 at The Eels Foot

The Eels Foot are offering a 2 for 1 meal during February and March - Sunday to Thursday evenings only. See page 3 for further details.

Rubbish Collections Resume
by Leah Hart

Rubbish collections began again in Deben Quay this morning. Rubbish not collected last week will also be collected this week.

Flowers for You
Special February discount on all bouquets ordered over £25
Tel: 275321

As if suddenly sensing that he is being watched, Mr Mortimer glances up, a look of puzzlement spreading across his face as he notices the two men standing on the path outside his front door. Looking dejected, Mr Mortimer places the paper onto the coffee table then disappears from view.

Mrs Mortimer, who is washing up in the kitchen when she hears the front door open, watches from behind the glazed pine door as her husband leads the two detectives into their sitting room, then turns her attention to making a pot of tea. Just as she is pouring hot water into a teapot, her husband soundlessly opens the kitchen door and shuffles into the room, closing the door quietly behind him.

'We have visitors my dear, the two policemen are here again,' Mr Mortimer says softly. It is only after he has spoken that he notices that a teapot and best cups have been set up on a tray – his wife must have already observed the arrival of their guests. Mr Mortimer picks up the tray and carries it through to the living room, with his wife following meekly behind.

Mrs Mortimer settles into the armchair furthest away from her guests, and watches as her husband sets down the tray onto the enormous glass coffee table that takes up a large proportion of the centre of the room. She then leans forward to set out cups, saucers and a sugar pot, which she leaves close to her guests, accompanied by a delicate stainless-steel spoon. Having stirred the tea pot to ensure that it has had time to brew properly, Mrs Mortimer expertly pours the taupe liquid into the four awaiting teacups.

With the cups of tea duly consumed and polite conversation waning, the two policemen waste no time in setting out the reason for their visit. 'I'm sorry to disturb you both again so soon, but we need to know more about Lucys friends,' Cook explains, almost sounding apologetic.

'I'm sorry, I don't really understand the relevance. As far as I know she hadn't been in touch with anyone from her childhood for years,' Mr Mortimer says, seemingly exasperated by the question. 'She didn't really have any close friends when she was a teenager, if that's what you want to know.'

'She always was a bit of a loner,' Mrs Mortimer chips in. 'She preferred to read quietly in her room rather than go out with friends.'

'Anything at all you can tell us might help,' Cook says. 'Is it possible that she met up with one of them again, perhaps when she was working at the Lamb Inn?'

'She hadn't been there long before she disappeared,' Mr Mortimer responds curtly.

'Were you happy about Lucy working in a pub?' Morgan says, gently placing the China cup onto the coffee table then settling back into the soft leather sofa. 'It seems a strange place to work for someone who was a loner?'

''I suppose so, I never thought about it like that.' Mr Mortimer sighs. 'No, we weren't happy about it. but as I've said before, it was only going to be for a few months until she'd saved up enough for her tuition fees. She valued the experience of working and managing her own finances. She worked very hard you know.'

Cook finishes his tea then sets it down a little more forcefully than he intended, wincing at the loud clanging noise that is made when the delicate teacup comes into contact with the glass table. 'Am I right in thinking that when Lucy was younger, she was a member of St Mary's church youth club?'

Mr Mortimer looks at Cook with narrowed eyes, wondering where the line of questioning is heading.

Cook assumes the silence to be one of affirmation. 'I don't suppose you met a volunteer from the youth club called Luke?'

'No, I did not,' Mr Mortimer replies in a clipped tone. Suddenly he seems to tire of the seemingly pointless questions, stands up and strides across the room to the large bay window that overlooks the neat front garden. Mr Mortimer stands with his back to the room then shoves his hands into his trouser pockets, staring out of the window.

'I think there was a Luke at the club who was a few years older than Lucy, but we don't really know anything else about him. Why do you want to know?' Mrs Mortimer interjects, her cheeks colouring a little.

'We're not sure yet Mrs Mortimer, we're just trying to get a clearer picture of who Lucy knew in the town,' Cook replies. 'Well, we'd better get back to the station. If there's anything else you remember, please phone me, any time of the day or night.'

'Thank you,' Mr Mortimer replies stiffly, his focus returning to the room. He strides across the plush beige carpet and into the hallway, expecting his guests to follow him.

Cook stands up and again expresses his gratitude for their time and promises to let them know if there are any developments. Morgan follows him out into the hallway, where Mr Mortimer is already waiting by the open front door. The front door closes again behind the two police officers, leaving them in no doubt that they have been swiftly ejected from the Mortimer's household. The question is why?

Chapter 15

The journey back to the police station begins in silence, with both men pondering on their next course of action. Eventually it is Cook who breaks the tension. 'What do you think then? Do you think it could be Luke Fields mentioned in Lucys diary?'

'Yes, I do and I also think that the Mortimers know exactly who he is,' Morgan says, turning to look at his friend.

'What makes you think that?'

'Because otherwise the mother would've kept quiet. They're churchgoers, they don't feel comfortable lying to us.' Morgan slows the car down a little to turn into the police station car park, then channels his concentration towards looking for a free space. It takes them a few circuits of the tiny car park to find a suitable space as it is almost full to capacity. Having had his car damaged quite a few times from other officers trying to park in the narrow spaces, Morgan is now somewhat choosier about where he leaves his car. Increasing the size of the car park is not something that could be easily solved, especially given the ever-dwindling budget from Government. Installing CCTV to catch any future culprits would also help of course to alleviate the risk but that too was unlikely to ever happen.

The sun is now rising up higher in the sky as the morning starts to slip away into the afternoon. Morgans stomach reminds him that he has not yet eaten breakfast, so he locks the car and gestures to Cook in the direction of a small café that is only a short distance away from the station.

Cooked breakfasts are served all day at the Honeypot and are a most welcome treat for a weary police officer, not to mention the strong coffee and iced buns that are freshly made onsite. Celia would be appalled if she knew how often her husband ate fried food whilst at work; only healthy, home cooked food is allowed to come out of her kitchen.

'We'd better let the team know what's happening, then do another press release this afternoon,' Cook says, munching his way through a bacon sandwich.

Morgan nods, too busy tucking into a fried egg to respond.

'Hopefully we'll have some more test results in soon,' Cook tries again to engage his friend in conversation.

Morgan grunts affirmatively, wiping a dribble of creamy yellow yolk from his chin with the back of his hand. He pushes the empty plate into the centre of the table then leans back into the chair, swigging down a large mug of strong, sugary tea. 'I wonder if the church youth club keeps records of their volunteers?'

'Good idea, I'll leave that one with you. Hopefully Marham police will have some news on Luke Fields. We could also do with talking to the neighbour again, see if he's seen Mr Fields,' Cook replies before pushing back his chair and standing up. 'Come on then, let's get back to the station.'

'Yes boss,' Morgan teases. He drains the mug of its' last dregs of hot sweet liquid then follows closely behind Cook, who is already making his way out of the door.

Cook notices the email as soon as his computer finally reboots and his email account loads. He clicks on the new email icon then opens the attachment, which contains the preliminary postmortem report for the body in the tearoom.

To: DCI.Cook@DebenQuay.Police.UK
From: DrLenBootle@PathLab.Suffolk.UK
Date: 26 February 2006

Re: Preliminary Findings

To DCI Cook,

The preliminary examination of the body found in the tearoom has now been completed. I can confirm that the body is a female in her late fifties to early sixties. The location of the blotchy purple lividity on the underside of the body confirms that she was not moved for at least twelve hours after death, making it very likely that she died where she was found.

There was no soot in the deceased mouth or lungs and no trace of carbon monoxide in her blood, which suggests she was already dead before the fire started. Her blood tests did not show anything abnormal, only traces of alcohol, paracetamol, naproxen and codeine, which were probably taken for the osteoarthritis that was evident in her knees, wrists and fingers. Initially I did not find any obvious cause of death but after examining her neck, I discovered a tiny fracture of the hyoid bone - she had been strangled. The skin was far too burnt to show any bruising on the neck to confirm but even so, the findings are unequivocal. Tests also confirmed that an accelerant had been poured over the body, though this was also obvious already from the acrid aroma across the centre of the corpse.

Once her dentures have been found or her son (who can provide a DNA sample), I will be able to confirm her identity, which is likely to be Mrs Fields.

Yours faithfully,

Dr Len Bootle

There is also a new email in the teams shared email inbox.

> To: SCS@DebenQuay.Police.UK
> From: Forensics@.Suffolk.org.UK
> Date: 26 February 2006
>
> Re: Results
>
> DCI Cook, We now have the results of the samples taken around the area where Lucy Mortimer's body was found - unfortunately there was little useful evidence from the fingertip search made on Sunday morning due to the high number of visitors to the area. No belongings were found which could be identified as being Lucys. A check on the tides for that weekend indicated that it was possible that if Lucy's belongings had ended up in the river, they could have been caught up in the current and taken down stream to the open sea, where there is little likelihood of them being washed up.
>
> No sig. evidence was found on the kayak either, which is not entirely unexpected given it had been in the water but at the moment there's also no link to Lucy.
>
> We also can't tell if Lucys body entered the water where she was found, or further upstream.
>
> Sorry its not better news!
>
> Forensics team

Whilst Cook and Morgan were visiting the Mortimer's, Fallow spent the morning sifting through seemingly endless hours of CCTV footage from the town centre cameras; hour after hour of scrutinising poor-quality images showing no trace of Lucy Mortimer. Fallow has however had better luck checking the criminal records database.

Name: Luke Fields.
Offence: Sexual assault against a minor.
Outcome: Caution given.

A complaint has been made by a Mr Mortimer that Mr Luke Fields, aged 22, who is a volunteer at a youth club in Deben Quay, has been having an inappropriate relationship with one of the youth cub members. The girl, Lucy Mortimer, denies the relationship but witnesses have reported seeing inappropriate behaviour by Mr Luke Fields towards Lucy Mortimer.

'Well, well, well,' Cook says gleefully. 'I think we need to go and have another chat with the Mortimers again and find out why they've been lying to us.'

Morgan shakes his head in disbelief. 'I thought all those god-botherers were against lying?' He says with his usual lack of tact.

'It would seem not,' Cook responds, resisting the urge to pull Morgan up for not being 'politically correct'. It's no wonder he was given promotion over his friend. Cook follows Morgan down the corridor towards the conference room, their return visit to the Mortimers will have to wait, first they need to address a room of journalists and give them the latest press release.

The conference room is filled with a larger number of journalists than would normally be expected at a small-town police station. The story of the tearoom fire has made national headlines and there are representatives from some of the national newspapers as well as the usual local ones. Cook strides confidently to the front of the room, where he pulls out a chair and settles down into it, nestling behind a metal table as if it is a security blanket. Morgan sits to the left of Cook, with Fallow standing close behind them to observe the proceedings.

Cook takes a sip from the glass of water that Fallow thoughtfully placed on the table when he prepared the room earlier. Quietly he takes in a deep breath to steady his nerves, then begins to read aloud the statement that the comms team have prepared.

Deben Quay Police Press Release - 26 February, 2006

A body has been found in the remains of Mrs Fields tearoom, which was set alight in the early hours of Monday morning. The body has not yet been identified, but it has been confirmed that it is a female in her late fifties to early sixties. Anyone who was in the area of the quayside on Sunday night or the early hours of Monday morning, should contact Deben Quay Police.

The brief announcement is immediately followed by a barrage of questions that Cook politely but firmly refuses to answer - there is nothing else he can tell them at the moment without potentially jeopardising the investigation. He cannot release the identity of the victim until Luke Fields has been found, not just because a sample of his DNA is needed but also because protocol forbids them from disclosing the identity of the deceased without first informing next-of-kin. The last thing they need is to give Luke Fields an excuse to make a complaint against them, especially given that he is currently their only suspect. Cook succinctly ends the meeting then waltzes out of the room with his entourage in tow, before any further questions can be thrown at him.

Chapter 16

Two hours of flicking through the remainder of the CCTV footage from the town centre is giving Morgan a throbbing headache. He decides that his time could be better spent visiting St Mary's church hall to find out whether or not they hold records on their youth club volunteers. Leaving Fallow to continue looking through the footage, Morgan pulls on his coat and steels himself against leaving the warmth of the station to make his way across the town centre to the place where the youth club meets on a weekly basis.

In less than fifteen minutes, Morgan is standing outside the church annex - mock Victorian building, surrounded by neat flower beds and well-tended shrubbery. Morgan pulls open the heavy oak door and walks into the narrow hallway to find three closed doors. The first two doors yield empty rooms, but the third, much larger space, is occupied by a group of older ladies who appear to be enduring, rather than enjoying, a rather energetic keep-fit class.

Morgan quietly walks around the edge of the class to reach the office, which is located towards the rear of the large hall. It is a cramped space, filled with piles of unfiled documents, most of which are on top of a small filing cabinet. Sitting behind a desk in the centre of the room, is an elderly woman, who has a look of confused frustration on her face as she tries to log onto an aging computer that seemingly does not want to cooperate. The woman looks up as Morgan quietly enters the room.

'I'm sorry to disturb you,' Morgan says. 'I'm DI Morgan from Deben Quay police.'

'Margaret Dickinson, youth club leader,' the woman replies officiously, standing up to shake Morgans outstretched hand. 'How can I help you?'

'I'm investigating a recent death that you might have heard about in the news. Unfortunately, a body was found in the river at the quayside at the weekend and she's now been identified as Lucy Mortimer. Lucy used to attend the youth club here and we were wondering if you had any records of children who attended the club and the volunteers who helped out?' Morgan explains.

'Ah, I see. Yes, I did hear about the discovery, poor girl. Well, I've only been working here a few months but I can take a look through the files and see what I can find out. I'm not sure what we would've kept but there should certainly be some paperwork for the volunteers. How far do you need to go back?'

'I'm not sure what age Lucy would have been when she was a member, perhaps the last ten years?' Morgan replies.

'Ok, let's take a look,' Margaret says, pulling open the top drawer of the filing cabinet. The drawer contains a multitude of green suspension files crammed into the narrow space, that by the looks of it, were not in any particular order.

'You look like you could do with some help in here,' Morgan says, leaning against the doorframe.

'I certainly could. I'm still trying to figure out how to do the accounts, let alone finding out how this filing cabinet is supposed to be organised,' Margaret says sharply, as she continues to rifle through the files. Having satisfied herself that there is nothing of interest in the top drawer, Margaret closes it and pulls open the one below. Part way through the middle drawer, she pulls out a file and begins to flick through its contents.

'Ah, this looks more like it. Here's a list here of all those who attended the youth club and also the names and contact details of the volunteers. Are you looking for anyone in particular?' Margaret asks.

Morgan indicates for her to hand over the file, skilfully avoiding answering the question. 'Thanks, I'll need to keep this.'

'I guess that's ok. Could I take a copy first though?' Margaret asks, indicating towards the oversized photocopier that occupies one corner of the room. Without waiting for a response, Margaret strides across the room and lifts up the lid of the photocopier, then places a page onto the flat surface, waits for a new copy to appear in the tray below, then repeats the process over and over again. Once finished, she passes the file to Morgan.

'Well, I'd better leave you to your work', Morgan says, buttoning up his coat. 'Thanks again for your assistance.'

Morgan carefully picks his way back around the perimeter of the room, where the exercise class is now finishing. Fleetingly Morgan wonders if this is where Celia comes for her yoga class. He has never thought to ask where his wife actually goes to on a Monday night.

Once back in the outer hallway again, Morgan quickly scans through the file, his heart thumping as he scrutinises the names on the list. Towards the bottom of the page is the name he has been hoping to see; Luke Fields.

'Bingo,' Morgan exclaims to himself. Pulling out his mobile phone from the inner pocket of his coat, Morgan messages Cook.

> **Fallow was right! Luke Fields did volunteer at the youth club!!**
>
> Good job! We need to get a positive ID of Lucy in Marham, see if the neighbour can identify her
>
> **Yes boss!**
>
> And go and speak to someone at TST, see if they have any old news reports from when the original complaint was made again Luke Fields
>
> **I'll see if that new one – Caroline Woods is about, she seems pretty keen to work with us**
>
> Good idea, let me know later how you get on

Morgan replaces the phone into his coat again, then pulls his scarf around his neck more tightly, bracing himself for the cold walk to the Suffolk Times building, a short distance from the hall. Hopefully the newspaper keeps copies of its old articles, Morgan thinks as he strides across the road to the front of the austere building. The case is starting to look a lot more complicated than they first thought.

The Suffolk Times building is surprisingly quiet for the time of day. The two administrators who are busily tapping away on their computers barely notice Morgan when he walks through the main door of the second floor.

'Hello, I'm looking for Caroline Woods. Is she here?' Morgan asks.

The woman looks up at Morgan and shrugs her shoulders, then returns her focus to the computer.

'Try in there,' says the other administrator, whose name badge identifies him as 'Russell Barker'.

Morgans gaze follows the direction that he is being pointed in, then he walks around the front desks and into the open plan office, where a handful of journalists and designers are busy working. Morgan immediately spots Caroline, who is sitting at a desk towards the back of the room, talking quietly into a mobile phone. As soon as Caroline notices Morgan, she quickly ends the call.

'Hello Caroline, I was wondering if you had anything new for me?' Morgan asks.

'Buy me a drink and I might tell you,' Caroline replies playfully.

Morgan grins at her, then motions towards the exit. He strides across the room to reach the door first, then holds it open for the journalist to pass through. Morgan cannot help but wonder what the delicious perfume is that Caroline is wearing. Whatever it is, it is having an effect on him. Or perhaps it is just from being in close proximity to such a beautiful and talented woman.

Morgan takes a deep breath and shakes himself from his thoughts, then quickly catches up to Caroline, who is already making her way out of the building and striding down the narrow, cobbled path that leads towards the town centre.

The nearest pub to The Suffolk Times building is the Cherry Tree. The pub occupies yet another one of Deben Quays eighteenth-century buildings, that was purpose built to supply the locals with a regular flow of alcohol. As expected for the time of day, it is quiet and they quickly settle into a secluded corner, furthest away from the few regular punters who as always, adorn the bar.

'I wondered if you've heard any new rumours or had any more information that might be of interest to us?' Morgan asks before taking a sip of his bitter shandy.

'Sorry, not anything of any use. We've had a few crackpot calls, as I'm sure you have, but nothing worth repeating. Any luck identifying the body in the tearoom?' Caroline asks.

'We think its Mrs Fields but keep that one to yourself as it hasn't been confirmed yet.'

'Sure! Being discrete is part of my profession,' Caroline teases.

'I'd like to believe that,' Morgan says a little less sincerely than he intended. 'I don't suppose you have access to the newspaper archives, do you? We wanted to look through articles from about ten years ago?' Morgan asks as he gulps down a third of the amber liquid then places the glass back down on the table in front of him.

'We certainly do. What are you looking for?'

'Anything on a church youth club that Lucy Mortimer went to, we think that she may have known one of the volunteers,' Morgan replies evasively.

"Ok...' Caroline replies, clearly intrigued. 'Any name in particular?'

'Yes,' Morgan takes a deep breath, uncertain if he should be divulging something so significant to a journalist. 'Luke Fields, but please keep that one to yourself for now as well.'

'You're kidding!' Caroline says. 'Any relation to Mrs Fields and her now cremated tearoom?'

'Her son as it happens and he seems to have gone AWOL, so we need to keep this quiet until we've found him.'

'Blimey, you find a suspect then lose him!' Caroline teases.

Morgan pauses to drink deeply from his glass again. 'Well at least we have a suspect this early on in the investigation,' he retorts, feeling slightly hurt by her comment.

'Sorry, I didn't mean to offend you. Can I get you another drink?'

'I'd better not, I need to get back to the work.'

Morgan waits politely for Caroline to finish her drink, then escorts her back out of the pub. 'When do you think you'll be able to look through the archive?'

'I'll try and take a look today. I'll let you know if I find anything,' Caroline replies, then turns around to head back up the street towards The Suffolk Times building.

Morgan watches as Caroline Woods sashays her way up the narrow street and wonders if she realises the effect she has on men; somehow, he suspects that she does. As soon as Caroline disappears from view, Morgan turns in the opposite direction to hurry back to the station where Cook should by now have returned.

Over a mug of strong coffee, Morgan relays the conversation that he has just had with Caroline Woods and in turn, Cook updates him on his latest findings after spending the afternoon at the Mortimers house.

'So, what happened when you confronted them,' Morgan asks, blowing on his mug to cool down the scalding liquid to a more drinkable temperature.

'Mrs Mortimer cried when I mentioned the allegation against Luke Fields. Her husband tutted and looked the other way and didn't say anything. Eventually Mr Mortimer said that they had thought it was all behind them and that's where they had wanted it to stay. They didn't think it was relevant as it had been so long ago.'

'What he actually means is he didn't want the scandal to come out again,' Morgan says.

Cook grimaces. 'They did eventually admit that they'd heard Luke and Lucy were more than friends but were never sure of the exact nature of the relationship. They made a formal complaint against him but Lucy wouldn't say if anything inappropriate happened and the so-called witnesses backtracked on their original statement. So, Luke Fields got a caution and the case was eventually dropped. He was made to leave the youth club and as far as the Mortimers knew, he wasn't in contact with their daughter again.'

'Well, they were wrong about that then weren't they. Makes you wonder what else they didn't know about their daughter.'

Chapter 17

As usual, Morgan is up and about early, whilst his wife is still snoring softly with the duvet pulled up tightly under her chin. Morgan has already showered, dressed and is making breakfast, when Celia finally emerges, just as her husband is setting out two mugs on the kitchen table for their morning tea. Morgan stands next to the kettle, lost in thought, as he waits for it to boil. He barely notices when Celia pours out two bowls of muesli and grabs a bottle of milk from the fridge.

Over the roar of the kettle, Morgan just about detects the sound of the morning newspaper being roughly pushed through their letterbox - an action that always riles him - the fragile plastic frame has already been broken once by an overly enthusiastic paper boy trying to feed too much through it. The sound is sufficient to stir Morgan from his thoughts and he heads off to the front door.

Having successfully pulled the now ragged paper through the metal flap of the letterbox without damaging its' plastic casing, Morgan discovers that a report on the tearoom has made front page news. Momentarily he closes his eyes as he realises his utter foolishness in revealing his inner thoughts to a journalist. There in black and white for everyone to see, is the implication that the body in the tearoom is Mrs Fields.

THE SUFFOLK TIMES

Friday, 27 February 2006

Body found in Burnt-Out Tearoom
by Caroline Woods

A body has been discovered in the burnt out remains of Mrs Fields tearoom. The body has not been formally identified but is believed to be that of Mrs Fields, the owner of the business. Relatives of the victim have not yet been located nor informed of her death. Coincidentally, it was Mrs Fields who first discovered the body of Lucy Mortimer whilst out walking her dog on Sunday morning.

A Murder is Announced
by Leah Hart

The Deben Quay Players are performing the Agatha Christie classic, A Murder is Announced at the town hall. The play will be on from Friday 27 February from one week. Tickets will cost £6 each and can be bought in advance from the Cobblers shop on the High Street. Tickets may also be available on the night if it has not sold out. This will be the second show by the Deben Quay Players, which was established one year ago.

Burglary in Deben Quay
by Russell Carter

A house was broken into on Finchingfield Drive yesterday morning between 8.30 to 9.30 AM. Any witnesses to the crime should contact Deben Quay Police.

Flasher in Town Centre
by Leah Hart

A man has exposed himself to three shoppers in the town centre on Tuesday afternoon, near to the recently closed Woolworths store. The man has been described as tall, with dark hair and wearing a dark blue wool hat.

Deben Sailing Club Offer

2 for 1 on all kayak and boat hire during February and March. Phone Sally at the sailing club (Tel: 276539) for further details.

Morgan emits an abundance of expletives before rapidly following this with a vehement chastisement of himself for the school-boy error. He will need to have a chat with Caroline Woods as soon as he can and give her a piece of his mind. He just hopes that the foolish disclosure will not come back to haunt him.

His bad mood now very apparent to anyone close by, Morgan stamps back into the kitchen and flings the newspaper into the bin. He decides to skip breakfast - he has now lost his appetite, instead, he will go straight to work, if he's going to get into trouble then he might as well get it over and done with as quickly as possible.

Just as Morgan is about to close the front door, his phone bleeps. It is Cook, who is already at the station and apparently sifting through the ever-increasing pile of emails.

> Morgan, can you go over to Glebe Cottage before coming in, SOCO found some tyre tracks. They've already taken impressions etc but would be handy to see where exactly they are and get a feel of what type of vehicle might have made them – you know how long it can take to get test results back

> Sure. I'm now on my way

Morgan lets out a sigh of relief at being given a brief reprieve even if it does not last long - Cook is certain to see the headlines soon when he reads the paper with his morning coffee. The unexpected detour will also take his mind off Caroline Woods - for a little while at least.

The frozen furrows on the unmade part of road are clearly visible now that the snow has dissipated. Morgan immediately spots them when he steps out of his car and observes how they stretch from the end of the tarmac road at the bottom of Ferry Lane to the grassy patch in front of Mrs Fields cottage. Morgan barely notices the damp mist that is beginning to curl around the lane as he follows the tracks. He continues past Glebe Cottage and onwards towards the quayside, still following the tracks. At the bottom of the muddy path is a slip way used by sailing boats, so that they can be launched into the grey, uninviting river. There are multiple tyre marks in the mud next to the concrete slipway, which is not unexpected, but they will all need to be investigated further. The area has been cordoned since the fire, so the tyre tracks must have been made before Sunday night. All of the police and fire vehicles that were parked in the area on both Sunday morning and evening will need to be checked even though it is unlikely any of them parked this far away from the tearoom.

Morgan stands at the edge of the river, whose low tide gently laps against the concrete wall and surveys the scene before him; it is easy to become distracted by the beauty of the area and forget that two bodies have recently been found nearby. The thought occurs to Morgan, that if Lucy Mortimers death was not accidental, then this could have been the point where she entered the water. A sobering thought to have so early in the morning.

Finding Luke Fields car must now be a top priority, along with Lucys car, which is still missing. A DVLA search revealed the car to be a black Honda Civic, just as Stan Smith already deduced. Lucys car was also confirmed to be registered at Luke Fields address in Church Lane, Marham.

Morgan begins walking again, following the path that runs alongside the river for a short way, then returning up back up the dirt track once again. He stops to gaze at the burnt-out remains of Mrs Fields tearoom.

The emergency call to report the fire came from a couple who were out late, apparently wanting to take a look at the place where Lucys body was found. Hardly a romantic gesture by a couple in love, Morgan supposes wistfully as he wanders up the path. As the river path had still been closed to the public, the couple had instead walked down the quayside path almost as far as the tearoom, where they spotted flames shooting up from behind the trees. The call was made to the fire service at 12.30 A.M.

Despite the dark clouds threatening to unleash their fury on him, Morgan decides to continue to walk up to Mrs Fields house and take another look inside the building. He unlocks the back door and steps inside, taking care to avoid a torn rubbish bag, whose contents are strewn across the path.

It is difficult to tell if there has been any disturbance inside the property given that its owner was clearly not one who lived in an abode of show-home status and of course the police searched the house earlier in the week, thus adding to the chaos. Perhaps Mrs Fields was in the tearoom when she was attacked ponders Morgan, as he wanders through the small kitchen. Or she could have looked out of the window and seen someone at the tearoom and decided to investigate? The whereabouts of Mrs Fields dog, Nutmeg, made infamous by the discovery of Lucy Mortimers body, is another loose end that needs to be tied up.

With nothing else to see, Morgan reluctantly returns to his car and heads to the station. Cook must have seen the headlines of The Suffolk Times by now and Morgan knows his friend well enough to know that he will be fuming.

In fact, DCI Cook is so incensed at the apparent disclosure of the deceased's identity to the local press, that he is on the verge of threatening the whole team with demotion. Morgan knows that this would never happen and that once Cook has calmed down it will likely all be forgotten, but even so, as soon as the team are dismissed, he decides to own up.

'Boss, can I have a quick chat?' Morgan says gingerly.

Cook looks up from his desk, which is almost buried in paperwork. 'Sure, what's up?'

'I think I may have accidently said something to Caroline Woods about the body in the tearoom. I told her it was to be kept quiet though,' Morgan says through gritted teeth.

'For goodness sake! I expect that sort of behaviour from a junior officer, not from you!'

'It was a really stupid thing to do, I don't need you to tell me that,' Morgan snaps.

'Yes, it was,' Cook retorts. He stares at Morgan for a moment then turns his attention back to the awaiting paperwork. The conversation is over.

Morgan slinks back to his desk and pulls the landline phone towards him, dialling a number that he now knows off by heart. His luck has run out though, as Caroline Woods does not answer. Morgan will have to find another way to deal with his anger at a situation that he could have avoided if he had not been so careless.

He takes a deep breath, still simmering, then turns his attention to helping Fallow, who has finished watching the CCTV footage of the town centre and has now been tasked with trawling through the remainder of Lucy Mortimers diaries. Morgan picks up one of the diaries and takes it back to his desk to read through it. It does not take long to discover another possible lead; several of the entries in Lucys diary mentions a friend at the church youth club named Anna. No surname is mentioned though so they will need to talk to the Mortimers again to see if they can shed any light on her identity.

Morgan meekly informs Cook of the development and is unsurprised that his still angry friend, immediately sends him, with Fallow in tow, to the Mortimers, knowing that the grieving couple will not be pleased by yet another visit.

Morgan always feels a little surprised when he receives little contact from the deceased's family, especially if the death may not be accidental but has to admit to himself that everyone handles grief in different ways. Perhaps, he surmises, the Mortimers think that it's best to leave the investigation to the professionals. Morgan does not feel convinced though, if it was his child who had died, he would have been constantly badgering the police for updates. Being a father though is of course not something that he will ever experience, Morgan recalls with a bitter pang as he walks up to the front path to the Mortimers house with Fallow following closely behind. Morgans instinct is telling him that something is amiss and he cannot help but wonder if perhaps the Mortimers do not want something to come out. It is time to put that particular theory to the test.

Morgan does little to hide his relief when he sees that it is Mrs Mortimer who answers the door, as she is likely to be much more forthcoming without her husband's presence.

As Mrs Mortimer politely shows the two men into the immaculate living room, Morgan apologises for the inconvenience of disturbing her yet again.

'Of course, officer I understand. How can I help you?' Mrs Mortimer asks sedately.

Morgan wonders if she has taken some kind of tranquiliser, which would not be entirely unexpected given the circumstances. 'Thank you for talking to us again, we appreciate anything you can tell us about your daughter.'

Mrs Mortimer smiles sadly, then wanders off into the kitchen, returning a few minutes later with a tray. She sits down in one of the floral covered armchairs then pours tea from the teapot into three mugs. When all three cups are filled almost to the top, Mrs Mortimer offers a cup to each detective.

Morgan takes a sip of the milky drink more out of politeness than his need for refreshment. He has always detested tea but understands that Mrs Mortimer may feel the need to fulfil her role as a host, if only to distract her from her daughter's death for a short while.

'We found a reference in one of your daughter's diaries to a girl called 'Anna'. It seems she was friends with at the church youth club and we wondered if you had any contact details for her?'

'Goodness me, that was a long time ago.' Mrs Mortimer looks up at Morgan in surprise. 'I'll go and look through our old address book, see if there's anything in there.'

Fallow waits for Mrs Mortimer to leave, then wanders around the room, inspecting the multitude of ornaments and pictures scattered throughout the lounge. 'Have you noticed there aren't any pictures of Lucy?'

'Yes, I have. There's nothing here to suggest they ever had a daughter, it's like they've cut her out of their life. But oddly her bedrooms not been touched since she was a teenager,' Morgan replies.

'Strange really, I don't know what to make of it,' Fallow says as he meanders his way back to the sofa.

At that moment Mrs Mortimer returns, clutching a black address book in her right hand, which she passes to Morgan with the appropriate page open so that he can copy down Anna Jackamans details. Morgan thanks Mrs Mortimer again for her help, then the two men retreat from the house, leaving the bereaved mother with a promise that she will be kept informed of any developments.

Both men are deep in thought during the short drive back to the station. Morgan thinks they should prioritise speaking to Anna Jackman – it is a long shot but every lead is worth pursuing. He is not certain however that Cook will agree with him and given his current mood, Morgan is not too keen to find out. Still, the first task he allocates to Fallow back in the warmth of the office again, is to check up on the address they have been given.

For once they are in luck - Anna Jackamans parents still live at the same address given to them by Mrs Mortimer and a quick phone call reveals that although Anna Jackaman is currently away, she is due to return home on Sunday evening. Fallow scribbles down Anna Jackamans address and phone number and passes it to Morgan.

Despite the breakthrough, Morgan is feeling more than a little fed up and decides that it is time to call it a day. He shuts down his computer and retrieves his coat from the stand.

The heavens open up just as Morgan steps outside the back door of the station. He mumbles a curse to himself for yet again forgetting his umbrella, which is hanging up in the porch at home. He will have to make a run for it, he decides, as the rain does not show any signs of letting up. Even so, by the time Morgan reaches the car, he is soaked through.

Once inside, Morgan tears off his coat and flings it onto the empty car seat beside him. With the engine switched on, the heater is soon blasting out hot air but it does little to dry Morgan and instead leaves him uncomfortably warm and wet all at the same time. He sits in the car for a moment, watching the heavy rain pelting large droplets down onto the windscreen. The weather perfectly reflects his mood he concludes, as he reaches over to turn up the radio.

The uplifting sounds from the local radio station manage to lift his mood a little by the time Morgan pulls out of the car park to join the rush hour traffic. The last thing Morgan needed at that precise moment was for the usually short drive home to be hampered by roadworks. He has barely driven half a mile when the car comes to a stand-still at the back of a long train of traffic. Morgan drums his fingers on the steering wheel, his left foot pumping up and down onto the floor, his mood worsening again despite the cheerful music blaring out of the radio. After what seems to be a very long time, the temporary traffic lights turn green and Morgan pulls out onto the other side of the road to bypass the roadworks. As Morgan passes by the workers who are diligently digging holes in the pouring rain, he even manages to allow a small smile to form on his tight face. At least he is dry now, unlike those poor people outside in the freezing torrent. By the time he pulls up outside his house, the rain has begun to ease along with his demeanour.

Celia Morgan is not usually the type of person to flap over preparing a meal for guests but given that their guests are DCI Cook and his wife, she is feeling a little under pressure to perform her duties well as a police officers' wife. Celia spends most of the day preparing for the evening ahead, deciding on the menu as well as which type of wine to drink with the dishes she has chosen. Planning a dinner party is something that she normally enjoys doing, much to the bemusement of her husband, who has neither the time nor the inclination to cook. For some reason though, on this occasion Celia is feeling a little apprehensive.

If he had his own way, Morgan would probably eat out every night and then die a premature death from heart disease considers Celia, as she peels and slices a bag of carrots. Having watched her own father die from a stroke, Celia is all too well acquainted with the long-term effects of a poor diet and lifestyle and is determined to save her husband from himself. At least Morgan seems to enjoy running so he does get some exercise, recalls Celia, though she has never quite understood the appeal of getting cold, hot and sweaty all at the same time. The thought reminds her of the need to chat to Morgan again about getting a dog. It will be company for her as well as also being a good way to encourage her to exercise, something she has a tendency to avoid rather than embrace. Maybe something like a King Charles spaniel would be ideal? There are always adverts in the local paper for dog training classes on a Thursday night, which would give her something to do other than sitting at home waiting for her husband to return home from work.

Celia often ate alone whilst her husband worked. Reheating his meal when he returns is something Celia intensely dislikes doing as she knows it will never taste as good as when it has just been freshly cooked but often she has no choice but to do just that. She wonders what she should do with her spare time now that she has no job to go to. Perhaps she should look for another job or even voluntary work, something with more meaning to it than just waitressing in a café?

Celia places a saucepan onto the hob then fills it with the sliced carrots and Brussel sprouts. As the colourless liquid begins to boil, she turns down the gas a little, then pulls out a kitchen chair and sits down heavily onto the hard surface. Celia allows her mind to wander, reminiscing about the time when she first met Morgan; she has never forgotten the first time she saw him across the playground, with his chestnut hair fashioned into a mullet and his school uniform too small for his gangly limbs - it had taken another three years before they had finally become an item. It seems so long ago now, Celia mused, she almost feels as if she is a different person from that young girl.

Wearily Celia rises from the chair to put a tray of potatoes that she prepared earlier into the oven. The first time she learnt to cook roast potatoes had been just before her wedding, when Morgan was still training to be a police officer. She had felt so proud the first time she had seen Morgan wear his uniform. Around the same time, Morgans friendship with Cook had blossomed and it seemed only natural that the two wives should also become friends. The lack of children in the Morgan household though has slightly driven a wedge between the two women, who are by now leading very different lives. Still, it is always nice to have some company Celia decides, as she sets out placemats and cutlery on the dining table then fusses over the place settings.

DCI Cook and his wife Sarah arrive promptly at seven o'clock, bringing with them a bottle of wine for Morgan and a box of chocolates for Celia. It is raining again and the couple are soaked through by the time the front door of the 1980's semi-detached house opens. Morgan tries and fails spectacularly not to smirk as he takes the dripping coats from his guests and hangs them up, inadvertently blocking his guests from leaving the porch and entering the house.

'James, perhaps you could actually let our guests into the house and make them a tea or coffee, they look as if they need warming up,' Celia says pointedly.

Morgan, bristling from the chastisement, ushers the Cooks through to the sitting room and positions them in front of the electric fire. Then he hurries into the kitchen, returning a few minutes later with two steaming mugs of coffee. Whilst in the kitchen, Morgan also opens the bottle of Merlot that Cook has brought with him, to leave it to breathe until the main course of roast beef is ready to be served.

'How thoughtful of Celia to serve soup as a starter, its ideal for this kind of weather,' Sarah purrs, her clothes still a little damp as she takes a seat at the mahogany dining table, with her husband sitting opposite her.

Celia moves to the head of the table and dips a silver-plated ladle into a large porcelain dish, from which she portions out a good measure of soup for each of them. Morgan, practiced in his wife's exacting requirements in dinner party etiquette, immediately passes around a large platter of sliced fresh bread to his guests.

Once the warming soup has been eaten, Morgan quickly clears away the bowls into the kitchen. Although he does not relish these occasions, he knows that his wife appreciates having company. Each time he is late home from work, he feels guilty that Celia is sitting at home alone. He wonders if there is anything else he could do to occupy his wife's time, perhaps he could look out for another job for her? Nothing too stressful, just something where she can get out of the house and meet new people.

Morgan hurries back to the dining room to relieve Celia of her hosting duties, so that she can return to the kitchen to tend to the main course. Ten minutes later, Celia has served up a huge plate of sliced roast beef, accompanied by two porcelain terrines of seasonal vegetables.

'This looks wonderful,' Cook exclaims as Celia passes him a plate, stacked high with the well-cooked meat.

Celia beams at her husband, then urges her guests to all help themselves to the steaming vegetables. It is moments like these that make all the other lonely times worthwhile, Celia concludes as she begins to tuck into the meal.

After a somewhat stilted start to the night, the conversation begins to flow more smoothly as the evening goes on, oiled by the copious amounts of wine that Celia has chosen for each individual course. The two wives manage to deftly steer the conversation away from the investigation and instead concentrate on more amenable topics, such as holidays and the weather.

It is obvious to Morgan that Cook is bored with the topic of conversation, so he deftly ushers him into the kitchen under the guise of helping to clear away the dinner plates, so that they can chat whilst they polish off the remainder of the beef that Celia had been intending on saving for another meal.

'I'm really sorry about what happened,' Morgan says sheepishly.

'Let's just forget about it, especially tonight. Anyway, the case seems to be progressing now at a good pace.'

'True, though I would feel a lot happier if we could locate Luke Fields,' Morgan replies.

Cook does not have the opportunity to respond as his wife enters the room, carrying two wine glasses in each hand. 'I hope you two aren't talking shop,' Sarah says as she places the glasses onto the work top next to the sink.

Cook reaches across to kiss his wife on the cheek. Sarah always seems to know just how to handle him - one of the many things he loves about her.

Celia has excelled herself in preparing four sumptuous courses to feed her guests with and by the time they finish the apple crumble along with the cheese and biscuits, they are all too full and sleepy to bother drinking the dessert wine Celia chose for the course. Even though it is only ten o'clock, the Cooks decide that it is time to leave, with the excuse that they need to get back to their children, as well as to catch up on some much-needed sleep - their youngest daughter is teething and waking them up at frequent intervals throughout the night.

Even though Celia feels a little put out by her guest's early departure, she is also gratified by the praise that has been lavished upon her and a warm glow of happiness rushes over her as she washes the remainder of the dishes, then sets them aside to dry on the draining board. By the time she creeps into bed though, with her husband already asleep, Celias good mood rapidly fades and the short-lived feeling of fulfilment is replaced by one of emptiness again.

Chapter 18

The weekend is looking promising for the Morgans, as they sit in their warm conservatory with a pot of tea, accompanied by a simple breakfast of warmed croissants and a large bowl of prepared fruit. Whilst they relax over their breakfast, the couple discuss their plans for the day.

'Let's go to the plant sale at the church hall,' Celia enthuses as she watches Morgan polish off the remainder of the pastries. As a keen gardener, she is always looking to add to her collection of plants and is especially keen on ornamental grasses and miniature Japanese maples. This time though she is looking for vegetable seeds to sow in time for the seedlings to be ready to plant outside once the bitter frosts have ceased.

Morgan has barely finished his second cup of tea when Celia removes the delicate China cup from his large hand and pulls him towards the front door like an excited puppy hoping for a long walk. Morgan takes one last longing look at the newspaper, which still lies unread on the conservatory sofa and concedes defeat. The paper can wait, Celias unbridled enthusiasm cannot.

The plant sale is being held at a church hall a mere five-minute stroll from the Morgans home. Celia quickly finds the plants that she is looking for on one of the stands then locates three novels as well as a coffee and walnut cake from two of the other stalls. With the desired items located, the couple are ready to head back home for lunch, where they enjoy a simple meal of homemade vegetable soup and granary bread from their local bakery. After the light meal has been eaten, Celia heads off outside to the small greenhouse located at the bottom of their garden. Morgan heads for the sofa, where his newspaper is still awaiting his attention.

After an hour or so in the garden, Celia is far too cold to bear being outside any longer and returns to the house, where she begins to plan their evening meal. Dinner will need to be something fairly quick to prepare as the couple have tickets for the evening performance of an Agatha Christie play that is being performed by the Deben Quay Players. Celia deftly prepares a garden salad, sirloin steak and homemade chips, ready to cook before their long-awaited evening out. It is at this point that their weekend goes awry - before Celia has even washed her hands in preparation of cooking the meal, the shrill tone of the phone interrupts the calm ambience of the Morgan household.

Morgan listens carefully to the news that another body has been found at the quayside, not far from where Lucy Mortimer was discovered. The body was found early afternoon by a group of teenagers, who were trying to get a closer look at the area where Lucy Mortimers body was discovered, now that the police cordon at the end of Ferry Lane has been removed. As soon as they had reached the quayside path, the group spotted a vagrant lying on the bench in the old bandstand; a torn sleeping bag wrapped around him and an empty bottle of cheap gin lying askew beneath the bench. The teenagers had quite understandably assumed the man was asleep, and less understandably, had proceeded to mischievously poke the old man in order to wake him from his apparent drunken snooze. Instead, they were the ones who were surprised, when they could not wake him up and eventually, they realised that the man was dead. Within half-an-hour of the phone call to the emergency services being made, a local GP had certified that the male was indeed deceased and the police duly notified of the situation. It was at this point that Chief Superintendent Bennett decided that DCI Cook should mobilise his team given that the area seems to have become rather too popular a place of late for dead bodies.

As Morgan reaches the river path, the areas either side of the bandstand are being cordoned off by a uniformed police officer. Morgan mutters loudly under his breath as he makes his way towards the officer then flashes his ID card at them as he ducks underneath the tape. Surely this is not something that warrants interrupting his weekend off and if it is, then the area should have been secured earlier before half of the town has had the chance to traipse through it. It certainly appears to be a straightforward death decides Morgan and not entirely unexpected given that a homeless person was sleeping rough during a bitterly cold winter.

Morgan stops on the concrete path just outside the bandstand to chastise himself; it is unlike him to be so uncharitable. Perhaps he should consider a career change if he has become so de-sensitised that he thinks so little of the demise of another human being.

The detective stands next to one of the peeling upper struts of the Victorian structure that is sorely in need of repair, and watches as a scene-of-crime officer retrieves an empty gin bottle from underneath the bench. Although the assumption is that cause of death will not be suspicious, an inquest could still be needed and so evidence must be gathered with the usual duty of care.

'What do you think then?' Morgan asks Dr Bootle, as the aging pathologist appears at the bandstand.

'Looks quite straight forward to me,' Dr Bootle shrugs his shoulders. 'We'll do a PM though in any case.'

Morgan smiles tight-lipped as the pathologist gathers up his bag from the ground, where he left it only moments before and strides off towards the town centre. It seems that Morgan is not the only one who is displeased at having their weekend interrupted.

Morgan stays at the quayside just long enough to ensure that everything has been put into place to secure any potential evidence, then makes his way back to the car, feeling thoroughly cold and irritated by the intrusion on a rare weekend off. He sits in the car for almost as long as the time he has just spent on the quayside, waiting for the car to warm up. When he can no longer delay putting off the inevitable, Morgan reluctantly makes his way back home, fully expecting that he will receive a frosty reception from his wife.

Morgan did indeed correctly guess the mood that Celia would be in when he returned home, which was by now too late for them to make the start of play. Celia barely brought herself to speak to her husband all evening, conducting dinner in near silence and only making the occasional polite comment to ease the tension. Once the meal was eaten, she went upstairs to have a long soak in a bubble-filled bath before going to bed early.

Although Morgan can understand his wife's disappointment at their planned evening going so awry, he does still feel slightly perplexed at her attitude, after all, she knew what his job entailed when she married him. The thought momentarily crossed his mind that he could go to the pub for a couple of pints and salvage what is left of the evening but he does not want to risk making the atmosphere at home any worse, so instead, Morgan settles down in front of the TV to watch the tedium of Saturday night television for a while before joining his wife, who is already asleep, in bed.

Sunday morning starts out bright and sunny, the glowing rays of the winter sun seemingly clearing the low mood the couple found themselves in the previous evening. The Morgans decide to make the most of the good weather and start clearing away all the autumnal debris that is littering their small but private, garden. Celia appears to have put aside her disappointment from the previous night and is humming a tune to herself as she rakes up the fallen leaves then dead heads the rose bushes. The couple managed to squeeze a small vegetable patch into their garden the previous summer and it is currently housing the bolted vegetables they forgot to dig up at the end of the season. Dealing with the patch is next on Celias to-do list. The old plants will need to be removed and the soil turned over ready for the new crop she will plant later in the year.

  Morgan detests gardening but it is a job that needs to be done and in his opinion, one that is best completed as quickly as possible. Celia, who is well aware of her husband's feelings, goes to considerable effort to keep her husband well fed, producing his favourite toffee apple sponge to help sweeten the tedium of the menial tasks.

  Although the sun is out, it is still chilly and after only two hours Morgan has had quite enough of being outside and instead retreats to the warmth of the sitting room. By the time Celia also decides to call it a day, Morgan is already snuggled up on the sofa underneath a huge fake fur blanket, snoring in front of the TV.

Dr Bootle volunteering to be on-call is almost unheard of, especially on a Sunday when he is usually found on the golf course. Certainly, it is not something that has occurred for many years, having always managed to find a locum to cover for him. But, having cancelled his plans for a romantic weekend away to Paris with his long-term partner Eric, Len Bootle decides it would be better to fill the empty hours with anything that could fully occupy his mind, even if that 'something' happens to be work. The couple have been in a relationship now for nearly ten years and never before had such a vicious row, leaving Len wondering if their relationship will survive - especially given that their row was over his ongoing reluctance to marry. The thought of conducting a postmortem however has cheered the pathologist up a little. He knows that it will take his mind off things for a while and hopefully divert him from the constant re-runs in his mind of his row with Eric. Perhaps a little distance between them will help to resolve things, Len contemplates wistfully, as he makes his way from his Jaguar XJS to the back door of the mortuary suite.

    The body from the bandstand was brought into the morgue the previous evening and Harry is already preparing it for examination. The elderly man's clothes, which have already been removed and checked for possessions, were incinerated last night due to their hazardous condition. It is clearly some time since the man last washed and the smell is so intense that Harry almost retches as he lays him out on the mortuary slab and takes fingerprints and hair samples.

Just as Harry is finishing preparing the body, the main door to the mortuary suite is flung open and Len Bootle waltzes in, pulling on a pair of rubber gloves as he approaches the table. He takes down a Dictaphone from a shelf and switches it on. It continues to irk Harry that he cannot persuade his boss to become more ofay with modern technology, but the pathologist will not budge, preferring instead to stick to tried and tested techniques.

Dr Bootle speaks out aloud as he works, 'The core temperature was recorded *in situ* as being 32 degrees, which suggests the body was discovered approximately three hours postmortem. I would like to note for the records that the GP who examined him at the bandstand noticed a slight rigour mortis, particularly to the head and neck, which were observed to be stiff and inflexible.'

Harry moves away from the table to allow Dr Bootle more room to manoeuvre around the cadaver. 'Do you see that the rigidity has spread further down the body?' Dr Bootle says aloud.

Harry momentarily loses concentration as he wonders if the pathologist is talking to him or to the Dictaphone. He quickly decides that it is the latter and therefore no response from him is needed.

Dr Bootle stops to look at Harry to see if he is listening, then continues on with his monologue. 'I can confirm that the estimated time of death is between 11 am and 1 pm. Some lividity is still present on the right-hand side of the body, so I can also confirm that the man died where he was found - on his side on the bench in the bandstand. Can you see the feint indentations from the wooden struts of the bench?'

This time Harry is certain that the question is being aimed at him. He nods in acknowledgment then takes a step nearer to look at the marks more closely. Fleetingly, Harry wonders why Dr Bootle no longer teaches at the local university, when it is clear that it is something he enjoys doing.

Dr Bootle continues with the examination, noting that the man was probably in his late sixties, but given his lifestyle, he may have been younger than his appearance. 'The cadaver has a slightly grey beard, deep wrinkles around his eyes and mouth, which stretches outwards towards his receding hairline. His nicotine-stained fingers suggests that he was a heavy smoker; his emaciated physique indicates that he had not been eating properly for some time before his death.'

Harry steps forward to take photos of several tattoos on the man's arms, which have faded to a mid-green and could be used as a search term in the police databases, a fact that has always fascinated Harry - it seems inconceivable that a body could be identified from art alone but it is something that occurs frequently with unidentified bodies. Harrys last task before opening up the body cavity is to take blood samples, which will test for anything such as viruses, bacteria, drugs and alcohol and he does so quickly.

With the external examination completed and samples retrieved, Dr Bootle turns his attention to the chest cavity. 'As I expected,' Dr Bootle tuts loudly, 'The lungs are blackened, though surprisingly there are no sign of cancerous tumours.'

The pathologist enlarges the incision, to open up the lower abdominal area underneath the emaciated rib cage. It is immediately apparent from the enlarged liver, that the deceased was a long-term heavy drinker. 'I expect it would not have been long before this gentleman experienced symptoms of cirrhosis of the liver, if he had not already done so before death,' Dr Bootle explains to Harry, who is once again leaning in closer so that he can take a better look.

'It looks as if the stomach only contains liquid. We need to take samples and test for food, alcohol and any other drugs that might have been ingested before death.'

Dr Bootle does not wait for a response from Harry before moving onto examining the head, which he carefully opens. Even Harry can see the adverse effects of alcohol without the need for yet another informative a monologue from the pathologist. Dr Bootle clearly thinks so as well, as he remains silent whilst he continues to examine the brain.

With the postmortem complete, Harry is left to clear up. As he wheels the body back down the stark corridor towards the cold storage room, he wonders how long it will take for them to receives the test results. One knock-on effect of the recession has been in the cost-cutting exercises within the NHS leading to the out-sourcing tests to private laboratories, who seemingly provide a reduction in service as well as in cost. Everything seems to be being privatised these days, Harry concludes and even more worryingly, he suspects that the process that began in earnest with the utility companies, would end with the privatisation of his beloved NHS.

Chapter 19

The sun is beginning to set as Fallow and Morgan drive across town towards the wealthier end of Deben Quay. By the time they reach Recreation Lane, the light is fading rapidly, with the sun sinking low behind the tree-lined recreation ground that stands adjacent to the small housing estate.

Morgan stands at the edge of the field for a moment to take in the beautiful, if slightly eerie scene, as the enormous poplar trees that circumvent the field are enveloped by a pink streaky mist that curls around the shrubbery at the edge of the football pitch. He continues to watch as the sun disappears from view, which would have left the quiet lane in complete darkness had it not been for the row of streetlamps that are dotted at regular intervals on the grass verge. As soon as darkness fully descends, Morgan turns his attention to Fallow, who is still waiting patiently next to the car.

The two men stride across a concrete parking area, ignoring a small group of youths who are sitting on the top of a brick wall that runs along two lengths of the parking bay then joins onto a block of garages. They continue up a narrow path flagged with fences either side, that leads towards Number 3.

Anna Jackaman looks nothing like Morgan has been imagining. His expectation of a plain, bespectacled cardigan-wearing spinster is very quickly dispelled when a svelte, well-dressed woman opens the door. Ms Jackaman clearly has money and lots of it by the looks of her designer jeans and carefully manicured nails.

'How can I help you?' Anna Jackaman asks curtly as she shows the two men through into the living room, which is adorned with pictures of herself in various photographic poses.

Morgan tries to avert his eyes from the more risqué photos as he walks across the room to sit down on the cream leather sofa. 'We're investigating the death of Lucy Mortimer who I believe you were friends with when you were teenagers?' Morgan says.

'My goodness that was years ago,' Anna Jackaman retorts. 'You said she's dead. How did she die? Stupid question, you wouldn't be here if it wasn't suspicious.'

'I assume you don't read the local papers Ms Jackaman?' Morgan asks.

'No, I don't, it's just a load of gossip as far as I'm concerned and I don't like gossip. What's this all about then?'

'Last Sunday Lucy was found dead in the river Deben and we're investigating how she died. You were friends with Lucy when you both attended a youth club run by the church, is that right?' Morgan asks.

'Yes, that's right, but it was so long ago, I don't see how this can be relevant?' Anna Jackman says, her forehead wrinkling in puzzlement.

'It seems that Lucy was living with Luke Fields at the time of her death,' Morgan replies, watching Anna Jackaman closely for her reaction. 'She left Deben Quay some time ago and was living with him in Marham. Do you remember Luke Fields? He was a volunteer at the Church youth club around the same time that Lucy was as a member?'

Anna Jackaman sits down heavily onto a nearby chair, a look of bewilderment spreading across her face. 'She was with Luke Fields?' She says softly, then coughs gently to clear her throat.

Morgan nods, allowing a heavy silence to descend, hoping that the uncomfortable silence will prompt further response from Anna Jackaman.

After a few moments, Anna Jackman sighs audibly, as if conceding to the inevitable. 'Lucy and I were friends when we were very young. We met at the youth club and went there most evenings. There was little else to do in those days and our parents didn't like us hanging around the parks or the river like the other kids. We were best friends. That was, until I found out she was seeing Luke Fields.' Anna Jackman says, looking across the room at Morgan to make sure that he is listening. 'I was also seeing Luke. I was in love with him and he was in love with me. Or so I thought. At the time I thought Lucy must have led him on, taken him away from me. That's why I told her parents they were seeing each other. They got the police involved and I never saw either of them again. Not long after, I left the town and starting a career in modelling. I've been in London since then and only returned recently.'

'I must ask where you were last weekend, in particular on Friday evening?' Morgan says.

'Oh, I see. I was here, at home for once. I often travel as part of my job, but I had a free weekend and was spring cleaning the house.'

'Can anyone confirm your whereabouts?' Morgan asks.

'Not really, I spent most of it by myself. I had a Chinese takeaway delivered on Friday evening about seven o'clock and I went food shopping on Saturday morning, but that's about it I'm afraid.'

'Ok thank you for your time. We'll get back to you if we have any more questions.' Morgan stands up and moves towards the door with Fallow following meekly behind.

'I'm sorry that I couldn't be of more help,' Anna Jackman says as she opens the front door then moves aside to allow the two men to squeeze past. 'It's quite a shock hearing those names after all these years, let alone finding out that Lucy is dead.'

'I'm sure it is, well please let me know if you remember anything else that might help,'

Morgan says before the front door is firmly shut behind him.

The two men make their way back to the centre of town to find the car park close to the Lamb Inn is nearly empty. Given that the pub is evidently quiet, it provided an opportune time to re-interview the landlord, Tom Baxter. One of the bar staff, a young woman called Jessica Stanbridge, had phoned the station earlier with the rather interesting news that Tom Baxter had been having an affair with Lucy Mortimer whilst she was working at the pub.

The detectives arrive to discover that the landlord is upstairs in his private apartment above the pub. After obtaining directions from the man pulling pints behind the bar, Fallow and Morgan make their way through to the residential part of the building and up into the back bedroom, which Tom Baxter is using as an office.

The slightly tubby man looks up in surprise at his visitors. Quickly he shuts down the laptop that is on a small table in front of him, leaving Morgan with the distinct impression that the pub landlord was looking at something he does not want the two police detectives to see.

'Can I help you?' Tom Baxter asks gruffly, his cheeks slightly flushed.

'Yes, there is something you can help us with. Why didn't you tell us that you were having a relationship with Lucy Mortimer?' Morgan snaps.

'Why do you think? I'm a lot older than her and I knew her parents wouldn't approve,' Tom Baxter snorts. He picks up the packet of cigarettes that are lying on the table next to the laptop and pulls one out. A chubby, nicotine-stained thumb flicks on a lighter with ease and Tom Baxter sucks deeply on the carcinogenic stick. He watches as an orange glow begins to creep up towards his fingers then flicks the ash-laden end of the cigarette into a nearby ashtray. It is only when he has smoked half of the cigarette that he turns around to stare at Morgan.

Morgan tips his head to one side and looks at the landlord, a slight smirk twitching at the corners of his mouth as he tries to suppress his delight at the man's discomfort. 'Well, now you mention it, it does seem a bit surprising that a young attractive girl like Lucy would have been interested in you. No offence meant of course.'

'Of course,' Tom Baxter responds, tight-lipped. He takes another deep drag on his cigarette, seemingly not noticing the column of ash that falls onto his now closed laptop. 'I can see why it would look a bit strange but the truth is she liked older men. I reckon she didn't get on with her father, he seems a rather pompous, stuck-up prick to me.'

'And you weren't worried when she disappeared?' Morgan asks.

'Nope, I told you last time, I thought she'd gone off with that customer. If you ask me, she already knew him before that night when he came into the pub.'

'What makes you think that?' Morgan asks.

'I don't know, she just seemed friendlier with him then she was with most of the other punters. She wasn't that good with people. Strange choice of a job for someone whose anti-social but I needed the help so wasn't about to turn her down.'

'I bet you weren't,' Morgan mumbles just loud enough for Tom Baxter to hear. 'Were you jealous?'

'Course I was, but as you say, she was a pretty girl and I knew she wouldn't stick with me for long.'

Morgan nods in agreement then wonders if the landlord was referring to Lucy working at his pub or having a relationship with him. Or both. 'Where were you last Friday evening?'

Tom Baxter sighs. 'I don't know, I can't remember. You don't think I had anything to do with her death, do you?' He says, sounding worried for the first time since Morgan met him.

'Where were you?' Morgan repeats. 'If you can't recall then perhaps you might remember down at the police station? It's amazing how quickly one's memory comes back after a few hours in a cold cell.'

Tom Baxter glares at Morgan, his eyes narrowing at the blatant threat. 'If you must know I was here, in the front room with five other men. We were playing poker all night.'

After a little persuasion, Baxter hands Morgan a list of the poker players names and phone numbers. At the top of the list is Fallows uncle, Chief Superintendent Bennett. An alibi could not get better than that though of course it would not look good for the Super if it was made common knowledge that he played cards with the likes of Tom Baxter. Morgan tries and fails to stifle a grimace as he realises that another avenue has just closed.

'Well, we'd better leave you to your work, we can see that you're busy,' Morgan says, dragging a slightly perplexed Fallow out of the door before he catches sight of the list. The card game was no doubt illegal and they would have been drinking in a licensed establishment after hours, but there was little he could do about it when the Super was one of them.

The temperature has already fallen significantly by the time Fallow drops Morgan off at home after what seemed to be a very long shift. Morgan holds back a retort at Fallows cheerful goodbye. It is very unlikely that Morgan will have a pleasant night given the mood Celia will probably be in, having been left yet again on her own. Morgan stands on the doorstep momentarily, key poised in the lock and pushes away the temptation of stopping off at the Eels Foot for a pint first – that might be pushing his luck too far. Perhaps he could take Celia away for a weekend soon to cheer her up, he decides - once the case has been closed of course.

Celia is indeed in a testy mood and barely acknowledges her husband when he walks through the front door. She is engrossed in an episode of a medical drama and Morgan knows far better than to disturb his wife when she is watching one of her favourite programmes. Instead, he heads straight for the kitchen to make himself a hot chocolate. It isn't his usual drink but given the chilly night and frosty atmosphere in the house, he is feeling the need for something warm and comforting. With his drink finished, Morgan showers and changes into his pyjamas, pulling his dressing gown tightly around him. He settles down onto the sofa, where Celia is still gripped by the drama of this week's storyline.

It is just when the credits are finally rolling up, that the phone rings – it is Cook, wanting to know how the interview with Anna Jackaman went. Morgan relays to him an annotated version of the conversation and suggests that however unlikely, Anna Jackaman should also be considered a suspect. He can tell from the quiet noises coming from the other end of the telephone that Cook does not agree, but before the call ends, Cook concedes that they should keep all avenues open for now.

Morgan replaces the phone and nestles back down into the sofa. Whilst he has been busy talking to Cook, Celia has switched the TV off and disappeared upstairs with a warm mug of cocoa.

Morgan allows himself a few minutes of solitude, enjoying the quietness that envelopes him, redressing the balance away from the chaotic noise of the station. There is something niggling at him - why did Anna Jackaman return to Deben Quay after all these years? And why did she come back just before her ex-best friend died? Perhaps Anna had planned to seek out Luke Fields again, not realising he had left town many years before, wondered Morgan. It is much more likely though that she had simply wanted to be closer to her parents again, something that often happened after the rebellious teenage years have passed and the fast pace of the twenty-something party girl has been left far behind. Yes, Morgan decides, that is the most likely explanation. Something is still bothering him though and he cannot quite work out what it is.

Chapter 20

Monday is looking as if it will live up to its reputation of being the worst day of the week. For one thing, it is raining again. Huge droplets are lashing against the bedroom windows, waking Morgan up before the sun has even had the chance to rise and making him feel depressed before he has even got out of bed.

Morgan has always hated this time of year, especially when the weather keeps him cooped up inside. He would much rather be out in the sunshine, as long as the outdoor activity does not involve gardening that is. He stares out of the bedroom window at the huge dark clouds that are dominating the skyline above the roofs and chimney stacks of the neighbouring properties. There is certainly no chance of a glimpse of sunshine anytime soon he concludes as he pulls back from the window and heads for the bathroom.

By the time he reaches the station, the rain has soaked through Morgans meagre jacket, leaving him damp and further depressed in the knowledge that there is little chance of his coat drying off again too quickly in the cold office. Morgans mood worsens considerably when he finds a mountain of urgent paperwork waiting for him on his desk. He still needs to begin typing up the notes from yesterday's interview with Anna

Jackaman, not to mention starting a new file for the cadaver found at the bandstand on Saturday. Hopefully once the PM report is finalised, he can pass the latter task onto uniform and they can be left with the unenvious task of trying to find out his name and locate the destitute man's relatives.

The morning only begins to improve when Morgan is summoned downstairs to the front lobby, where a not entirely unwelcome visitor in the guise of Caroline Woods is waiting at the enquiry desk.

'Hello James. I hope you don't mind me dropping in like this, but I heard that another body has been found. I thought I should let you know that I was in the area on Saturday morning, interviewing homeless people on the quayside and saw a man in the distance hanging around. I just thought he was gawping at the tearoom, but now I'm not so sure.'

Morgan momentarily blanches at the completely inappropriate and very public usage of his first name, then reddens a little as he recalls that he has not yet given Caroline Woods a piece of his mind over the newspaper article. He sighs loudly and rolls his eyes theatrically, looking in the direction of the enquiry desk, where the officer smirks then return's his attention to the newspaper lying open on the enquiry desk.

'You'd better come in and make a statement,' Morgan says, holding open the security door to allow Caroline Woods into the dark corridor beyond. Morgan opens the first door on the right, flicks on the light and gestures for Caroline to step inside the room.

The journalist removes her damp beige mac and sets it down on the back of one of the chairs, then pulls up another one next to Morgan, who has just sat down. 'I was looking for witnesses for the fire at the tearoom and thought I'd try the two tramps who usually sleep in the bandstand. The woman wasn't there, so I just talked to the old guy. He didn't really make much sense and didn't seem to have seen anything of any use, so it was all a waste of time really,' Caroline says, flicking a section of her shoulder-length hair behind her shoulder, splattering a near-by wall with moisture in the process.

'Can you remember what time you were there?' Morgan asks as he reaches across the desk for the notepad and pen that is always left in the room.

'I think it was about 10 am. I'm wondering if the man I spoke to could have been the one that was found dead that afternoon? There's an article in this morning's paper about it,' Caroline says proudly as she opens up her oversized handbag and passes a newspaper article to Morgan.

THE SUFFOLK TIMES

Monday, 1 March 2006

Controversy Over New Homes Planned
by Russell Carter

Plans have been submitted for ten homes to be built on a small plot of land near Candlet Road. Nearby residents are up-in-arms at the proposal, as garages belonging to three existing properties would need to be demolished to make way for an access road for the new development.

The proposal by a local architect is to build six, three-bedroom houses and four, affordable two-bedroom terraced houses. The terraced houses would be partially owned by Heritage Housing to give first-time buyers the opportunity of owning their own home.

More Car break-ins
by Russell Carter

Six cars have been broken into around the Walton area over the weekend. Items such as Satellite Navigation systems and radios were stolen from five of the vehicles. Local Police warn drivers not to leave any valuables on show and to always ensure that doors are locked and windows fully closed. Residents are reminded that valuables should be locked in the boot of the car or removed from the vehicle when it is left unattended.

Another Body Found by the Quay
by Caroline Woods

The body of a homeless man has been found at the Quayside on Saturday afternoon, close to where the body of Lucy Mortimer was recently found. The identity of the man has not yet been discovered, but is thought that he has died from natural causes.

Another Store Closes
by Leah Hart

Another high-street store has become a victim of the recession, closing after just six months of trading. Size Up, a plus size women's clothes shop was located on the High Street near to the Bakers Oven.

DEBEN QUAY BUTCHERS
For all your local meat supplies
Tel: 27435

Morgan begins to read Carolines article in earnest. He is a little surprised by how much detail is in there, especially as they have not yet released a formal statement. He wonders if Caroline would take offense if he asked her where she is getting her information then quickly decides that she probably would. He briefly smiles at the journalist, then places the paper onto the table in front of her before making notes of their brief conversation.

'Ok thanks, that will be enough for now. I'll get this witness statement typed up for you to sign before you leave.' Morgan pushes back his chair and opens the door, indicating for Caroline to file back out into the reception area again. Further along the corridor from the interview rooms is a small office used for hot-desking, where he can type up the statement quickly and ask Caroline to sign it - he knows she will be keen to get back to the Suffolk Times headquarters.

By the time Morgan finishes typing up the statement, Caroline seems more relaxed than when she first arrived at the police station. 'I'm sorry about disclosing Mrs Fields identity in the paper on Friday - a draft of the article got printed by mistake. I don't suppose you'd allow me to buy you a drink later to make up for it?' Caroline asks sweetly, re-crossing her slender legs, which are encased in sheer black stockings underneath her pencil skirt.

Morgans gaze is instantly drawn down her long legs to her black high heels, which compliment her shapely figure. 'I'll probably be tied up today I'm afraid. As you can imagine we're very busy with all the bodies that keep appearing,' Morgan replies, torn by the invitation.

'I can imagine. It would be a shame though if we didn't have time to meet up. Maybe if we put our heads together, we might be able to figure out some of this mess? I'll be in the Eels Foot about seven tonight if you change your mind.'

Morgan watches as the attractive woman sashays across the reception area. He cannot help but admire the slim figure that is accentuated by the tightly fastened narrow-waisted coat. Quickly he follows and overtakes so that he can open the outer door for Caroline to pass through. Morgan stands at the entrance to the station and watches as Caroline elegantly climbs into her car and drives off without so much as a second glance.

As soon as Carolines car has disappeared from view, Morgan marches back past the enquiry desk, ignoring the smirking custody sergeant. He heads towards the back stairs that are located behind an innocuous teak door, then takes the steps two at a time onto the next level. Morgan bustles his way through as group of officers who are almost entirely blocking the corridor, then continues down to the end of the cramped space, where a security door prevents anyone who is not part of the team from entering. Morgan swipes his key card through the door lock then pushes it open. He is immediately greeted by Cook who is rushing out of his tiny office towards him.

'Morgan, we've had a call about Luke Fields, he turned up at his house a little while ago. I've sent the local police to arrest him, so we need to get to Marham now,' Cook says, breathless with excitement. 'SOCO went round yesterday and found a pair of boots at his house with mud on them and some paint thinner in his garage. Samples have gone to the lab and they're checking tyre prints from Lukes's car against those we found near the tearoom. Apparently, they also have some paperwork from his office which is going to be of interest to us!'

'I'm ready to go whenever you are,' Morgan replies, equally as eager to finally have the opportunity to question their prime suspect.

Marham police station is located in a squat, dark building that was probably built sometime in the twentieth century. There is only just enough space for a few holding cells, none of which yield any comfort to their occupants who have been heard to describe them as more of a dungeon than a prison cell. Morgan cannot help but ponder on whether the design of the cells was on purpose, after all, even a short stay at Her Majesties establishments were meant to be a deterrent of some sort.

Upon his arrival at the station, Luke Fields is duly stripped of his clothes, swabbed and fingerprinted, then left to perch on the uncomfortable metal bench in cell number 1.

The suspect is still shivering in a thin paper suit when Cook and Morgan arrive at the front desk. Having made the two officers sign into a hard-back visitors book that looks as if it has been there for many years, the Duty Sergeant duly disappears from the front desk to retrieve the suspect and take him to the interview room, where it is at least a little warmer, even if not much more comfortable than the holding cell.

In the Duty Sergeants absence, Cook and Morgan are shown through to an interview room by a passing officer, who clearly does not bother to adhere to the Duty Sergeants well thought out procedures for visitors to the station. En route to the interview room, the detectives are encouraged to grab a coffee from the small kitchen area, which they gratefully take advantage of. By the time Luke Fields arrives, the two detectives are already seated on plastic chairs at the far end of the interview room and sipping their bitter coffees whilst they wait eagerly to interview the suspect.

Cook watches as Luke Fields slinks through the doorway and heads towards one of the unoccupied chairs, seemingly unconcerned by the potential gravity of the situation and vastly more interested in the opportunity of sitting next to a storage heater, which offers only a meagre amount of warmth.

'Well Mr Fields, we finally meet,' Cook says.

Luke Fields stares at Cooks intensely, his attention briefly drawn away from the heater. 'Why am I here?'

'Why don't we start with where you've been for the past week,' Cook asks.

'I've been helping out on a church youth club holiday in Wales. What's this all about?'

'You went on holiday knowing that your mother is missing?' Cook replies astonished.

'I didn't know she was missing, I thought she'd just gone to see a friend or maybe gone on holiday herself.'

'Have you ever known your mother to just disappear?' Morgan snorts in disbelief at the suspect's attitude.

'No, I suppose not,' Luke replies sheepishly. 'I take it she's still missing then?'

'Oh no, not now, we've found her alright. The only problem is she's dead,' Morgan interjects bluntly, his patience already worn thin by Luke Fields flippant attitude.

Luke leans forward and rests his elbows on the table, then clasps his hands in front of his mouth. 'Dead, are you sure? How did she die?'

'She was found in the remains of her tearoom, which was destroyed by fire,' Morgan continues.

'When exactly did you go to Wales?' Cook interjects.

Luke shuffles back into his seat, pushing his back into the stiff plastic chair. 'We left on Monday evening, stopped half-way at a B and B that night to break up the journey. I don't understand. There was a fire at the tearoom? So, she was killed in the fire?'

'Not unless she poured paint stripper over her own body, strangled herself and then set fire to her own business premises,' Morgan retorts. He narrows his eyes as he carefully watches

Lukes's reaction, which seems to be genuine, but then again, he could just be a very good actor.

'We'll need to take a swab from you to check your DNA against the body, just to make sure that it's your mother. She was too badly burnt to be able to identify any other way,' Cook says bluntly. He too has taken an instant dislike to the suspect.

'There's no point, I'm adopted. My mother couldn't have children, so they adopted me and my sister when we were very young. We don't know who our real parents were, we never felt the need to find out,' Luke replies.

Cook grimaces then glares at Luke Fields, silently wishing that the young man was not so smug. 'What time exactly did you leave for Wales on Monday evening?'

'It was about six forty-five. The coach left the church at seven,' Luke replies.

'What did you do after my colleagues visited you at your home?' Cook asks, making notes at the same time.

'Well, after the visit I had from your lot, I was busy tying up loose ends, you know how it is.'

'And you weren't worried about your mother whilst you were away?' Morgan says, shifting back into the hard, plastic chair and crossing one knee over the other.

'Not really. We hadn't spoken for a long time.'

'I take it you didn't have any access to the news whilst you were away?' Cook asks.

'No, we were camping on the coast near Milhaven. The point of it was to get away from it all.'

'I bet it was,' Morgan says, tight-lipped.

'So, you don't have any alibi for Sunday night then?' Cook asks.

'I didn't realise I needed one.'

'Why don't we talk about Lucy Mortimer,' Cook says, changing tactic.

'What about Lucy? I haven't seen her for about a week or so. She drove off in her car last Friday and I haven't seen or heard from her since,' Luke says with a look of confusion on his face.

'You weren't worried when she didn't contact you? You seem to have a habit of losing contact with all the women in your life,' Morgan retorts.

Luke Fields stares at Morgan, his eyes narrowing in anger. 'She said she wanted some time to herself. She's been acting a bit strange recently, distracted, not really herself. I wondered if she'd met someone else.'

Cook cocks his head to one side, mulling over Lukes last statement. However plausible it seems, there is something that just does not seem to ring true. Perhaps it is the instinct he has developed over the many years of police work - something is telling him that Luke Fields at the very least is a liar.

'As you know, your mother found a body in the river Deben, it's taken us a while to discover the identity of the deceased as she didn't have any identification on her. We have identified her though; her name was Lucy Mortimer.' Cook tries to suppress the acutely inappropriate smirk that is trying to form on his lips.

The colour instantly drains from Lukes's cheeks, the hand that is resting on the table, begins to shake. 'I don't understand. Both Lucy and my mother are dead?' Luke closes his eyes momentarily and lets out a slow controlled breath.

'You're very good. You almost look upset by the news. We've also had a look at the accounts from your business - they're not good, are they? And guess who inherits your mother's assets? We know you've been to the tearoom recently; we matched your tyre prints to those found at the scene,' Morgan lies.

'How did Lucy die?' Luke asks, ignoring Morgans implicatory comment.

'She drowned. The only problem is, she was also drugged before she died,' Morgan replies bluntly. 'Let's stop with this pointless charade. We all know what's going on here. We all know who caused the deaths of these two women.' Morgan roughly pushes back his chair and shoves his hands into his trouser pockets then begins to slowly pace the length of the room.

'Let me ask you again,' Cook interjects a little more forcefully than last time. 'Were you not worried when Lucy disappeared? Even though she was pregnant?'

'She didn't tell me,' Luke says feebly then closes his eyes, trying to hold back his emotions.

"Where's Lucy's car?' Cook asks, changing tack again.

'I don't know. How could I know? I thought she'd left me.'

'So now you thought she'd left you? Earlier you thought she'd just gone to stay with a friend. Which is it?' Morgan snarls.

'I don't know. I suppose I hoped she'd gone for a break and was going to come back. We'd had a few arguments recently. I thought she'd gone to cool off, but it did cross my mind that she might not come back.'

Morgan stops pacing for a moment to stare at the suspect but holds back a retort.

'What did you argue about?' Cook asks, standing up to stretch his legs.

'Money mostly. As you already know, my business is in a lot of debt. She wanted to enrol on a course and I needed her to get a job.'

'Things are that bad?' Cook asks.

'Yes,' Luke replies meekly.

'Babies are expensive,' Morgan says, returning to his seat.

'Is that why you killed your mother and set fire to her business? You would have inherited everything, including her life insurance,' Cook asks.

Luke shifts in his seat, looking a little unnerved. 'I want a solicitor, I'm not saying any more without one.'

The interview is suspended to allow Luke time to instruct a solicitor. As it is already late, Cook and Morgan decide to head back to Deben Quay. Why the budget could not stretch to allow them to stay overnight perplexes Morgan. He wonders if it is not just the budget that prevents them from staying, Cook is after all in charge of the investigation and needs to get back to check on his team's progress and unlike Morgan, he also has a family who needs his attention.

Chapter 21

The first thing Cook notices when he logs onto his email account is the toxicology report the lab sent through the previous night. He clicks on the email attachment to open the document and begins eagerly flicking through the report.

To: DCI.Cook@DebenQuay.Police.UK
From: Toxicology@SuffolkLab.co.uk

Date: 28 February 2016

Re: Test Results

Dear DCI Cook

Please find below the test results analysed from the stomach contents from unknown John Doe found at Deben Quay bandstand.

- Samples taken from the stomach contained high levels of ethylene glycol.

Cook already knows what ethylene glycol is used for and therefore why it could have conceivably been found in the stomach of the vagrant – he has heard of previous cases where anti-freeze has been inadvertently ingested by desperate alcoholics, though in some cases they have managed to somehow survive the poison.

Given the lifestyle of the vagrant, this is not incomprehensible and a cause of death that Cook is eager to accept as the last thing they need is another unexplained death on their hands.

An email containing the results of the fingerprint analysis has also arrived.

To: DCI.Cook@DebenQuay.Police.UK
From: Forensics@SuffolkLab.co.uk

Date: 1 March 2016

Re: Test Results

Dear DCI Cook

Please find below confirmation of identity following fingerprint analysis of the unknown John Doe found at Deben Quay bandstand and further information retrieved through database searches of medical and police records.

- Terry Smith, aged 61.
- Discharged from the armed forces on medical grounds due to assault on an unknown recruit.
- Terry Smith suffered from PTSD, which developed after the death of a fellow soldier whilst they were both serving in the Middle East. A roadside IED had blown up the vehicle they had been travelling in whilst out on patrol and a soldier had burnt to death trapped in the vehicle. Subsequently Terry become very volatile.
- After discharge from the army, Terry Smith acquired several convictions for affray, common assault and breach of the peace. More recent arrests were mainly for drunken disorderly behaviour and he was cautioned on 5 occasions for urinating in a public place and for breaking into local graveyards (presumably looking for somewhere to sleep).

It riles Cook to hear of someone who is clearly mentally ill being left to fend for themselves, especially when they often end up in a downward spiral of alcohol and drug abuse. He firmly believes that it is time the armed forces took responsibility for their ex-soldiers, especially those who have been damaged physically, emotionally or mentally whilst serving their country.

Cook continues to read through the report, which details that no relatives were listed on Terrys records, though a note on his police records was made that he had been arrested in the company of another vagrant called Betty (surname unknown). Cook updates the case notes in their system then moves the email into the team's shared inbox under 'In Progress'. Once the inquest has confirmed that the death is accidental, then it will be filed along with all the other closed cases. Cook cannot help but morosely wonder what will happen to Terrys remains. Certainly, the government will pay for a cremation but who knows what will happen to his ashes, perhaps they will remain on a shelf unclaimed at the funeral directors. Perhaps if no one claims them, he could scatter them on the quayside, close to where Terry died.

After such a long day, Morgan and Cook feel completely justified in stopping off at the Eels Foot to unwind a little before heading home. Normally a chance to catch up on the station gossip, Cook and Morgan instead focus their chat on the recent investigations. The two men are so engrossed in their conversation that they fail to notice Caroline Woods walk through the door of the almost empty pub.

The journalist smiles at them as she walks past then continues towards the end of the bar, where she pulls up a stool. 'Would either of you like a drink?' Caroline shouts across the room.

'Thanks, very kind of you, but we just got a round in,' Cook responds, holding up his almost full glass for the journalist to see.

'Would you like to join us?' Cook asks.

'Thank you,' Caroline replies, collecting her drink from the bar and settling into the chair next to Morgan.

'You two look like you've had a hard day,' she says, picking up her half pint of bitter and sipping the cool dark liquid.

'We've been interviewing someone,' Cook replies, not wishing to give too much away. Caroline Woods may be attractive and friendly, but she is still after all a journalist and he is not about to fall for the same trick that Morgan did.

'So, you've found Luke Fields then?' Caroline laughs.

Cook stares at Morgan with a bemused look on his face. It is swiftly becoming clear to him how the journalist is obtaining up-to-date news of their current investigations. Cook sighs, returning his focus to Caroline. 'This is off the record of course,' he eventually responds. 'But yes, we've arrested Luke Fields. We'll do a press release tomorrow, but we won't be giving out much at this stage.'

'Sure,' Caroline replies. 'I know how it is with these things. By the way, I went through our archives and found some articles on Luke Fields from when he was a youth club volunteer.'

'That's great, thanks,' Morgan says gleefully, smirking at Cook. Just because Caroline Woods is a very attractive female, it does not mean that their relationship is any different to the symbiotic relationship that benefits DCI Cook and Phil Wattle.

'Could we have some copies of the articles?' Cook asks, conceding defeat. 'It will help us to build up a picture of him.'

'Sure thing. So, you think he's responsible then? Off the record of course!'

Cook laughs at the audacity of her question. Given that she has already disclosed information to the public without their consent, he decides not to respond and instead focusses on drinking the remainder of his pint. When his glass is empty, he politely excuses himself to his drinking partners – it is time for him to head home.

'So, do you come here often?' Caroline asks Morgan as soon as they are alone.

Morgan is not quite sure if she is flirting with him or asking a serious question. 'When I can, it's my local,' Morgan replies tersely.

'And your wife doesn't mind?'

'It's part of the job, winding down after a stressful day. Sometimes you just need to de-brief, especially when you have to cope with some of the stuff we deal with. We don't like to take our work home with us. Anyway, I'd rather not talk about Celia.'

'Oh ok, what would you like to talk about then?' Caroline smirks. 'How about where we go after this drink?'

'I should go home really, it's been a long day,' Morgan replies sternly, tiring a little of the charade.

'Well, you know my motto - life's too short. You should grab opportunities when you can as you never know what's around the corner.'

'All the same, I'd better not. Celia will be waiting for me.'

Morgan picks his coat up from a nearby stool. 'Maybe another time,' he says, almost as an after-thought, hoping that he has not offended her.

'We'll see,' Caroline replies, clearly miffed that her advances have been rejected.

Morgan smiles apologetically, then walks across the room and pulls open the main door, allowing a bracing chill to enter the warm pub. Before he steps outside into the dark night, he briefly turns around to look at Caroline again, but she is busy texting on her phone and does not notice.

Allowing the heavy outer door to slam shut behind him, Morgan pushes thoughts of the journalist to one side and begins the walk home to his wife. It has begun to snow again. Morgan pulls up the collar of his coat to cover his ears then quickens his pace as he strides down the lane towards home.

The house is encased in darkness, with Celia already in bed asleep. Morgan fleetingly wishes that he had been bolder and taken up Carolines offer. He pulls off his damp coat, which he hangs up in the porch, then heads into the kitchen. After opening the fridge door, Morgan immediately spots a covered plate of food that Celia has left for him to reheat in the microwave. Morgan ignores the food and instead grabs hold of a can of beer, which he takes into the sitting room then he sits in complete silence in the dark, drinking the entire contents of the can in less than five minutes, wondering why it is that he feels so alone.

Morgan must have fallen asleep on the sofa, as the next thing he is aware of is the sun peeping through the thin curtains. He rubs his eyes, trying to wake himself up, wondering what time it is. Morgan stretches out an arm and fumbles about on the coffee table, where he knows he must have placed his watch the previous night. They are due to interview Luke Fields again today and he needs to go to the station first to check over the paperwork.

As it turns out, Morgan did not need to stress about being late – in fact he is so early that he is the first to arrive at the incident room. Morgan pulls up the blinds then flicks on the kettle to make a strong black coffee. He settles down at his desk and begins sifting through all of the evidence they have collated so far, trying to get it all straight in his mind. Most of it is circumstantial and they will need something more than that if they are going to convince the Crown Prosecution Service to charge Luke Fields with the murders of his girlfriend and mother. Morgan hopes the test results from Lukes shoes and car tyres do indeed show what they are hoping to see, otherwise they will have to release Luke Fields from custody without charge.

Cook turns up half-an-hour later, looking as dishevelled as Morgan did when he had first awoken. Unlike Morgan though, Cook has been up most of the night with his eldest daughter Cassie, who has picked up a stomach bug from school, and he is in no mood to interrogate a suspect, especially when the suspect just happens to be Luke Fields.

Cook needs little persuasion to allow Morgan to drive them to Marham, even after three strong mugs of coffee he is still struggling to keep his eyes open. The traffic is light and it takes them just over an hour to reach the small, semi-rural police station where they discover that Luke Fields solicitor has already arrived and is briefing his client in the interview room. The conversation abruptly halts when Cook and Morgan enter the room, leaving an uncomfortable silence that is quickly replaced by Cook introducing them to the solicitor.

Morgans gut instinct was telling him before they even reached Marham that the trip would be a waste of time, a feeling that is quickly confirmed as the presence of the solicitor results in Luke Fields saying little other than 'no comment' to any of their questions. There is little point in continuing with the interview until they have some strong evidence to at least prove that Luke Fields was in Deben Quay at the time of the two deaths, so the interview is quickly abandoned. Neither detective is in a good mood as they drive back to Deben Quay police station, both equally as frustrated as the other by the lack of progress.

Chapter 22

Caroline Woods is feeling rather smug about being assigned to the murder stories. She has only been at the Suffolk Times for a few months, so by rights the job should have been given to one of the journalists who have worked for the newspaper for longer, such as Leah or Russell. She puts her good fortune down to her great skill in ferreting out stories, though other more cynical observers might have supposed that she has flirted her way to the top. Caroline cares little for gossip though and would strongly refute any such rumours – if anyone dared to suggest them. Phil Wattle is old enough to be her father and even she would not go as far as to flirt with a man of his age. Whatever the reason for the assignment, Phil Wattle seems to be pleased with her coverage of the story so far.

THE SUFFOLK TIMES

Tuesday, 2 March 2006 ✓

Shock Mugging in Town Centre
by Leah Hart

Three elderly women have been mugged in Deben Quay town centre over the last five days. Two of the women were shaken but unharmed by their attacker but a third woman was taken to hospital with a suspected broken wrist after being pushed to the ground and her handbag stolen. The victims had all been to the post office to withdraw money from their accounts and Police warn that it seems likely they were watched doing so. Residents have been urged to take care when withdrawing money and not to carry large quantities of cash on them. The man is described as having black hair, 5 foot 8 and wearing a navy blue coat. Anyone with any information about these attacks should contact DI Harrold at Deben Quay police.

Ricky's Autos
For MOT's services and all types of body repairs.
Tel: 286795

Businessman Questioned Over Deaths
by Caroline Woods

A man is being questioned by the town's police over the deaths of Lucy Mortimer and Mrs Julia Fields. The unnamed suspect is not believed to be currently living in the area but is thought to have originally come from Deben Quay. Deben Quay police are appealing for witnesses from the weekend of 21st February, who may have seen someone acting suspiciously in the quayside area.

Open Day at Hemley Hall
by Leah Hart

A spring fair and open garden will be at Hemley Hall on 22 March. All proceeds from the event will go to Guide Dogs for the Blind.

Cherry Farm Shop
Locally grown fruit and vegetables.
Located on Deben Quay High Road

Caroline flicks through the latest edition of the paper as she waits for Phil Wattle to begin the morning briefing. As the office door bangs shut, heralding the arrival of last member of the team, Caroline slaps the paper down onto the desk beside her and turns her attention to the editor, who is impatiently pacing up and down in front of the large metal-framed window.

'I'd like to start today's meeting by congratulating Caroline on her coverage of the murders. You seem to be getting on well with it, so I want you to continue with it and follow the trial, if and when it happens. I hear you've made a friend of DI Morgan as well. Not a bad thing to keep in with the police, we get a lot of scoops that way.' Wattle ignores several of the team who are rolling their eyes and making vomiting gestures at his praise for the newest employee. 'Leah, I want you to attend the Hemley Hall open day. There's going to be a dog show and a small animal competition, so see what stories you can get out of that. Take Russell with you as well and get some pictures, maybe interview the winners and their pets.'

It is little wonder that rumours are spreading quickly through the small enterprise Caroline decides, as she is yet again assigned the top story, an act which can only fuel dissention amongst the other journalists. It does not bother her though – she's used to having few friends and participating in the office gossip is something she can easily live without. She does however like to eavesdrop on other people's conversations as you never knew what you might hear. For instance, when she was last at the police station, she overheard Morgan telling Cook that his wife would be away for the week on a yoga retreat in Andalucía – and that it would be an opportunity for her to holiday without her relaxation time being cut short by the confines of her husband's job. Caroline also overhead Morgan, before the two men moved out of earshot, say that he would also enjoy the break, as his wife had become clingy and demanding of late. It occurs to Caroline that she has not yet given Morgan copies of the newspaper articles that he wanted and that perhaps this would provide her with an excuse to contact him.

The investigation suddenly seems to be picking up pace Morgan mumbles to himself as he puts down the phone. He has just learnt that another woman has come forward to disclose that Luke Morgan had an inappropriate relationship with her when she was a minor.

    Morgan gathers up his belongings and hurries out to interview the woman, anxious to get a statement in case she changes her mind about making one. His curiosity is soon satiated, as he is told a similar story to that of Anna Jackaman; Luke had professed to be in love and had persuaded Charlotte Turner to have sex with him. She revealed that at the time, the Fields had an old caravan in their garden, which the children played in. Luke persuaded Charlotte to skip school and meet up with him at the caravan whilst his mother was at work. It was only when Charlottes sister read entries in her diary revealing the secret liaisons, that the relationship ended. Charlotte was immediately removed from the local school and sent to a boarding school for young ladies.

    Morgan is not surprised by this new allegation and cannot help but wonder how many more victims of Luke Fields will turn up before the end of the investigation; it is usually the way that once these sorts of stories get into the papers that it prompts even more victims to speak out.

The thought of returning to an empty house keeps Morgan at work until a little after seven, when he can no longer ignore the pressing need for food and sleep. The house seems so empty without Celia. Feeling the weight of the oppressive silence that has descended, he showers and changes before turning his attention to finding something to eat. He has never been very interested in cooking and is too tired to bother to learn now, so instead, Morgan picks up the phone in the sitting room to order a takeaway pizza. Just as he is dialling the number, there is a knock on his front door. Intrigued, Morgan replaces the receiver and hurries to the porch. He pulls open the front door to reveal a drenched Caroline Woods standing in the rain, holding a bottle of wine and a Chinese takeaway in one hand and a large beige envelope in the other.

'I thought you'd want these as soon as I got them,' Caroline explains, handing him the unsealed envelope. 'They're the articles on Luke Fields - I think you might find them interesting.'

Morgan raises his eyebrows, then takes the damp envelope from Carolines dripping hand.

'I thought I'd drop them off to you on the way back from getting a takeaway. Theres enough here for two if you're hungry?'

Morgan smiles, then pulls open the door wider to allow Caroline in out of the rain, which is now pouring into the porch. He relieves the drenched journalist of the sodden plastic takeaway bag and wine bottle, then takes her saturated mac from her to hang up in the porch. Before Morgan has even shut the front door, he eagerly peeks inside the envelope.

Youth Worker Leaves Church Under Cloud Of Suspicion

A volunteer who was working at a local church youth club in the centre of Deben Quay, has left unexpectedly. Luke Fields, 27, was working with teenagers at St Mary's Church youth club but left suddenly four weeks ago. It is thought that the volunteer had been having an inappropriate relationship with one of the youth club members.

Ricky's Autos
For MOT's services and all types of body repairs.
Tel: 286795

Although she is not named explicitly, Morgan assumes the article is referring to Lucy Mortimer. It seems a little strange by today's standards that Luke was not arrested for the offence, but that was the way they dealt with problems like that, even up to a few years ago; they simply moved people like Luke Fields onto another location.

'Do you think the article is about Lucy Mortimer?' Caroline asks, echoing Morgans own thoughts.

'Probably, although it seems she was not the only one he was having an inappropriate relationship with,' Morgan replies, teasing the journalist who raises her eyebrows, a slight smile forming on her soft cherry-coloured lips. Morgan is struck by her relaxed mood, in comparison to her usual brusque manner. She seems gentler, perhaps even vulnerable considers Morgan. Perhaps recent events have struck a chord with her own life.

Morgan offers Caroline a glass of the chilled Chablis that she brought with her, then rummages around in the kitchen cupboards for plates for the takeaway. 'How did you know that chicken chow mein is my favourite?'

'It's my favourite. too,' Caroline replies as she dishes out some of the noodles first onto one plate, then the other. 'So, do you think you have the suspect then?'

'It certainly looks that way, the evidence is starting to stack up nicely,' Morgan says, pausing to suck up a greasy noodle.

'He does seem a likely culprit for murder and as you say, the evidence is stacking up against him. He has motive as well, from what I've heard.'

Morgan stops eating to look at Caroline, intrigued to know how she is managing to obtain her information. 'He certainly has a preference for young girls, but whether or not any of them are happy to give evidence in court is another matter. We often find in these cases that someone will come forward and make a report but when it comes to actually giving evidence in court, they drop the case.'

Caroline nods her head thoughtfully. 'I can imagine. Maybe there have been some other more recent cases? I could take a look if you like, see if I can find anything out from the newspapers? Perhaps he has been in the news in Norfolk?'

'Thanks Caroline, that would be really helpful. There seems to be a pattern of behaviour here and it's unlikely he will have diverged from it.'

'What about the murders though, they weren't sexual were they?' Caroline picks at her food for a moment, then places her fork down onto the plate.

'If they were committed by Luke, then they could have been motivated by his financial problems. He's in a lot of debt and would have inherited enough from his mother's estate to clear it.'

'But what about Lucy? Maybe they argued and he killed her in rage? Or maybe she wouldn't have sex with him and he lost control?'

'I don't think that's likely as she was drugged and seemingly unharmed. It seems a bit odd, it's almost as if he was putting her out of her misery, like a dog that has cancer. Maybe he was planning to kill himself as well and wanted to take his girlfriend and mother with him? Maybe he changed his mind at the last minute? Who knows what goes on in someone else's mind.' Morgan finishes his glass of wine then pours another one for himself, topping up Carolines glass at the same time.

Caroline pushes away her plate then excuses herself from the table. She heads towards the porch to have a cigarette, where she can shelter from the worst of the rain. Caroline sucks greedily on the cigarette then exhales the smoke out through the open door, a thin trial of vapour leading into the front garden. With the cigarette finished, she flicks the lit ember out into the rain and watches as it is extinguished by the continuing torrent of water. It is only then that she seems to notice the cool chill from the open door and quickly slams it shut before making her way back into the warmth of the kitchen again, where Morgan has made coffee. Caroline follows Morgan into the sitting room and settles down onto the sofa next to him. She takes a steaming mug from his outstretched hand then sips it cautiously before stretching her legs out as close to the fire as possible.

'What do you think happened to the tramp? Perhaps he saw something he shouldn't have and was killed as well?' Caroline asks, breaking the comfortable lull that has descended.

Morgan is slightly taken aback by the rapid change in topic, which immediately destroys the sleepy ambience that he has been enjoying. He is also more than sightly irked that what Caroline has just said, had not yet occurred to him; that the death of the homeless man could be connected to those of Mrs Fields and Lucy Mortimer. 'We're certain that it's natural causes and not expecting the inquest to say otherwise,' Morgan says carefully, suddenly feeling a little more guarded than he did earlier in the evening. He takes a sip of the steaming liquid, then places the mug onto a coaster on the side table nearest to him. 'What makes you think Terry Smiths death could be connected to the other cases?'

'I don't know, just instinct I suppose. It just seems too much of a coincidence to me,' Caroline says thoughtfully.

'You could be right but we're not going to look into it any further, resource implications and all that. We've identified him but don't know if he has any living relatives, certainly no one's come forward yet. Maybe you could run an article in the paper, see if anyone has heard of him?'

'Sure, no problem. Give me his details and I'll see what I can do.'

Morgan gives Caroline a brief description of Terry Smith then changes the topic of conversation - she is after all still a journalist and has already proved untrustworthy. Instead, they talk about what they like to do in their free time when they're not working.

After they finish their coffee and the remainder of the bottle of wine, Morgan rummages through the kitchen cupboards to try to find another one, eventually locating a bottle of Shiraz Rose that Celia has been saving for their next dinner party. He makes a mental note to buy another one before his wife returns home and notices that it is missing. 'So, how did you know that Celia is away?' Morgan asks the question he has been wanting to know the answer for since he opened the front door to find Caroline Woods standing on the other side of it.

'A journalist never reveals her sources I'm afraid,' Caroline teases.

Morgan nods then sips his replenished glass of wine. He nestles back into the sofa, listening to the wind outside, which has now picked up and is howling around the back door, rattling the loose fence panel he has been meaning to fix for months. He's glad that he does not have to go outside again tonight. As soon as the thought enters his mind, he chastises himself as he realises that Caroline will need to go out again. In fact, neither of them has considered how she will reach home, both of them have drunk far too much wine to drive. Perhaps he could phone for a taxi for her he decides, trying to stifle a yawn. The overindulgence of food and alcohol, not to mention the hypnotic flames of the fire are making him feel both relaxed and sleepy.

Caroline draws up her legs and curls herself up further into the sofa, her cheeks reddening from the heat of the flames. They sit in silence, both of them mesmerised by the flames, bewitched by the intensity of the flickering colours that are creating shadows against the wall.

'Well, I suppose I should get going,' Caroline says at last, breaking the silence. 'I can see my company is sending you to sleep.'

'Sorry, it's the long hours I'm afraid. I can't handle late nights and early starts anymore, I must be getting old,' Morgan replies. 'Can I phone for a taxi for you?'

'Thanks, but I like walking, it makes me feel alive.'

'I'll come with you,' Morgan says, instantly regretting his act of chivalry.

'Don't worry, I'll be fine. You look settled in for the night,' Caroline replies softly, bending over to kiss his cheek. Morgan curls his fingers around her neck to pull her closer to him, kissing her fully on the lips. He can feel her responding to him as they sink down onto the carpet in front of the fire.

It is only much later that Morgan wonders what came over him and how he will be able to face Celia when she returns. What will he say to her? Should he say anything at all? Caroline, as if reading his thoughts, answers for him.

'You won't tell anyone will you?' she says softy, turning to look at Morgan.

'No, of course not,' Morgan responds, with more than a hint of relief in his voice.

'I really should go this time, I've got a lot of work to do.' Caroline pulls on her jeans and jumper before moving towards the front door. 'When's Celia back?'

'Wednesday evening,' Morgan replies, unsure of where the conversation is going.

Caroline collects her still damp coat from the porch and puts it on. Standing in the porch, she smiles at Morgan one last time, then shuts the door behind her.

Guilt immediately washes over Morgan, not only about what has just happened but also for letting Caroline walk home alone. It could be the dreadful weather instigating his reluctance to act chivalrously, but it far more likely that he just wants Caroline Woods to be as far away from him and his house as possible. The house he shares with his wife.

A sudden wave of nausea washes over Morgan and he cannot tell if it is the result of too much alcohol or the realisation that he has just broken his wedding vows. His heart thumps loudly behind his rib cage as he clears away the empty wine glasses from the floor, where they were abandoned a little while earlier. Perhaps the wine clouded his judgement he considered, as he placed the glasses in the sink. It's certainly not something he ever thought that he could do. How could he betray Celia like that?

Morgan switches off the downstairs lights and makes his way upstairs - the washing-up can be left for the morning. Right now, his mind is in a torrent of turmoil, wondering if he will ever see Caroline again and more importantly, whether or not he should. If he does then it could herald the end of his marriage but he also knows that right now, he does not wish to say goodbye to Caroline Woods either.

Chapter 23

Luke Fields was transported from Marham police station to Deben Quay early morning, to be formally charged in the County where the misdemeanours have taken place. He is looking a lot less arrogant than the last time he saw him, Morgan considers, as he watches one of the custody officers lead him into the interview room. Morgan is feeling more than a little smug as he observes Luke from across the table; the pale-skinned suspect seems to have developed a nervous habit of picking at the skin on his chin, which he does with vigour as he stares at the table in front of him where a forensic report is lying temptingly within reach.

Cook switches on the recorder, noting the time and date, as well as who is present in the room. 'So, here we are again Mr Fields. I hope this time you will be a little more cooperative than the last time we met.' Cook stares at the suspect, waiting for a response. Luke glances sideways at his solicitor, then nods his head.

'When was the last time you saw your mother?' Cook asks, shuffling back into his chair, his arms resting across his slightly protruding abdomen that is rising and falling rhythmically.

'I don't know, several years at least. We fell out and didn't speak very often after that, just the odd card at birthdays and Christmas,' Luke replies, still staring at the document on the table.

'So, you haven't been to her house recently then?' Cook asks.

'No, of course not, I just told you.' Luke looks up, his brow wrinkling in puzzlement, wondering where the line of questioning is heading.

'So, how come your footprints were found at both your mother's house and business premises?' Cook continues, watching carefully for any reaction from the suspect.

Luke closes his eyes momentarily. 'Whatever I say will be taken the wrong way won't it. If I say I was there you will think that I killed her and Lucy, if I don't then you will think that I'm lying.'

Cook turns to the left and raises his eyebrows at Morgan who is smirking. 'Correct. So why don't you just tell us the truth?'

Luke opens his eyes and looks at his solicitor again, unsure of how to respond. Morgan leans forward, straining to hear what Luke's solicitor is whispering to his client.

'I went to see my mother on the Thursday evening. It was her birthday so I thought I would surprise her,' Luke eventually says after deciding the best way to answer.

'So why not tell us that before? And why did you still go on the youth club holiday, even though we informed you that your mother was missing?' Cook asks.

'I didn't want to let the children down.' Luke barely spoke above a whisper.

'I bet you didn't,' Morgan snorts, eliciting a glowering look from Luke Fields solicitor, warning him not to go too far down that particular line of questioning.

'Did you go into your mother's house?' Cook asks.

'No. There wasn't any answer when I rang the doorbell, so I went to the tearoom to see if she was there.'

'What time was this?' Morgan asks, sitting upright with renewed interest.

'I don't know exactly. It was dark, so I guess it must have been early evening? I was back home in time to watch Midsomer Murders, so it must have been about seven when I was in Deben Quay.'

'And no one else was with you or saw you to corroborate this?' Cook asks.

'No,' Luke says dejectedly. 'Well, there was a couple in the bandstand, I could hear them talking when I went to see if mother was in the tearoom but I didn't see them, so I doubt they saw me.'

Cook makes a note of it. 'So, you didn't go inside either building then?'

'No. It didn't look as if anyone was there, so why would I?' Luke says, becoming exasperated by the line of questioning.

'So, how come we found your fingerprints on the door frame of your mother's tearoom?' Cook asks.

'I don't know! This is ridiculous, I can't remember everything I've done and everything I've touched,' Luke snaps.

'I'm sure you can't,' Morgan retorts. 'You seem to have forgotten killing your girlfriend and mother.'

Luke's solicitor leans sideways to whisper loudly to his client, urging him not to say anymore for now. Cook promptly halts the interview to allow Luke and his solicitor time to discuss the situation before pulling Morgan out of the room before he can protest.

The break gives Cook and Morgan the opportunity to grab sandwiches from the small canteen and take them back up to the incident room, which is virtually empty as most of the team are embroiled in work. Morgan perches on the edge of his desk to eat his sandwich, leaving Cook to take up residence in the chair. Cook leans across the desk and switches on Morgans computer, then logs into his account and discovers that the latest forensic report has arrived.

To: DCI.Cook@DebenQuay.Police.UK
From: Forensics@SuffolkLab.co.uk

Date: 4 March 2016

Re: Test Results - Tearoom

DCI Cook,

The following results have been obtained:

- Impressions of the footprints taken from near the tearoom are a perfect match for a pair of Luke Fields trainers that SOCO found at his house.
- Mud samples taken from the bottom of the trainers are still being analysed and will be checked against the samples taken from the quayside.
- Fingerprints taken from the door frame at the tearoom and from the doorbell at Glebe Cottage match those taken from Luke Fields.
- A discarded Marlboro Light cigarette found outside the tearoom contained Luke Fields DNA.
- The tyre tracks found close to the tearoom and slip way did not match the tyres on Luke Fields car. Lucy Mortimers car is still missing and cannot be discounted.

Cook sighs in relief as he reads through the email for a second time. 'We got it! The evidence we need to put that bastard away.'

'Just in time as well,' Morgan smirks as he reads the email over Cooks shoulder. He will enjoy telling Luke Fields the good news.

Cook smiles thinly, they may have enough evidence to arrest Luke Fields but they will need more than that to secure a conviction. He turns around to locate Fallow, who is busily typing up a report on a neighbouring desk.

'It looks like there were a couple in the bandstand on the Thursday night before Mrs Fields died, I need you to look into it, they might have witnessed Luke Fields going to his mother's tearoom,' Cook says to Fallow. He pauses for a moment to take another bite of his soggy BLT. 'It might also be an idea for you to go through the witness statements as well, just in case anyone else mentioned the couple. After you've done that, we'll need to organise a press release asking for more witnesses to come forward.'

Fallow nods in acknowledgement, then shuts down his computer and roughly pushes back his chair, the sound of it scraping against the floor echoing through the room. He reaches behind the door to grab his coat from the hook just as the door flings open to reveal Bennett, who has chosen that particular moment to check up on the team's progress. He ignores his nephew who is politely holding the door open for him and instead makes a beeline for Cook, who swiftly follows him into his office.

Morgan takes up residence in the newly vacated chair and gulps down the rest of his sandwich. He allows himself a few moments of respite to read through the daily news. A jolt goes through him as he spies Caroline's name, which is as ever, adorning the front page.

THE SUFFOLK TIMES

Friday, 5 March 2006

Arrest Made Over Quayside Deaths
by Caroline Woods

Norfolk businessman Luke Fields has been arrested for the deaths of two people. Lucy Mortimer, his former girlfriend, was found dead at Deben Quay on 22 February this year. She was drugged before being killed and dumped in the river. Luke Fields mother was found dead in the remains of her tearoom, which was also destroyed by fire.

Mr Fields originally came from Deben Quay but moved out of the area many years ago. Neighbours near his current home of Marham, describe him as a quiet man who mainly keeps to himself.

Body at the Bandstand Identified
by Caroline Woods

The body of a homeless man found at the bandstand on Deben Quay, has been named as Terry Smith, aged 61. Any relatives of Terry Smith should contact DC Fallow at Deben Quay police.

Mumps Outbreak at Suffolk School
by Leah Hart

An outbreak mumps has been confirmed at a school in Suffolk. Twelve pupils at Middleton High School have been diagnosed with mumps as well as two teachers. The school has been closed until further notice.

Lorry Overturns on Main Road
by Russell Carter

A lorry which overturned on the A14 yesterday caused havoc for commuters in the Westleton area. Both lanes of the carriageway were shut for two hours after the accident, which occurred at 3.10 pm yesterday afternoon. An ambulance was called and checked over the driver who had escaped through the window of his cab. The lorry was righted by crane and one lane of the carriageway reopened again by 5.30 pm. Nearby residents were shocked at yet another accident happening on this stretch of the road.

Morgan discards the paper on the desk and goes in search of two officers who can go to Marham and speak to Luke Fields neighbours - hopefully it might shed some light on the suspects whereabouts during the weekend of his mother and partners deaths. As he is making his way back to the office, Bennett is then leaving Cooks office. Morgan presses himself up against the wall to make way for Bennetts ever-expanding girth that is now making its way through the doorway.

'I hope you're keeping an eye on my nephew,' Bennett barks as he squeezes past. 'He might seem tough, but really, he's quite sensitive. Being bullied at school didn't help of course, which is why I thought it would be good for him to be part of a team.'

'Yes Sir, of course,' Morgan says, feeling a little guilty that he has not shown much kindness to Fallow.

'Let's get back to the interview room,' Cook says as he appears from his office.

'Yes boss!' Morgan replies cheekily, hoping that Bennett is not still in earshot.

Just as the two men are about to step into the corridor, the phone on Cooks desk begins to ring. Cook sprints back to grabs the phone and receives some welcome news.

'A black Honda Civic has been reported parked in a country lane half-way between Deben Quay and Marham. A local dog-walker noticed that the car hadn't moved for several days so decided to report it as an abandoned vehicle. Local police have carried out a PNC check and guess who owns the car?'

'Please tell me its Lucy Mortimers,' Morgan says hopefully.

'You got it in one!'

'Where's the car now?' Morgan asks.

'It's in the forensic workshop. Can you go there now?'

'Sure thing, boss.'

Morgan last visited the voluminous workshop when he was training to become a detective. The huge sterile warehouse is located on the outskirts of Deben Quay and just as Morgan expected, nothing has changed. He quickly locates the workshop foreman, who takes him through to a cramped office at the far end of the building.

'Well, as I'm sure you remember from your training, we have carried out the usual checks - dusting the car for fingerprints and checking for fibres and hairs. We've also made impression of the tyre treads.'

'Anything you can give us the heads up about now?' Morgan asks hopefully.

The workshop foreman, whose badge on his jumper helpfully tells Morgan his name is 'Steve Fulcher', explains to Morgan their initial findings. 'It's looking promising, several fingerprints have been found on both the passenger and driver's side as well as mud in the driver's side footwell.

'That does sound promising, obviously we need the results as soon as you get them, we've got a rather nasty bloke that we want to charge.'

'Sure thing, I'll mark the tests as 'urgent'. Hope you get to catch your guy.'

Morgan hopes so too but he also knows that it is not that easy to get a case past the Crown Prosecution Service. There is nothing else that he can do now though but wait and hope that they get the results back soon.

Chapter 24

Morgan is lying in bed awake listening to the dawn chorus, thoughts of Caroline running through his mind. He has slept little, his mind going into overdrive as he tussles with his emotions. As the sun begins to break, he finally gives up the pretence of sleep and hauls himself out of bed, pulling on the clothes he discarded onto the bedroom floor the previous night. The house is cold without Celias excellent organisational skills - Morgan has forgotten to set the timer on the heating once again and is now paying the price for his ineptitude.

Even a strong cup of coffee does little to warm him as he waits for the radiators to spring into life. He can't face breakfast with feeling so unsettled without the company of his wife, so he decides to make a start on the long list of jobs that Celia has left him. He cleans the bathrooms with vigour, scrubbing the bath enthusiastically as if trying to cleanse all thoughts of Caroline from his memory. Once finished, he decides he should go and buy some food, as even he cannot eat takeaways every night.

The local supermarket is always busy on a Saturday morning, making the distasteful task even more odious than usual. Morgan meanders up and down the crowded aisles, trying to decide what he can actually manage to cook, as much as what he would like to eat. As he is picking his way through packets of rump steak, trying to decide which one to choose, someone taps him on his right shoulder. Morgan looks behind him to see who it is.

Caroline is standing in the aisle behind him, peering over his shoulder to see what he is doing. 'You look like you need a hand,' she teases.

Morgan almost blushes, which is not a good look for an almost forty-year-old male. 'I'm not used to shopping, as I'm sure you can tell,' he replies, feeling embarrassed at his ineptitude of such a simple task.

'That one looks a good one,' Caroline says, pointing to the packet that Morgan is holding. 'I'm going to buy the same thing for tonight. Why don't you bring it round to my flat and I can cook both of them. It would save me from worrying that you might burn your house down.'

Morgan smiles sheepishly at her. She has correctly deduced that he is in fact a liability to both himself and to others when in the kitchen, which is why Celia does not usually allow him in there. Celia has left him some home-made casseroles in the freezer, but Morgan has forgotten how to cook them and he cannot ask her as no phones are allowed at the retreat.

'That would be great thanks,' Morgan replies gratefully. He memorises Carolines address then heads off towards the wine aisle to find something suitable for the meal. It is after Caroline has left that Morgan realises that he never gave Caroline his address. How did she find out where he lives?

Late afternoon, Morgan receives a dinner invitation from Cook, which he manages to put off until Sunday. He hopes that he sounded less guilty than he felts when he informed his friend that he was already busy that evening, whilst deftly avoiding revealing his actual plans. He could tell by the tone of Cooks voice that he was suspicious of the spiel but given that his wife was probably listening into their conversation, Morgan correctly guessed that Cook would not openly question it. For now, at least, he was in the clear.

    Morgan managed to do little else during the remainder of the day other than put on a load of washing and even then he was uncertain that he had done it correctly - he had taken a deep breath, loaded the washing machine with a jumble of dirty clothes, added some badly measured detergent into one of the drawer slots and switched it on, hoping for the best. With the task completed, Morgan settled down onto the sofa to read the newspaper, which had been pushed through the porch door earlier. It made a nice change for him to have time to sit down and read, without Celia constantly nagging him to finish one job or another.

    On the front page of the paper is one of Carolines articles. She is still covering the murder cases and Morgan feels an unexpected tinge of pride that he knows the talented journalist.

THE SUFFOLK TIMES

Saturday, 6 March 2006

Two Die on Death Road
by Russell Carter

Two people died on the A12 last night in two separate accidents. The first accident happened at 11.10 pm at the Rookery Crossroads, involving a motorbike and a Land Rover. Witnesses reported seeing the motorbike overtake the Land Rover on a bend and skid off the road, hitting a tree. The motorbike rider was taken to hospital with severe head injuries but later died. The driver of the Land Rover was unharmed.

The second accident occurred at around 1.15am and involved three cars at the Ingham turn off. A Peugeot was thought to have come off the slip road straight into the paths of two vehicles on the A12. The driver of the Toyota Yaris died at the scene whilst the driver and passenger of the BMW were taken to Hemley Hospital with serious injuries. The driver of the Peugeot has been arrested for driving whilst under the influence of alcohol.

Deben Watersports

For all your water sport needs, including wetsuits, kayaks, kite-surfing and canoe repairs.
Tel: 38965 for details.

Businessman Charged with Deaths
by Caroline Woods

Norfolk businessman Luke Fields has been formally charged with causing the deaths of his partner and mother.
Luke Fields will be held on remand at Feering prison until the trial, which is likely to be conducted early next year. Anyone who was in the Deben Quay area last weekend and may have seen something, should contact local police.

Missing Dog Found
by Caroline Woods

A valuable greyhound which was taken from a racing kennels in Stockholt has been found alive and well. A concerned dog walker reported seeing the dog at a remote farm near Minsmere. The resident had become concerned after seeing the dog tied to a fence post when she walked her dog yesterday morning. The dog, which seemed distressed, was still in the same place when the woman walked her dog again that afternoon. The RSPCA have now collected the animal and, having checked it for a microchip, returned it to its rightful owner.

By early evening, Morgan is not only very hungry but also feeling slightly nervous in anticipation of the evening ahead. It is a twenty-minute walk to Carolines flat in Maybush Drive and by the time he is ready to set off from home, he is also feeling more than a little uncomfortable about what he is about to do. As he opens the front door, Morgan takes a deep breath and quashes the feelings of guilt to one side, almost managing to convince himself that there is nothing wrong with him spending the evening with an attractive young woman whilst his wife is away.

It is a pleasant evening in comparison to those they have had of late, though still a little chilly. Morgan sets off with time to spare so that he can go via the riverside and revisit the crime scenes again. When he reaches the quayside, he notices that the crime scene tapes have now been removed. A few curious onlookers are walking up and down the river path, trying to catch a glimpse of the burnt-out remains of the tearoom, which has been fenced off to prevent anyone from entering the unstable building. Morgan wonders what will happen to it if Luke Fields is convicted. He cannot imagine the building will endure many winters before it completely collapses.

Morgan strolls along the river path until he reaches the spot where Lucy was found, which now seems such a long time ago. The path is so peaceful in comparison to the last time he was here - when there was a bustle of police and forensic officers scouring the area for evidence. Now it is all but a distant memory, almost as if it never happened. He continues up the path to stand next to the cluster of reeds and rushes where Lucys body was discovered. Here too, it looks as if nothing sinister ever happened; sailing boats are moored up in the middle of the murky grey river as if tucked up for the night and being rocked to sleep; the gentle incoming tidal river, which is lapping against the decaying boat peppered by algae and limpets, is silhouetted by the fading winter sun. Morgan pauses for a moment to listen to the soft caws of seagulls who have travelled upstream from the nearby coastal waters and the rush of water as it swirls onto the sandy riverbed below the coastal path that he is standing on. It is as if nothing ever happened here, as if nature itself has washed the bitter memories away again; cleansed it. It is hard now to ever imagine there was a body here at all.

It is beginning to get dark, with the sun sinking lower behind the poplar trees that run around the perimeter of the sheep fields that lie adjacent to the river path. Morgan takes one last look at the fading light shimmering on the surface of the river, then begins to stroll back up the path again but this time, heading in the direction of the town centre. As he passes the Victorian bandstand where Terry Smith was found dead, he notices a light on at Glebe Cottage. Intrigued, he makes his way up the path to the house.

Morgans heart thumps as he creeps around the shrubbery towards the rear of the property, his shoes crunching audibly on broken twigs and autumnal detritus, loud cracks echoing through the stillness. The only other sound he can hear is the low hum of a busy road some distance away. Morgan reaches the back of the property and peers in through a small low window, where there is a chink in the net curtain. Inside, he can see a figure moving about in the living room. A figure who is rummaging through the drawers of a sideboard. It is a silhouette that he recognises - Caroline.

Morgan storms over to the back door, the need for quiet surprise discarded, then flings open the partially glazed door, which has been left ajar. 'What are you doing here?' Morgan booms.

Caroline slams shut the drawer she has just opened. 'Oh my god, are you trying to scare me to death?' She looks both shocked and mortified at the same time. 'I was going for a walk and saw someone in here. The back door was open, so I thought I'd take a look. I was just about to call you,' Caroline replies smoothly. 'What are you doing here?'

'I was a bit early, so I thought I'd stop off on the way. I saw the light on so thought I'd better investigate,' Morgan says.

'Ah I see. Maybe we should get going, the beef casserole is probably ready by now.'

'I thought we were having steak?' Morgan asks.

'Well, seeing as it's so cold I thought a casserole would be nice. You don't mind, do you?'

'Sure, that's fine. There doesn't seem to be anything missing from the house and the door hasn't been damaged so it looks ok to leave. Maybe a friend of Mrs Fields stopped by to check up on the house and forgot to lock the door?' Morgan ponders.

'That sounds plausible, shall we go?' Caroline says quickly. She moves towards the door, ushering Morgan out of the cottage.

Morgan cannot help but wonder why Caroline is in this part of Deben Quay when she is supposed to be at home cooking their dinner, but he keeps his thoughts to himself as they meander their way through the narrow, cobbled streets that lace through the centre of the town. Ten minutes later, just as the last of the sunlight fades, they reach the Victorian building where Carolines lives.

The aroma of slow-cooking meat assaults their senses as soon as Caroline unlocks the front door. Morgans stomach rumbles, his need for food overriding any questions he still has over Carolines unexpected presence at Glebe Cottage.

After taking off his coat and hanging it up on a hook near the front door, Caroline leaves Morgan to explore the small lounge. Morgan watches as Caroline busies herself in the kitchen, placing saucepans containing new potatoes, cabbage and peas onto the hob to boil. Then, he peruses the small attic room, nosing through the well-ordered DVD and CD collection, before moving on to the tall pine bookcase that dwarfs the sloped attic room.

Feeling slightly guilty after all the snooping he has been doing, Morgan decides that perhaps he should make some contribution towards the meal. He locates a corkscrew in the kitchen and expertly opens the bottle of Merlot he has brought with him. He pours out two large measures of the fruity liquid into over-sized wine glasses then hands one to Caroline, who is still hovering in front of the oven in case one of the saucepans boil over.

    By the time Morgan has consumed his first glass of wine, the vegetables have been cooked and served up by Caroline alongside the succulent beef stew. They sit at the oval teak table that has been squeezed into the corner of the living room and chat about anything other than the cases that they are both working on. Morgan tells Caroline about his life, his childhood and how he ended up as a police officer. Caroline says very little, seemingly content to listen to his soothing voice above the dulcet tones of Jose Gonzalez, whose music is gently playing in the background.

    'Where did you grow up?' Morgan asks before taking another large gulp of wine. 'You haven't mentioned your family?'

    'I'm not in touch with them anymore, anyway I'd rather concentrate on the present then the past. Tell me more about your childhood, it sounds idyllic, with holidays on the beach and home-cooked meals every night.'

    'I was very lucky. I think that's what made we want to become a police officer, to give something back to the community. My parents are dead now, but I know they would've approved.'

They finish the meal and Caroline takes the plates through to the galley kitchen, discarding them into the sink to wash-up tomorrow. Morgan replaces the CD, which has now finished playing with another equally as soothing, then makes himself comfortable on the sofa, where he periodically sips from his half-empty glass. With perfect timing, Caroline returns from the kitchen with another bottle and tops up Morgans glass before she curls up on the sofa next to him and closes her eyes. The excess of food and alcohol is clearly making her feel sleepy, as she relaxes back into the soft cushions scattered across one end of the sofa. Morgan leans over and kisses Caroline affectionately on the cheek. She opens her eyes and smiles sleepy at Morgan then takes hold of his hand and leads him into the bedroom without so much as a murmur of protest from him.

Chapter 25

After being formally charged with the murders of both his mother and girlfriend, Luke Fields is remanded in custody without bail at Feering Prison. Given his history of inappropriate relationships, the prison warden decides that it would be safest to segregate him from the other prisoners, who may not take too kindly to finding out that their fellow prisoner has a preference for young girls; there are many long-term prisoners on the wing who have children that they will not see for years and therefore feel that it is their duty to protect them in any way that they can. Conversely, it is the prison administrator's job to keep Luke Fields safe, until the trial at least, a role that many members of the public openly contest, perhaps preferring a vigilante solution for certain types of crime.

It is never silent at night in a prison - something that Luke Fields discovers on his first night in Feering Prison - as he listens to the banter between the other prisoners and the footsteps of prison officers pacing up and down the corridors, making frequent checks to ensure he has not harmed himself - not that he would have the opportunity to do so as they have stripped him of anything that could be used as a weapon against himself or others. All he can do is wait for the dawn to break and wonder what will happen next.

This is not how he expected his life to pan out and he cannot help but wonder how long he will be able to tolerate these claustrophobic conditions. As a child, his father had locked him in the cupboard under the stairs as punishment for some minor misdemeanour or other and the experience had left him fearful of enclosed spaces. The tiny, obscured window, which is now his only source of natural light, is too high up for him to peer out of, leaving him with only four blank walls on which to gaze. Luke lays down on the thin mattress, feeling the coiled springs beneath the inadequate wadding poking up into his shoulder-blades. He stares into the impenetrable darkness, listening to the cat calls from the other prisoners and all the other unfamiliar sounds that surround him.

Luke sleeps fitfully, drifting in and out of consciousness, waking every time he hears an unfamiliar sound, which occurs frequently during that first, long night. At some point though he must have fallen into a deeper sleep, as the next thing he is aware of is the six o'clock buzzer jolting him from his restless slumber.

Sunday is normally a quiet day at the prison. Visitors are not allowed and many of the prisoners attend the church service, in part to relieve some of the tedium of the non-working day. There is also another reason for the high attendance rate at the service; many prisoners have miraculously 'found god' whilst inside and the more cynical person might deduce that this has been done to appear 'reformed' in the hope of securing an early parole. Religious services at Feering Prison are well attended by all accounts.

As a newcomer and a suspected sex-offender at that, Luke is only let out of his cell for meals, where he is carefully watched by staff and fellow prisoners alike. All are equally curious about their new inmate, but only the former have concrete knowledge of his alleged crimes. As a remand prisoner, Luke is not allowed the privilege of a job within the prison, so will have to find some other way to occupy the long days and nights to come. The thought of trying to fill the empty hours until the trial was a painful one, but the idea of being found guilty and not leaving this establishment for many years to come, was not one that Luke could currently stand to contemplate. All he could do for now was to sit on his meagre bed and think about anything that he could to occupy his mind and try to stop himself from going slowly insane.

Morgan is bored. Without his wife nagging him to finish the DIY jobs he started months ago, he feels underwhelmed with motivation to undertake anything, let alone something he detests doing. He has arranged to go to Cooks house for dinner in the evening, but at ten in the morning, the evening seems a long way off. Time seems to go by very slowly when you are waiting for something to happen.

Caroline has not contacted him since he left her flat in the early hours, leaving Morgan wondering if she is upset with him. He cannot decide if he should phone her, then feels guilty at the idea, when he should instead be missing his wife. Guilt wins out and Morgan pushes all thoughts of Caroline aside and sets to completing the tasks of putting up the shelves and bathroom mirror Celia bought nearly three months ago. At least she will be happy with him when she returns Morgan decides. He wonders what would happen when she does. Will she notice the change in him? Should he leave her? No, he is getting ahead of himself now. It's just an affair, nothing more.

Morgan cannot get used to the silence in the house, so delves into the under-the-stairs cupboard to retrieve an old radio that once belonged to his father. To his surprise, the radio still works and soon fills the empty house with jovial music. Spurred on, Morgan quickly finishes the bathroom, before moving onto tackling some of the cleaning tasks he knows Celia would ordinarily have done at the weekend.

The remainder of the day passes more swiftly than Morgan expected and before he knows it, it is time to shower and change. Wiping the condensation from the mirror he hung above the sink earlier, Morgan stares at his reflection, noting the grey hairs that are beginning to creep in as well as a few more wrinkles around his eyes. He cannot help but wonder what it is that a young, vibrant journalist would see in him.

The sound of the phone penetrates through Morgans thoughts, bringing him back to the present. He grabs a towel from the floor and wraps it around his waist then leaps down the stairs, two steps at a time. He grabs the receiver just before it stops ringing; it is Cook wondering where he is, checking if he has forgotten their plans. Morgan apologises profusely before slamming down the phone and running back upstairs to retrieve his clothes. Luckily Cook only lives three streets away and less than ten minutes later, Morgan is outside his friend's front door, albeit breathless and still with wet hair.

Cook immediately notices a difference in his friend as they eat a well-cooked roast beef with an assortment of roasted vegetables, accompanied by the bottle of Australian Shiraz Morgan purchased from the local corner shop. Morgan seems to be troubled by something and instinct tells him that it is not being caused by either the investigation or Celias absence. Cook diplomatically volunteers them both for washing up duties whilst his wife puts the children to bed, thus engineering an opportunity to converse with hid friend alone.

'So, what have you been up to whilst Celias been away?' Cook asks directly, as he takes hold of a greasy roasting tray and plunges it into the soapy washing-up bowl. Morgan blushes, then mumbles something that sounds like 'nothing', reminding Cook of his teenage son.

'Nothing at all, that's a bit boring. What did you do last night then, you said you had other plans?' Cook persists, handing over a wet Yorkshire pudding tray for Morgan to dry.

'I went to a friend's house for dinner, that's all.' Morgan says as he dries the tray then stacks it to one side.

'Was this friend by any chance a young, pretty journalist?'

Morgan stops drying to stare at Cook. He knows there is little point in lying to his oldest friend. 'So, what if it was, we're only friends. She's helping with the case.' Morgan finishes drying the saucepan that he is holding then hands it to Cook so that he can return it to the correct cupboard.

'I hope so. Celias a lovely woman and doesn't deserve to be badly treated.' Cook turns to look at Morgan. 'Did I ever tell you that I once had an affair?'

'No, you didn't. When was that?' Morgan stops what he is doing, astonished by the confession.

'It was after we'd had Harry. Sarah had gone off sex and was too busy with a screaming baby to give me any attention. It was stupid of me, I know. She forgave me eventually.'

Morgan looks at his friend and nods. He is about to speak when Sarah comes into the room with the wine glasses from the table. 'Would you like another drink?' Sarah asks Morgan.

'I'd better not, we've got an early start tomorrow. A prison visit is bad enough without adding a hangover into the equation.'

Morgan thanks his hosts for the meal and makes his excuses to leave. It is only a short walk back to his dark, empty house but by the time he reaches home he has made a decision; Cook is right, it has to stop now before anyone gets hurt. The problem is, he already has feelings for Caroline and cannot contemplate never seeing her again.

Chapter 26

Her head is pounding. A constant throbbing above her left eye, interjected by sharp, stabbing pains in the back of her optic nerve that will not ease, no matter which way she lays. She has given up trying to get up, as waves of nausea force her back down onto the sofa. The tablets the doctor have given her are no longer working. She will have to go back again and see what else she can take. She has had migraines before, but these seem different, much worse and lasting longer. The last time she'd had one of these heads she had tried having a hot bath and instantly vomited the minute she sunk into the water, the heat making her head throb harder than ever. She will not make that mistake again.

It is no good, she will have to phone in sick. She hates that more than anything; her job is her world. Caroline closes her eyes and nestles back into the soft cushions on the sofa, wondering what Morgan is doing and if he is thinking of her at all.

The thought of Morgan spurs her into action. Caroline takes a deep breath and hauls herself up off the sofa, feeling for the wall for support as another wave of dizziness shoots through her. She staggers into the bedroom and flops down onto the bed, grabbing hold of her mobile, which is still on her bedside table where she left it the previous night. Gingerly she lies back then carefully turns onto her side, allowing her senses to adjust for a moment before switching on her mobile, her pupils constricting in protest at the harsh light. Caroline punches out a short message to Phil Wattle, letting him know that she will not be at work. The usually simple task has used up the last of her energy reserves, still holding the mobile in one hand, Caroline pulls the duvet up over her shoulder and closes her eyes.

Morgan sleeps restlessly, waking frequently in a cold sweat. He dreams that Celia has left him, that Cook found out about his affair and sacked him; that he has lost everything for something that was never going to go anywhere. By the time his alarm clock beeps, Morgan has only managed to sleep for a couple of hours.

     A cool shower and a mug of strong black coffee energises him enough to still get into the office earlier than most of the other officers. They are interviewing Luke Fields again and Morgan wants to go through the paperwork to see if there they have missed anything or if there is a new angle they can use. The newspaper articles Caroline has given him could help, as they show that Luke has a history of inappropriate behaviour along with a preference for young women. Morgan wonders if perhaps Luke killed Lucy as she was too old for him or because a baby would remind him that she was no longer a child. Lucy looked very young for her age and Lukes sexual preferences show a strong pattern.

Morgan flicks through the latest forensics report that is lying on Cooks desk, which details the test results from a letter found in Lucys car - a partial fingerprint and a single hair found in the envelope were positively identified as belonging to Luke Fields. Morgan extracts the letter, which is still enclosed in a plastic evidence bag. He opens up the white envelope to reveal a short note nestled within, which he retrieves then unfolds. The letter is signed 'Lucy' and is dated the day she disappeared. Morgan carefully reads through the letter then places it back into the plastic evidence bag.

Luke looks as if he too has had little sleep. His dishevelled appearance shocks the two detectives, who are accustomed to seeing his well-groomed hair and neatly pressed clothes. Luke sits down quietly opposite them, patiently awaiting his solicitor who is running late.

'So, how are you finding prison life then?' Morgan asks as he sips on his third cup of coffee of the day.

Luke momentarily glares at Morgan through narrowed eyes, before looking the other way to continue staring at the wall in front of him. The tense atmosphere in the room is only broken by the arrival of Lukes solicitor, who is clutching a takeaway coffee in one hand and a black briefcase in the other.

Cook drums his fingers on the table, waiting for the solicitor to retrieve some documents from his briefcase and settle into the chair next to his client.

'Why did you kill your mother and girlfriend?' Cook begins, clearly not feeling in the mood for making small talk.

Luke looks at his solicitor then replies, 'no comment', before returning his gaze to the wall behind Cook and Morgan.

Cook stares at the suspect for a moment before continuing with his questioning. 'We've been doing some research on you and it seems that you have a preference for young girls. You first met Lucy when she was a teenager. So why did you start up a relationship with her again? Was it because she still looked young? Did she dress up as a schoolgirl for you?' Luke snorts and shoots Cook a look of sheer contempt.

'What about Anna Jackaman? Did you not want to start seeing her again now that she's back in Deben Quay? Or is she not your type anymore that she's grown up?'

Luke smirks, whilst his solicitor tries to control the look of surprise on his face when Cook shows him the newspaper articles Caroline has copied for them.

'What has this got to do with my client's charges?' The solicitor asks, sliding the newspaper clippings across the table towards Cook.

'Motive. Lucy was pregnant when she died, ergo she was no longer a child. And your client likes young girls,' Morgan says confidently. 'Of course, a pregnant girlfriend would also be a drain on his already difficult financial situation. Babies cost a lot of money and I get the impression that Lucy was not the sort of person to be happy living in a council house and shopping in Iceland.'

'You're wrong. She didn't care about the money,' Luke spits. 'I insisted on buying all her clothes and the car.'

'I'm glad you mentioned the car. We found a letter in it supposedly written by Lucy the day she died. It said that she was leaving you and that she was pregnant. The strange thing is, only your DNA and fingerprints have been found on the letter. Do you have a computer in the house?' Cook asks.

'Well of course I do, you know that, you've searched my house. I would've handled the paper in any case as it's my computer. Lucy rarely used it, only occasionally to do some shopping online,' Luke replies.

'That's right, we've searched your house and yes, there is a computer in your spare room. And guess what, the ink from your printer matches the letter. We also found a copy of the letter on your computer. The only problem is, the Word file containing the letter was created the day after Lucy died.' Cook stops to stare at Luke, who matches his gaze.

Luke takes a sip of water and clears his throat. 'I didn't write that letter,' he sighs, shoulders dropping a little, tiring of the cat and mouse game.

'You must have done. You just said that Lucy didn't often use the computer and only your DNA and fingerprints were found on the paper.' Cook decides to change tactics. 'When did your mother change her will, leaving everything to you?'

'I don't know. I didn't know that she did. I suppose after my father and sister died?' Luke picks up a glass of water from the table, drinking greedily from the vessel to moisten his dry mouth. 'As I've already said, I hadn't seen her for a while.'

'Oh yes of course, which is why your footprints were outside her house and business premises and why recent fingerprints were found at both places,' Morgan retorts.

'It was her birthday, I thought I'd visit her. But as I've already said, she wasn't there,' Luke replies.

'So why visit her now, after all this time?' Cook asks.

'I don't know. I hadn't seen her for a long time and wondered if she was alright.'

'How touching. I'm sure she would've been pleased to see you. So why kill her? Was it because she was going to change her will again?'

'I didn't kill her,' Luke says softly.

Luke pauses to stare at Morgan, his gaze steady as he seemingly probes into Morgans thoughts. Morgan shivers involuntarily.

Cook begins to speak again, diverting Lukes's attention away from Morgan once more. 'Your mothers' solicitor informed us that she was going to change her will and that she was leaving everything to the RSPCA. That dog of hers meant more to her than you did; the wayward son with a fetish for young girls. You would've lost everything, wouldn't you?' Cook challenges. 'What did you do with the dog? We didn't find his body in the tearoom, so he must be somewhere else?'

Luke closes his eyes, tiring of the accusations. Silence descends over the room until Lukes's solicitor breaks it with a request that they take a recess, so that he can counsel his client. Cook follows Morgan, who is already charging out of the interview room at great speed in search of a strong coffee.

No further progress is made when the detectives return from their break, with Luke continuing with his now familiar stony silence. Rather than waste any more of their time, Cook and Morgan terminate the interview and return to the station so they can begin to prepare the mountain of paperwork that the CPS will request for the trial. Morgan also wants to talk to Anna Jackaman again, to see if he can persuade her to make a formal complaint against Luke Fields for sexual assault from when she was a teen. He thinks it unlikely that he will succeed as she seems the type who will want to avoid any negative publicity damaging her modelling career, but it is always worth a try.

Before going to see Anna Jackaman though, Morgan needs to pluck up the courage to phone Caroline. They need to talk and soon - before Celia returns.

Morgan ploughs through his paperwork, procrastinating as long as possible, but as the office gradually empties, leaving him alone, Morgan can put the task off no longer. He takes a sharp intake of breath and dials Carolines number, his heart thumping with indecision as to whether or not he wants to talk to her. The choice is made for him, Caroline is not in the office - she is at home with a migraine. He now has no choice – he will have to stop off at her flat on his way to see Anna Jackaman.

Chapter 27

The door tentatively opens on the third knock. Caroline peers around the half-open door, blinking against the bright light in the hallway. She looks as if she is in a lot of pain, making Morgan immediately feel uncomfortable - he has never been very good at dealing with sick people.

'I tried phoning you at work and they said you weren't well. I hope you don't mind me dropping by,' Morgan says gently.

Caroline smiles weakly then opens the door a little wider to allow Morgan in. The flat is encased in darkness; the closed curtains keeping out any light that may have been emitted from the weak winter sun. Only a dim lamp is visible in the corner of the sitting room.

'Sorry it's so dark in here, the light hurts my head,' Caroline says quietly, as if even the sound of her own voice is causing her pain.

It is Morgans turn to smile tentatively. He rarely knows what to say in these circumstances and feels more than a little uncomfortable. 'I thought you'd like to know that we're getting more and more evidence against Luke Fields. The case is looking really strong. I'm just on my way to go and talk to someone he knew when he was younger who also claims she had a sexual relationship with him when she was fifteen. I wondered if you wanted to come? I want to try and persuade her to prosecute him for sexual assault but she's worried about the publicity harming her career.'

Caroline nods, trying not to wince as the movement causes a sharp pain to shoot though her head. 'I'll just go and get dressed.' She leaves Morgan in the lounge and carefully manoeuvres herself into the bedroom to retrieve some clothes.

Morgan watches through the open door as Caroline takes off her dressing gown and pulls on a pair of jeans and a t-shirt. 'Maybe we could get a takeaway later?' Morgan calls after her, hoping for the opportunity to talk to her about their relationship, or whatever they should call what was happening between them. Caroline does not answer and Morgan quickly drops the subject, realising a little too late that now really is not the right time.

Caroline seems a little stronger as she moves into the kitchen to grab her handbag from the worktop. She pauses in the doorway for a moment, then motions for Morgan to follow her out of the flat. Morgan follows behind as they traipse down the steep, half-turn staircase, which widens out as they near the bottom. The outer security door has been propped open, making Morgan snort at the irony. Through the doorway, he can see his very dirty car on the gravel driveway - it is covered in so much grease and grime that the front number plate is almost obscured. Morgan grimaces as he realises that he could be pulled over for such an offense and makes a mental note to go via the car wash on his way home later.

The car is parked close to the front of the building - an ornate structure that once housed a prominent member of the community. The house had been left to fall into decay by the previous owner, who inherited the property but none of the necessary funds to maintain such an elegant house. By the time the house was sold to a property developer, almost all of it had fallen into disrepair - the sash windows were beyond saving and the remainder of the house needed to be completely re-roofed, re-wired and re-plumbed. To make the development viable, the builder had squeezed in as many flats as the planning department would allow at the lowest possible cost, despite the detrimental effect to both the aesthetics of the building and the quality of housing for the new occupants.

Morgan traverses the driveway to unlock the car doors then helps to ease Caroline into the passenger seat, selfishly hoping that the motion from the car does not make her vomit. If there is one thing he cannot abide, it is vomit - especially in his car. Even the thought of it makes his stomach queasy. Morgan gets into the driver's seat then leans over the gear stick to turn the radio off in case the noise makes Carolines migraine worse.

They remain in a comfortable lull until they reach Anna Jackamans house. The jet-black

Audi TT in the driveway indicates that the glamour model is at home. When she opens the door, Anna Jackaman seems surprised by the identity of her visitors, especially when Morgan introduces Caroline as a local reporter.

'I thought it might help if Caroline talked to you about any possible press coverage,' Morgan explains as Anna looks curiously at his female companion, who is still looking rather pasty.

The model nods in agreement, then shows them through to the lounge, where she indicates for them to sit down on one of the white leather sofas. She offers them a drink and pours out the requested glasses of mineral water, placing them onto the coffee table in front of her guests.

Morgan politely takes a sip of his water, not wishing to offend his host though he would have preferred something a little stronger. He explains to Anna that they are planning to arrest Luke Fields for sexual assault against a minor and that another woman has also come forward who had a sexual relationship with Luke when she was underage. Marham police are also interviewing members of the church youth club which he recently joined as a leader. The fact that the assaults occurred over a long period of time is sure to be taken into consideration, as is the fact that he was in a position of trust when the allegations occurred. Annas contribution could be crucial to the case. Even if she herself does not want to press charges; she could still be a witness to Lukes's relationship with Lucy Mortimer when she was still legally a minor.

Anna sits quietly listening to the policeman's speech, carefully contemplating her response. 'How exactly do you think you will keep my name out of the paper?' She demands to know. 'I can't afford to ruin my career and it seems as if you already have enough evidence and witnesses to put him away for a long time. Why do you need my statement as well?'

'Because sometime in the future he'll be released, and he will carry on abusing young girls, grooming them, making them fall in love with him and having sex with them. He won't stop, they never do,' Caroline spits.

Morgans attention is instantly diverted to Caroline, shocked at the sudden outburst. Perhaps the case has touched a raw nerve he wonders.

Anna Jackaman looks unamused at the outburst. She stands up and asks the pair to leave. 'I'm sorry but I can't do it. I don't want the world to know my business. It was a long time ago and I'm sure I was quite happy to go along with it all. I can make a statement to say that I knew he was having a relationship with Lucy Mortimer but that's it,' Anna says as she ushers them out of the house.

Morgan storms over the threshold and strides off at speed towards his car, fists clenched at his sides. He slams the car door shut and angrily clips on his seat belt with a loud clunk then takes a deep breath, steading his heart rate again as he waits for Caroline. As soon as she has fastened her seatbelt, Morgan turns to glare at her. 'You could have reassured her that her name would be kept out of the paper.'

'Lie you mean? I can't promise her that. I don't own the paper, it's not up to me what's printed,' Caroline answers, equally aggravated by the whole situation. 'Just take me home would you, this is making my migraine worse.'

Morgan swings the car around at the end of the road and heads back to Carolines flat. The roads are quiet as he races along, barely noticing the speed bumps at the top of Carolines road. He screeches to a halt at the kerbside, not bothering to turn into the drive. Caroline slams the door behind her, then strides off towards her flat without even saying goodbye.

Just as Morgan is about to take his foot off the brake, he spots a maroon handbag laying in the footwell. He pulls up the handbrake and switches off the engine, ready to run after Caroline, but she has already gone. Morgan grabs the bag and chases up the stairs after her, taking two steps at a time. When he reaches her flat, he can see through the open door that Caroline is sitting on the sofa crying. Morgan quietly enters the room and sits down on the sofa beside to her, leaving his arm around her until the tears stop.

'I'm sorry if I upset you, I just really want to put this man away for as long as I can. He's clearly lost control and is a danger to young girls.'

'You're going to end it with me, aren't you?' Caroline sniffs, wiping her face with a tissue that Morgan has extracted from his coat pocket.

'I'm sorry. 'Celia will be back soon and I can't hurt her too. She doesn't deserve to be treated like this.'

Caroline nods then stands up. 'I'd like you to go. Obviously if I hear anything useful about the case, I will let you know.' A cold steely tone entering her voice.

Morgan leaves without saying goodbye, confused by Carolines sudden transformation in demeanour. He has never really understood women and however much he likes Caroline, he instinctively knows that she is far too complex for him. The entire episode is making him realise just how much he prefers his simplistic, familiar life with his wife.

Morgan has never seen Cook so angry as he meekly informs him that not only has he failed to get a statement from Anna Jackaman, but that he also took a reporter with him.

'What on earth were you thinking?' Cook shouts at Morgan, who is standing on the other side of the oversized desk that dominates the office. The door is wide open, with the rest of the team pretending to diligently work at their desks as they listen into the conversation.

'I thought I could reassure her about potential press coverage. She didn't want to make a formal complaint against Luke Fields as she was worried about her name getting in the paper.'

'And did it work?' Cook snaps. 'To actually take a journalist with you and without my permission! Did you manage to reassure Anna Jackaman? Was it worth it?' Cook slowly shakes his head, astounded by his friends' action. He has always known that Morgan is headstrong, but to go behind his back like this is something he never expected.

'No, it didn't,' Morgan replies sheepishly.

'I suppose you're still seeing her then?' Cook lowers his voice a little as he pulls out a chair and sits astride it, his left leg pumping up and down.

'It's over,' Morgan says quietly. 'I just thought it would help the case.'

'Well, luckily for you, Marham police have taken statements from two under-age girls who've been having sex with Luke Fields, so we've got the concrete evidence we've been waiting for. We need to get back to the prison and interview him again, but seeing as you can't be trusted, I'll take Fallow with me and leave you to finish off the paperwork.'

Morgan storms out of Cooks office, slamming the door behind him. Ignoring the open stares from his colleagues, he strides across the room and sits down heavily on the chair behind his desk, which is nestled in the corner of the room closest to the radiator. He reaches across the desk to grab hold of the tepid mug of coffee he poured out earlier, knocking it over in the process. Swearing under his breath, Morgan stares momentarily at the beige liquid that is seeping across his paperwork towards the keyboard before he grabs hold of a wad of tissues from his top drawer and begins to dab at the liquid, trying despondently to prevent any more damage before he finds himself in any deeper trouble.

With the mound of sodden tissues discarded to one-side, Morgan logs onto his computer and starts to noisily type up some of the reports they need for the case. He has only managed to bash out a few lines before a movement in the corner of the room catches his attention. He looks up from his keyboard to see Cook striding across the incident room towards the door, Fallow following closely behind.

Morgan stares at the closed door for a few seconds, his heart racing with anger. He never thought his friend would pull rank on him, but he supposes that's what happens when your friends are promoted above you. If only he could have brought himself to schmooze with the bosses, he too might have enjoyed a top promotion – but it's not something he could ever bring himself to do.

Perhaps he should start looking for a different career.

Luke Fields is looking a little more rested than the last time Cook saw him, leaving him wondering if he is beginning to adjust to prison life. He certainly needs to, with a little luck and a lot of hard work, Luke Fields will be spending a long time behind bars, Cook mutters to himself as he sits down opposite him.

Cook reaches across the desk to hand Lukes' solicitor the statements that Marham police collected from the two fifteen-year-old girls Luke allegedly slept with. They were both members of the same church youth club where Luke was a volunteer and have provided formal statements accusing Luke of persuading them to have oral sex with him. It transpires that he told each girl that he was in love with them and neither girl was aware of the other as Luke had ensured that they kept their 'relationship' a secret. He had apparently persuaded them that they needed to keep quiet until they were sixteen when they would be able to 'be together properly'.

Luke glares at Cook as he reads aloud the statements from the two girls. Lukes' solicitor is stifling a yawn as he casually watches the proceedings, only occasionally interjecting to remind Cook that his client will not be commenting on these new allegations. The plea hearing for the murder allegations will now need to be postponed so that Luke can be formally charged with these two additional accounts of sexual assault on a minor. All of the allegations will then be dealt with at the same time. The team at Deben Quay will lead the murder investigation, but Marham police will shoulder most of the responsibility for the sexual assault charges, as the allegations had largely occurred within their jurisdiction. Cook assumes that the solicitor will try to persuade his client to plead guilty, given the ever-increasing volume of evidence against him.

Cook shuffles the mound of papers on the table in front of him then pushes his chair back, preparing to leave. Just as Cook begins to stand up, Luke decides to speak.

'I don't know what you expect from me. A signed confession perhaps?' Luke says sarcastically. 'Well, you'll be waiting a long time for that. I've done nothing wrong, nothing to be ashamed of."

Cook turns around at the sound of the suspects voice, returning Luke's heavy stare.

Luke momentarily stops talking to ensure that he has a captive audience, before resuming with his perceptibly prepared speech. 'I've only ever been friendly and supportive to the kids I've worked with. A lot of them have problems you know. That's why they're there. These girls are looking for someone to blame - some way of channelling their anger at the world. I'm not going to try and defend myself against these ridiculous accusations.' Luke turns his head to one side to glance at his solicitor who looks as if he is literally biting his tongue, whilst silently wishing that his client would do the same.

Luke leans back into his chair, a slight smirk on his face. 'At the end of the day, you've no evidence. It's their word against mine. Who do you think the jury will believe? A couple of kids from broken homes, who get drunk at the weekend and have sex with anyone who asks? I don't think so, you're deluding yourself.'

'No, it is you who are the one who is deluded.' Cook slams his fist down onto the table. 'If it had been just one girl you might have gotten away with it, but it isn't and we can prove that you've been sexually assaulting young girls for a long time.'

'Can you?' Luke says softly, intrigued by the threat. 'Has someone else made a complaint against me?'

'We know there are others and with time, more will come crawling out of the woodwork. They always do. Especially now your names in the papers. Yes, some accusations will be false, but we will wheedle those out. We will find more, I'm sure of it. You don't start interfering with little girls overnight. It takes time to develop that sort of confidence, to learn how to handle them. How to groom them.'

Luke snorts and rolls his eyes, seemingly unconcerned by Cooks threats. His solicitor however has a few more deepened creases on his brow then he had at the start of the interview.

'You will of course be sharing any new evidence against my client with us?' The solicitor says pointedly.

'Of course. We wouldn't jeopardise the case by making such a basic mistake as not sharing evidence.' Cook spits as pushes his chair back to stand up.

'Good luck,' Luke calls after Cook, who has almost reached the door. 'You'll need it with such a flimsy case.'

Cook turns around to face him. 'We won't need it. We've enough evidence to put you away for a very long time for the murders of Lucy and your mother. You're the one who'll need a lot of luck. I've heard that paedophiles aren't too popular in prison. Watch your back, especially in the showers, you never know who'll be there.' Cook watches as Lukes's face fleetingly blanches before the steely look returns to his eyes.

Cook allows the door to bang against the wall, then strides through the doorway without glancing back. He follows the prison warden back through the long corridor and into a small room to collect his belongings, with Fallow following closely behind him, his ever-present shadow. They stand next to the main door in silence, listening to the jangling of prison keys as the warden opens the door to the outside, followed by the clanging of the metal door as it closes behind them. Cook has never felt so glad to get out of a cold, dark prison and get back outside into the relative warmth of the weak winter sunshine.

Chapter 28

Morgan is still sitting in the incident room, quietly seething as he sifts through reems of paperwork, when the office door opens and Cook and Fallow file in.

Cook has by now calmed down and updates Morgan on the interview with Luke Fields. 'We seem to have reached an impasse. Luke refuses to answer and we might not have enough evidence yet to get a conviction,' Cook complains.

Morgan grimaces. 'It's not looking good is it.'

A tight smile appears across Cooks face. 'No, it's not. But we can't give up. I know it's him, we just need to prove it.'

'I can't see us getting any further with trying to make him confess though, can you?'

Cook shakes his head. 'No, I can't either. We'll just have to rely on cold hard evidence then won't we.' Cook slaps Morgan on the shoulder.

'I think we'll need a bit of luck as well,' Morgan responds with a grin.

Cook smiles warmly at his friend. The moment of gloom has passed, they are now ready to resume the battle again of making sure that Luke Fields spends a very long time banged up.

By lunchtime, progress is being made with finding more of Luke Fields victims. As predicted, the Suffolk Times has received multiple calls from women who knew Luke through the youth club and church groups. It will take time to sort out all of the genuine claims but at least a few can be taken forward. The influx of new information is not only creating a mountain of paperwork for the team but is also needing copious amounts of time to be spent interviewing possible victims to weed them out from the bogus attention-seekers who always crop up. It is a positive step forward though decides Cook, who is sitting at his desk trying to digest all of the new information.

Cook wishes yet again that he has more resources and decides that this is an opportune moment to ask Bennett. His timely plea to the portly chief results in a bitter-sweet conquest, with the promise of three further officers to assist with the investigation but once the trial is over though, they will return to their normal duties. This means that in the long-term, Cook will be left with the same original small team and no reduction in workload. It is not often that he ponders on why he chose to take on a more senior role but this is one of them. He is feeling more than slightly overwhelmed by it all and the worst of it is that he doesn't even feel that he can trust his closest friend anymore to share his concerns.

Cook wonders if Caroline Woods was the one to contact station over the phone calls. The journalist seems to be quickly ingratiating herself with Morgan and is the entire reason why Cook can no longer trust him. Cook sighs then turns his attention to the ever-growing number of urgent emails in the team inbox. He locates several emails relating to the Luke Fields case then calls Fallow and Morgan to come into his office.

'As you both know, the local rag has had a number of phone calls about Luke Fields. They've emailed over the details, so I'd like you both to crack on with contacting them all. Find out if the stories are genuine and get statements if they are.'

'Yes boss,' Fallow says cheerfully.

Morgan looks sullenly at Cook, making it obvious that he feels the task is beneath him. 'Sure, we'll get on with it,' Morgan says after an uncomfortable pause.

'Go on then, crack on with it,' Cook snaps, his patience wearing thin.

The afternoon passes in a blur until at last Cook emerges from his office and claps his hands together to gain the teams attention.

'Right, it's time for a beer. Who's coming?' Cook asks, plastering a beaming smile across his face.

The team does not need asking twice. Cook swiftly herds them out of the office and locks the door behind him.

The evening goes as expected, with copious amounts of alcohol consumed, accompanied by raucous laughter, earning the group of detectives the occasional disapproving glance from the landlord. By the time Morgan leaves the pub it is long past normal opening hours. One of the perks of being in the police force, is that their local landlord is reluctant to throw them out however much disturbance they are creating, or whatever time they deign to leave the premises.

All in all, a good evening is had by all and Morgan even manages to not think about Caroline for a few hours. By the time he rolls up the stairs, making full use of the banister as he sways about, bumping into the wall as he climbs, Morgan has little thought for anything other than getting into bed; fully clothed, without even taking off his shoes.

Less than two hours later, Morgan is abruptly awoken from his drunken slumber by the sound of the front door clicking shut. Always alert to unexpected noises, he races downstairs to discover his wife standing next to the front door, a suitcase on the floor beside her.

'I thought you were coming back tonight?' Morgan says grumpily, kicking off his shoes and throwing them into the porch.

'The flight was changed at the last minute. Sorry I woke you,' Celia says evenly, trying not show the mixture of feelings that are washing over her; guilt for waking up her husband and sadness that he is not more pleased to see her.

Celia leaves the suitcase where it is and removes her damp coat and shoes, leaving both in the porch. Morgan watches her for a moment then heads towards the kitchen.

'Did you have a good week?' Morgan asks as he flicks on the kettle. He opens up the cupboard door above him and pulls out two mugs, setting them out on the worktop in front of the kettle.

'Lovely thanks, very relaxing. I met a few women who live nearby and want to start coming to the same classes as me. How was your week?' Celia asks, pulling out a chair and sitting down next to the kitchen table.

'Tiring. We've charged someone with the two murders and it turns out he has a preference for young girls as well, so you can imagine the amount of paperwork we've got.'

Their stilted conversation is interrupted by the sound of a newspaper dropping onto the front door mat. Morgan retrieves it and begins skimming through the headlines, his heart skipping a beat when he spots Carolines name in print. He wonders who else she has been speaking to, he hasn't spoken to her since Monday so could not have been the one to tell her about these latest allegations, which are there in the newspaper for all to see.

THE SUFFOLK TIMES
Wednesday, 10 March 2006

Murderer Charged with Sex Offences
by Caroline Woods

Luke Fields, the Marham-based businessman who has been charged with the murders of his mother and partner, has now also been arrested for the sexual assault of two under-age girls. It is thought that the two girls are part of the church youth club where Mr Fields volunteered. Mr Fields was also a youth club volunteer in Deben Quay until he was asked to leave due to having inappropriate relationships with underage girls, although he was not charged with any offences at the time. Do you know Luke Fields? If so, email the Suffolk Times.

DINE OUT FOR TWO OFFER

Special offers at two local restaurants will be launched every Friday morning.
See page three for details.

Fallen Tree Blocks Road
by Leah Hart

A tree was blown down during the night and has blocked one end of Ferry Lane. The emergency services were called out in the early hours to deal with the incident, which brought down a power line and crushed a parked car.

Local MP Resigns
by Russell Carter

Local MP Stephen Monk has resigned from his position due to allegations that he has spent public money repairing the roof of his second home in Deben Quay. The politician claims that he spent the money as agreed by the Government and that no offences have been committed. The story comes as no surprise as further similar claims have been made by other politicians.

Ricky's Autos
For MOT's services and all types of body repairs.
Tel: 286795

Celia puts some bacon under the grill and places a saucepan of water on the hob to poach some eggs, whilst chattering on incessantly about her holiday. Morgan is only partially listening, he is wondering how Caroline is and if he should contact her. His ears prick up though, tuning back into the conversation when his wife mentions inviting the Cooks around for dinner at the weekend. Morgan quickly suggests that it might be better to wait for another weekend, to allow her time to settle back into the routine. The last thing he wants is Cook letting something slip about what he has been up to whilst his wife has been away. In any case, his friend is still annoyed with him over the incident with Anna Jackaman.

There seems little point returning to bed now, so Morgan decides he might as well get an early start at the office and try to get back into Cooks good books. He eats his breakfast with gusto then pushes the plate away with a clatter. Nursing his rapidly cooling coffee, Morgan watches his wife who is ravenously eating. He chuckles, wondering if the retreat enforced a strict diet amongst its guests - he has never known Celia to eat a fried breakfast before, let alone wolf one down at such a rate.

Morgan pours the dregs of his mug into the kitchen sink and sets it to one-side to wash later, then takes the stairs two at a time up to the bedroom to change into his work clothes. When he returns, Celia is still in the kitchen, sipping a strong cup of tea. Morgan sits down on the sofa to pull on his shoes, then grabs his coat from the porch, which is still a little damp from the previous night. Just as he is fastening his coat the phone rings.

'Morning, just thought you'd like an update on the latest,' Cook says far too cheerfully for such an early hour. 'You'll be glad to know that Anna Jackaman has changed her mind. She saw the charges against Luke Fields in the paper and decided to make a statement.'

'That's brilliant news,' Morgan says.

'I've agreed with her that she probably wouldn't be needed in court, but her statement could help support the allegations made by the other two girls. She seemed pretty happy with that.'

Morgan smiles to himself as he listens to Cooks excited chatter. He hears the floorboards creak behind him and half-turns to see Celia standing behind him, gesturing for him to pass her the phone. Morgan shakes his head but before he has the chance to replace the receiver, Celia has grabbed it from him and is asking DCI Cook over for dinner at the weekend. Morgan tries to hide his annoyance as he stays at Celias side, listening in on the conversation. From what he can deduce, Cook is pleased by the invitation but insists that they play host as Celia has only just returned from holiday. Morgan suppresses a chuckle when he hears Celia promise to bring her holiday snaps with her, which she is planning to get printed later in the day. He can imagine his friend rolling his eyes, trying to sound enthusiastic at the prospect of viewing hundreds of pictures of the landscape and local wildlife Celia normally took when she visited somewhere new.

For a brief moment Morgan feels content, their lives have resumed to a steady normality and he steels himself against contacting Caroline again. As much as he has enjoyed her company and conversation, his life with Celia is far too comfortable, too familiar, to leave for another life with someone he barely knows.

Chapter 29

Morgan spends the day writing up reports, checking statements and compiling evidence, ready for the committal hearing, which has been set for the following week. It makes a nice change to be able to stay in the warmth of the office and to his surprise, Morgan is enjoying work he would normally have found tedious. Not only does he manage to leave work on time, which is a rarity in itself, but he even finds time to stop off at a local supermarket on his way home, to pick up some wine to accompany dinner.

Celia is already dressed in a calf-length beige skirt and black blouse and is waiting patiently on the sofa when Morgan returns. After a quick shower and change of clothes, he is ready and the couple begin the short walk to Cooks home.

There is a slight chill in the air as they walk towards Estuary Close. Morgan is glad that he picked up his warmer coat from the porch rather than his light-weight jacket. Celia is equally as well wrapped up against the cold, with a matching grey wool hat and gloves to accompany her waterproof jacket. It is still a pleasant walk though thinks Morgan, as he reaches for his wife's hand, covering the warm wool fingers with his own. The couple lapse into a contented silence as they traverse the quiet residential streets that separate the two couple's houses.

The Cooks live at the end of a quiet, suburban cul-de-sac. The 1980's detached house is adorned by a sweeping block-paved driveway. A small flower bed underneath the large bay window, displays the crocuses and snowdrops Celia planted for them as a house-warming gift when they moved in fifteen years earlier. The two large, welcoming led-lined lanterns mounted on the exposed brickwork, light up the white opaque front door with a yellow glow and illuminate a small push-button doorbell. Morgan takes a breath then presses his finger onto the buzzer for a few seconds, listening to the sound resonating through the building.

'Hallo,' Cook says cheerfully as he opens the door and welcomes his guest into his house. Cook takes their coats, then leads the couple straight into the living room. 'Take a seat.' Cook indicates towards the dark brown leather sofa, which is ideally placed in front of the large flat-screen TV dominating one corner of the room.

Morgan hands over the bottle of wine that he is still clutching in his hand. Cook turns the bottle over and grins when he sees the label, appreciative that his friend has thought to bring his favourite bottle of Australian Shiraz. 'I'll just go and find a corkscrew for this. Make yourself at home.'

The evening unfolds much as Morgan expected, with the two men ending up talking about the investigation, whilst Celia bores Sarah with a multitude of photographs of the area surrounding the Spanish retreat where she was staying.

Celia is clearly enjoying the opportunity to recount tales of delicious vegetarian meals and early morning yoga sessions, which have apparently relaxed her beyond imagination and seems not to notice her host trying to stifle yawn after yawn. As usual, she tries to persuade Sarah to join her weekly yoga class and as ever, Sarah reminds her that she has children to attend to and a husband who is at work more than he was at home, making it difficult for her to attend any regular social event. Even the offer of finding a childminder will not sway Sarah, who in truth thinks that standing in uncomfortable poses and chanting is more than a little strange and not something she wants to experience for herself.

The ambient chatter continues as they dine on roast beef, roast potatoes and a selection of vegetables. Cook ensures his guests are not short of wine, topping up their glasses at every opportunity, until Celia eventually removes hers out of Cooks reach and sips on a glass of tap water instead. After the meal, Sarah brings in a tray laden with a cafetiere and her finest coffee cups that are normally reserved for Christmas.

Eventually Sarah excuses herself on the pretext of checking that the children are still asleep, though in truth she needs a break from Celias incessant diatribe about her holiday. As soon as she reaches the top step though, Sarah feels a pang of guilt at her uncharitable thoughts. She should really pity Celia as it is clear she is bored and lonely without the tearoom to occupy her. Perhaps she should make more of an effort to keep Celia company occasionally Sarah decides, as she tiptoes into her eldest child room then pauses for a moment, listening to the soft rhythmic breathing coming from within.

Left unattended for a few minutes, Celia grabs the opportunity to interrupt her husband's conversation and steer it away from work and onto more agreeable topics of conversation for a dinner party, such as holidays. Celia does not notice her host suppressing a smirk behind his hand but the action does not go unnoticed by Morgan, who covertly rolls his eyes at Cook. Both men are thoroughly bored with the topic of Celias recent holiday.

The Morgans stay until almost midnight, then eventually concede that it is time to venture out into the bitterly cold night for the short walk home. Celia seems happy and much more relaxed than Morgan has seen her for a long time. He wonders if she is coming to terms with their inability to have children and has accepted that she will never become a mother. The idea of Caroline as a mother fleetingly enters Morgans mind - a thought he instantly regrets. He chastises himself for thinking about her and makes a promise to himself yet again to forget about Caroline Woods. It will be difficult to keep himself in check though if they keep bumping into each other through work, but he's sure they will be able to act like adults and retain a good working relationship. They will have to - in a small town such as Deben Quay, gossip spreads like wildfire.

Thoughts of Caroline are still firmly upmost in Morgans mind when he arrives at the courtroom early on Monday morning. The court is unusually quiet. Perhaps the early hour and day of the week is an unpopular time wonders Morgan, as he effortlessly locates the room allocated to Luke Fields case then makes his way towards an unoccupied seat at the far side of the balcony.

Luke Fields looks calm as he enters the room, resigned to give his plea for the charges of murder and sexual assault. Cook sits down next to Morgan just as Luke is seated at the front of the courtroom. Morgan strains to hear his friend as he speaks quietly into his ear, above the idle chit-chat of a group of local residents and journalists who are sitting behind them. Morgan turns to see what Cook is looking at and immediately spots Caroline amongst the group. Their eyes momentarily meet before she looks the other way and resumes conversing with her work colleagues.

A tense hush falls over the court as the judge enters room. He motions for the accused to stand up and enter his plea. A gasp of surprise is audible across the room as Luke pleads not guilty to the murders of his mother and girlfriend, but guilty to the lesser charges of sexual assault. This will mean he will go to trial for the two charges of murder, but luckily for the women who have made statements against him, they will not need to testify in court. The trial will be set for later in the year to give sufficient time to allow both parties to compile evidence. As expected, Luke is to be remanded in custody until the trial. There are no relatives or friends to offer bail money, and even if there were, the judge would not allow him his freedom given the seriousness of the charges. Morgan is sure there will be other cases to occupy him until the trial, but this case is different and will be in the forefront of his mind until they can secure a conviction. It also reminds him of Caroline, someone else who continues to haunt his thoughts. He hopes that with time, that particular episode of his life can also be locked away.

Chapter 30

The trial date is set for almost a year after the deaths of Lucy Mortimer and Julia Fields. Morgan and Cook prepare thoroughly - checking and re-checking their paperwork; practising what Cook, as officer in charge of the case, will say in court. Neither of them has played such an important role in a murder trial and neither man wants to let themselves or the police force down. They have worked too hard over the last year for the case to collapse due to a minor error on their part.

Morgan has seen little of Caroline during the last few months and wonders if she will be at the trial given how interested she has been in the case. He is therefore surprised to discover in the morning paper that the trial is now being covered by Phil Wattle. Perhaps Caroline has moved on Morgan wonders as he flicks through the paper. He has seen fewer and fewer news articles written by Caroline in the local paper of late, which have left him wondering if she is even still living in Deben Quay. He cannot of course ask though without setting gossiping tongues wagging.

THE SUFFOLK TIMES

Monday, 12 January 2007

Body in The River Trial Begins
by Phil Wattle

The trial begins today at Hemley Crown Court of the murders of Lucy Mortimer, 23 and Mrs Julia Fields, 64. Ms Mortimer was found in the River Deben last February and was initially thought to have drowned in a boating accident. It was later discovered however that she had in fact been suffocated before being left in the river. Luke Fields, 45, was arrested a few weeks later after it was discovered that he had been living with Lucy Mortimer in Marham, Norfolk. The post-mortem revealed that Lucy Mortimer was nine weeks pregnant at the time of her death.

Luke Fields is also being tried for the death of his mother, whose body was found in the burnt-out shell of her tearoom in Deben Quay. Mrs Fields coincidentally found the body of Lucy Mortimer prior to her death. Luke Fields is also being questioned over the death of his father and sister who were killed in a boating accident fifteen years ago. Mr Fields body was found in Kirton Creek in spring, 2003, but his sister Charlotte was never found.

Curry King
Traditional and contemporary Indian food. Parties catered for in the function room
Tel: 26543

Closure of Local Butchers
by Russell Carter

Deben Quay Butchers has closed suddenly, amongst rumours that they are yet another victim of the economic down-turn.

Former Teacher Found Dead
by Phil Wattle

A teacher who worked at a local girl's school has been found dead in Seaton Park. The teacher was found late last night by a dog walker who found the man inside his car. It is thought that the man knew Luke Fields, who is now on trial for the murders of his girlfriend and mother and has been convicted of several counts of sexual assault.

Cherry Tree Farm Shop
Now Open.
Suppliers of local fruit and vegetables.

Morgan folds the newspaper in half, then places it into his briefcase just as a heavy silence descends on the thronging court room. He looks up to see Luke Fields enter the room, still handcuffed to a prison officer. It is the first time he has seen the defendant in months and Morgan is shocked at his appearance; gone is the youthful, round face and steely eyes, replaced by a much thinner version, whose bony shoulders sag. The defiant look is all but gone.

The jury, who has already been chosen and sworn in, are seated close to the witness stand. There are a mixture of men and women amongst the group, of varying ages and backgrounds to reduce the chance of bias against the defendant. Many of the jurors have been taken from outside the local area for the same reason, to try to prevent any pre-formed prejudices surrounding the case resulting from the extensive coverage by the local media. These days though even this is not often enough, as nationwide media coverage of these high-profile cases often reaches far and wide across the Country.

As a witness, Cook is not allowed into the court room until after he has given evidence. Instead, he is sitting on a plastic chair in the long corridor outside the court room with the other witnesses, who are all anxiously waiting their turn. Once he has given evidence though he will be able to join Morgan in the viewing gallery at the back of the court room.

The first person Morgan spots as he enters the seated viewing area is Phil Wattle, who is already sitting at the back with a group of journalists. Morgans heart leaps as he quickly deduces that Caroline is not amongst them. Perhaps he could ask the editor of The Suffolk Times where she is, if they get a moment alone, he wonders as he locates a spare seat towards the front of the viewing balcony.

The first witness to be called to give evidence is Dr Bootle. Despite his many years of experience, the pathologist still feels a slight flutter of nerves as he takes the witness stand. He hides his feelings well though, as he confidently gives his evidence, providing the jury with the facts that Lucy had been drugged and subsequently drowned, whilst Mrs Fields had been manually strangled before paint thinner had been poured over her body, which was then set alight. The pathologist makes it clear to the audience that if the intention to cause Lucys death could be proven, this would constitute murder rather than manslaughter. The difficulty will be trying to prove both the motive and the intention of the suspect at the time of death.

A senior member of the forensics team is called up next to give evidence. He succinctly explains to the jury that Lukes's footprints, fingerprints and DNA were found at both Mrs Fields house and the tearoom. They also found Lukes's footprints in the area of the quayside, where they believe Lucys body entered the water and where tyre tracks from Lucys car were discovered. Both Lukes and Lucys DNA were found inside the car, though this was not unexpected given that the two were known to be co-habiting. Lukes fingerprints were also found on the steering wheel, but it is impossible to tell when this occurred, only that at some point he had driven Lucys car. No other DNA, footprints, fingerprints or fibres were found in Lucys car, making the likelihood of a third person being in the vehicle improbable, though not impossible.

With the forensic evidence heard, DCI Cook is next to be called to the witness stand. Morgan can see from where he is sitting that his friend is nervous and notices Cook wipe a sweaty hand down his trousers the way he always does when he is anxious. Even from this distance, Morgan can also see that Cooks right hand is shaking a little as he places it on the bible for his affirmations.

'DCI Cook, will you please tell the jury who is the beneficiary of Mrs Fields estate, as named in her last will and testament,' the barrister for the prosecution, Laura Watts, asks without any unnecessary preamble.

Cook stands up and clears his throat, then looks at the jury with a steady gaze. 'The sole beneficiary of Julia Fields estate is her son Luke Fields. He stood to inherit both his mother's cottage and the tearoom.'

'Was there any evidence that Mrs Fields intended to draw up a new will?'

'Yes, there was, there was speculation that Mrs Fields was intending to do just that so that she could make a local animal sanctuary the beneficiary of her estate.'

'In your opinion, what reason could Luke Fields have had to kill his mother?'

'The tearoom was well insured and her son would have gained a healthy pay out from this alone. In addition, the life insurance his mother took out many years ago would have provided Luke Fields with enough money to bail out his failing business and to start up again.'

'Objection your honour, the witness is speculating,' the defence barrister interjects.

Everyone in the courtroom turns to look at the judge in anticipation, with not a single sound heard across the room. 'You may continue as it could have relevance as a motive for Mrs Fields death.'

Cook shows the jury the note that was found in Lucys car, which was forensically proven to have been written on the computer at Luke Fields home. An examination of the documents on the computer proved that the document containing the note had been created after Lucy died.

'In your experience, what did you deduce from this note and from the forensic examination?'

'It is my opinion that the note was created to look like Lucy had committee suicide but the fact that it was created after she died suggests that it was not written by Lucy. The fact that the note was written on Luke Fields computer at his house, suggests that Luke Fields wrote the note after Lucy died.'

'Thank you DCI Cook, no further questions.'

Cook had expected the defence barrister David Anderson to grill him thoroughly, so is pleasantly surprised when it turns out not to be the case. He wonders if Lukes legal representatives know that their client is guilty and are simply providing him with the minimum effort they are legally obliged to deliver.

In a little over half-an-hour, Cooks ordeal is over and he is now at liberty to join Morgan in the viewing gallery, where he quickly settles into a seat, just in time to observe the next witness Dr Lea, a forensic psychologist who examined Luke whilst he was on remand.

Dr Lea begins by explaining to the judge and jury the rationale behind one of the possible motives for murdering Lucy; that some men do not want children as they do not want their partners attention to be deflected from them and they can also resent the financial burden of having a child, especially if did not want children in the first place.

'It is also possible that Luke did not want his partners body to change with the pregnancy, particularly as he seems to have a preference for young pubescent females.' Dr Lea pauses for a moment as if to ensure that the entire room is listening. A quiet gasp is heard in the gallery, somewhere to the left of Morgan and Cook.

Dr Lea looks at the judge, who nods for her to continue. 'Perhaps Luke Fields was unable to persuade Lucy to consider a termination? The use of a drug to subdue and calm the victim could indicate that he cared for them and did not want to hurt them unnecessarily. Lucys murder also shows planning and forethought - her death was made to look like an accident. Her car was disposed of in a remote location and a fake note concocted to hide the fact that Lucy was killed.'

Morgan notices that a number of jurors are listening intently to the witness, seemingly absorbing the possibilities in a sponge-like manner. He wonders if this could be the turning point of the trial.

Dr Lea continues to voice her opinions in a loud, clear voice, addressing the judge, jury and audience in turn, ensuring that the room is captivated by her performance. 'The death of Mrs Fields was much more violent and less organised. Money is an obvious motive for her death but perhaps she was also a witness to Lucy Mortimers demise. The use of strangulation may indicate a last-minute decision or could reflect on anger or frustration felt by the murderer - the need to literally squeeze the life out of her. The presence of forensic evidence in the case of Mrs Fields suggests a lack of planning, implying that this was an impulse crime. The fact that the body was burnt may have been to cover up the crime or else as an additional act of anger against the victim; wanting to eliminate all traces of the person she once was. The very act of trying to cover up the crime does however prove that the murderer was thinking clearly at the time, dispelling any rumours that the perpetrator may have momentarily lost control of their faculties. He would have had to find something to start the fire with, if he had not brought it with him. The fact that the paint thinner that was used by the murderer was left at the scene, suggests that he found it in the tearoom and used whatever was to hand to start the fire.'

The defence barrister, David Anderson, declines to cross-examine the witness and a tense silence descends on the room, broken only by the judge discharging the witness from the stand. As Dr Lea is the last witness of the day, Judge Browne dismisses court until the next morning. The audience waits for the jury and defence team to depart, before they too leave the room.

Morgan catches up with Cook, who is waiting for him outside the court, on the top step of the elegant, glass-fronted building, which houses several court rooms, jury rooms and holding cells.

'How do you think it's going?' Cook says as Morgan approaches.

'It seems to be going well, but it's difficult to tell at this stage.' Morgan shrugs his shoulders.

'I suppose it's a bit early to be making any bets on the outcome. Tomorrow should be interesting with Luke Fields taking the stand. I'm looking forward to seeing how he copes with it.' Cook smiles to himself at the thought of Luke Fields being bullied and manipulated by the prosecution barrister, who is renowned for her viciousness, especially when facing a murderer or sex offender.

Morgan is also visualising tomorrow's court proceedings but in a different light; he is determined to speak to Phil Wattle to find out what has happened to Caroline. the not knowing is more than he can bear. However hard he has tried, he has not been able to put her out of his mind.

The two men say their goodbyes and head for home, dismissing the fleeting notion of a few pints at the pub as they need to be up early to prepare for another day in court.

Chapter 31

Despite the sun shining through the arched window nearest to the defendant, Morgan sees Luke Fields shiver slightly as he makes his way to the stand to swear an oath before the court. The prosecuting barrister Laura Watts waits impatiently for the accused to be examined by his own barrister so that she can begin her examination. 'How long were you in a relationship with Lucy Mortimer?' Laura Watts asks, standing directly in front of Luke.

'About six months,' Luke responds. 'We bumped into each other in the pub - the Lamb Inn - where she was working. I'd been visiting a client and decided to go for a drink there before heading back to Marham.'

'And how long was it after that drink before Lucy left Deben Quay with you and moved to Marham?'

'It was only a few weeks,' Luke admits quietly.

'That was quick work. She must have really fallen for you,' Laura Watts retorts.

'We knew each other when we were younger - we attended the same church youth club.'

'I see,' Laura Watts responds, walking back towards the prosecutors table, momentarily turning her back on the defendant. 'Do you mean the one where you were a volunteer and Lucy Mortimer was a fifteen-year-old schoolgirl?'

Luke looks downwards, squirming in his seat. 'Yes.'

'And was that the same church youth club where you were also having a relationship with another fifteen-year-old - Anna Jackaman?' The barrister says as she checks through the notes on the table in front of her.

A gasp is heard from the back of the room. Lukes's cheeks redden as he nods in agreement of the statement, prompting a reminder from Judge Browne to reply audibly for the records.

'And how many other young girls have you had relationships with since then?'

'Two.' Lukes's response is barely audible, prompting the judge to ask the defendant to speak more loudly.

'You expect us to believe that you've only had two inappropriate relationships in the last ten years or so with females under the age of sixteen?' Laura Watts asks, glaring at Luke.

'Yes.'

'And were those two girls also in church youth clubs?'

'Yes.' Luke takes a sip from the glass of water in front of him then clears his throat.

'How did you get these young impressionable women to have sex with you?'

'They wanted to,' Luke sneers. 'I cared about them and they cared about me.'

'And what about Lucy? Did you stop caring about her? Or was she starting to look too old for your taste. Or perhaps it was the fact that your girlfriend was pregnant that made you look for sex elsewhere?'

'No!' Luke says uncomfortably. 'I can't help it if I'm attracted to other women.'

'But they aren't women, are they? They are children in the eyes of the law.'

Judge Browne calls a halt to the line of questioning and reminds the barrister to stay within the realms of the current case. Laura Watts responds that she is trying to build up a picture of the defendant's life at the time of the murders and the judge agrees that she can continue.

'Did you visit your mother whilst you were in Deben Quay becoming re-acquainted with Lucy Mortimer?' Laura Watts asks acerbically.

'No. We weren't on good terms.'

'And yet you decided to drop in on her the night before your girlfriend disappeared?'

'Yes,' Luke answers sullenly.

The prosecution barrister continues 'Why were tyre marks from your car not found at your mother's house, only those from your girlfriend's car?'

Luke Fields takes another sip of water before placing the glass down again. 'I parked further up the road where it wasn't muddy. I wasn't a hundred percent sure I wanted to see my mother, so I parked out of sight of the house.'

'And no one saw you arrive or leave?'

'It was dark and there was no one else about, so I'd be surprised if anyone saw me.'

Laura Watts nods, then turns towards the jury. 'Why did you decide to visit your mother on that particular day?'

'It was her birthday. I sat in the car for a while then decided that I would see her and knocked on the door but there was no one in. I went to the tearoom to see if she was there, but it was closed.'

'So,' Laura Watts turns to look at the defendant again. "You went home again, having driven all that way to see your mother?'

'Yes. What else could I do. She wasn't there.'

'You didn't think perhaps she was taking her dog for a walk and would return home again?'

'I didn't know she had a dog,' Luke admits. 'I hadn't been in touch with her for a while.'

Laura Watts cocks her head to one side as she digests this information. 'How long had you been having financial problems at the time of your mother and partners deaths?'

'A while. I was hoping the business would pick up but with the recession it's hard for any business these days.'

'What were you going to do?'

'I was trying to find a job. I knew the business wouldn't last much longer.'

'But you did not find a job, instead you decided to kill your girlfriend who was pregnant and would not consider having a termination.

Then, you decided to kill your mother to receive your inheritance. It had to be that same weekend because it was your mother who found the body of your girlfriend and you were afraid that she might have remembered who Lucy Mortimer was when she found out her name,' Laura Watts says, addressing the court room.

'No,' Luke shouts. 'I didn't kill either of them.'

Morgan has a good view of the jury from where he is sitting in the gallery and it is obvious to him that many of them do not believe Lukes's protestations of innocence. His attention is momentarily diverted from the scene as the low rays of the weak winter sun begin probing through the tall glass windows, flooding light into the dark space, reminding him that the day is drawing to a close. Judge Browne who must also have seen the sun's rays streaming through, looks at his watch and deftly halts the session. Court is duly dismissed for the day.

It is cold, foggy and drizzly, typical weather for the time of year but depressing none-the-less decides Morgan, as he winds a scarf around his neck and heads out of the front door. In his hand, he grips tightly onto a plastic bag containing his packed lunch, which Celia made up for him the previous night. Morgan sits in the car, waiting for it to warm up, thinking about the case and all that had happened a year ago. He wonders what the day will bring - will Luke Fields confess or will he continue to deny any involvement in the deaths of his mother and partner? Morgan enjoys the opportunity to mull over the possibilities as he listens to the rhythmic sound of his car engine turning over. As he clips on his seatbelt, he allows himself another fleeting thought – will he see Caroline today?

Less than twenty minutes later, Morgan is pulling up in the car park nearest to the court building. The small car park is already half-filled. Morgan notices the presence of the wealthier cars at the far end of the plot, vehicles that must belong to the well-paid legal team. Those cars closest to him are clearly owned by the witnesses and visitors, who evidently earn a great deal less than the professionals.

The rain has almost stopped by the time Morgan pulls up next to a Mercedes A class. Morgan figures that his car will be safer next to the more expensive automobiles, than parking next to a disgruntled defendant - not that his car is in any way pristine, but he would prefer not to add to the already damaged paintwork.

Morgan pulls up his collar up around his ears, shielding himself a little from the drizzle that has become torrential, just as he opens the car door. He grabs his packed lunch from the passenger seat, then jogs towards the glass atrium at the front of the court building, which was only opened two years ago, after a formal ceremony led by the town mayor and numerous other significant dignitaries.

The reception area is bustling with members from the legal world, witnesses, defendants and observers alike. Morgan checks that today's hearing will still be in the same room as before, quickly finding out from a list pinned to a gigantic notice board close to the unisex toilets - another innovative idea of the architect. He meanders down the glass-roofed corridor towards court room number 3, where both legal teams are already assembling below the viewing gallery. Morgan pushes open the door and threads his way through the narrow line of chairs that are filling up fast and onwards towards the far end of the room then chooses a seat at the end of the row where he removes his sodden coat, laying it onto the chair beside him.

A few minutes later, Cook jogs along the row of seats and promptly moves Morgans coat again so that he can take up residence next to his friend. Morgan scowls as the wet item is plonked onto his lap, which he quickly shoves onto the floor next to his packed lunch. Suddenly a commotion in the room below diverts Morgans attention away from his now damp trousers; Luke Fields is being brought into the court room.

The defendant looks as if he has slept little. Morgan wonders how immensely difficult it must be to sleep when your life is in the hands of twelve strangers. Morgan found it hard enough to sleep last night himself and it is not his life that is about to change forever. He watches as Luke traipses across the room towards his seat, his shoulders sagging; clearly a night in the courtroom cells has done nothing to raise the defendant's spirits.

The prosecution barrister, Laura Watts, picks up where she left off the previous afternoon. She goes over Luke's story in depth, picking at any holes in his statement and deftly demonstrates the reasoning for her conclusions to the jury before the defendant is dismissed from the stand.

Next to be called up is Luke Fields elderly neighbour, Stan Smith, who seems pleased to have been called up as a witness.

'I hadn't seen Lucy for several days before the police spoke to me and told me that she was dead,' Stan Smith begins confidently. Morgan wonders what Stan Smith did as a job before he retired, he certainly seems to be comfortable on the witness stand.

'How well did you know the couple?' Asks David Anderson, the defence barrister.

'I used to speak to Lucy quite a bit, but not so much with Luke. Lucy didn't have a job as she was hoping to do a college course, but she wasn't sure that they'd be able to afford it. I used to hear them arguing a lot, especially the week before she died. I heard on the grapevine that Luke had money problems and assumed that was what the rows were about. I wondered if she regretted moving here as she often looked sad and lonely.'

There was little else that the elderly neighbour could add and with his testimony complete and the prosecution team deciding not to cross-examine him, Stan Smith leaves the witness stand. The only other witness for the defence is the leader of Marham church youth club, where Luke was a volunteer until his arrest. Simon Flaxton gives a glowing account of the good work that Luke had undertaken, especially with the more disadvantaged children.

The church leader's impression of Luke Fields has clearly not been swayed by the recent accusations made by two fifteen-year-olds who were part of his youth club., leaving Morgan wondering at the stupidity of some people. Perhaps Simon Flaxton did not want to admit that he had taken on someone without checking their credentials first, or perhaps he thinks that the two girls are lying. It is also possible that the church leader was aware of the abuse. Morgan makes a note on the jotter that is resting on his knee, to check the church leader for any criminal activity, particularly relating to children.

No further witnesses take the stand. Noone had seen anything relevant on the weekend of the murders. The only potential witness was the homeless couple in the area that weekend, but Terry Smith is dead and Betty is nowhere to be found. Morgan wonders wistfully if Caroline could be right in that Terry Smith died because he saw something. Perhaps Betty is also dead considers Morgan, though he knows there is little point pursuing this line of thought at the moment - if Betty is indeed dead, her body has not been found and no one has reported her missing.

With the final witness duly dismissed, the two barristers sum up their conclusions of the case and then the jury retires to an adjoining room to deliberate.

Morgan watches the Mortimers leave the gallery then follows them out of the court building and onto the front steps where he catches sight of them talking to Laura Watts.

'They think it went well and that it'll go our way,' Mr Mortimer says confidently to Morgan as he approaches.

'Yes, it did seem to go well, but you never know with a jury. It's the waiting that's the hardest part, not knowing how long it will take and what the outcome will be,' Morgan replies. Although he can empathise with the couple, he does not want to bolster their hopes when he is all too aware that the case could go either way.

They barely have time to start the conversation, let alone for it to conclude, before a court official makes his way towards them to inform them that they should all leave. It is nearing the end of the day and the jury will need to be put up in a hotel for the night. There is nothing else the Mortimers can do now but to go home and wait it out. They have a very long night ahead of them.

Morgan offers the Mortimers a lift home, which they graciously decline, so he decides instead to stop in at the Eels Foot. Cook is already there and has bought Morgan a drink in anticipation of his arrival. Perched up at the bar, the stress of the last few days shows on the two detectives faces as they try to steer the conversation away from the trial.

'How about a fishing trip later in the year?' Morgan asks before drinking deeply from his pint.

Cook nods. 'Sounds good to me, but I'll have to check with the boss first.'

'Fair enough. I'm sure Celia won't mind helping Sarah out for a couple of days if that would help smooth things over?'

'That might just swing things in our favour. We could camp overnight near the river, make the most of the weekend. It would certainly be a welcome break.' Cook puts his empty glass back down onto the bar then indicates to the woman standing behind the bar that he would like a refill.

The two men chat for a while longer, planning their forthcoming trip. Eventually Cook drains the dregs of his fourth pint and waits for Morgan to follow suite. They can put off the inevitable no longer, it is time to go home and endure a very long and fitful night.

Chapter 32

The house is in darkness when Morgan arrives home, staggering slightly as he tries to focus on putting the key into the lock and turning it as quietly as he can. Not wanting to wake Celia, Morgan heads for the spare room and falls asleep before he has even undressed.

As predicted, Morgans night is a restless one. Eventually he pulls back the thin polyester duvet encased in a floral cover and gets out of bed to switch off the overhead light that is still on. With the room encased in darkness, Morgan clambers back into the cramped single bed and tries to get back to sleep, but the events of the day are still on his mind with his thoughts churning around in circles without respite, preventing him from sleeping. By dawn he finally gives up any notion of sleep and decides to go for a run.

It is a fresh morning, with the sun that is already beginning to push back the dark night, promising a warm, sunny day ahead. Morgan jogs around the perimeter of the town, running past Cooks house and out into the countryside, where he plods along the quiet rural roads. He runs for about half-an-hour until his mind feels clearer and his body is drenched in an icy sweat. The sun is rising higher now above the trees as he turns around and heads back home where

Celia is still sleeping. Quietly he showers in the ensuite and dresses in his work clothes, before creeping back down the narrow staircase and flicking on the kettle.

After scalding his mouth on a mug of strong black coffee and leaving a cup of coffee on the kitchen table for Celia, Morgan collects his coat and car keys then heads out the front door. He drives slowly through the quiet meandering roads that separate his house from Cooks, who is already waiting for Morgan to collect him. The rest of the Cook household is still in slumber, making the most of the half-term break.

The sun has almost fully risen by the time the two detectives drive past the front of the court and locate an empty space in the car park. Morgan goes straight to the room allocated to the case and finds two seats at the front of the viewing gallery, whilst Cook heads off to a nearby coffee shop for take-outs. Morgan is surprised to see Caroline sitting at the back of the court room, a scarf and hat pulled tightly around her head. Even from this distance Morgan can see that Caroline is ill. His heart pounds as he wrestles with himself, trying to decide if he should go and talk to her. By the time he has made up his mind it is too late; Phil Wattle is now occupying the seat adjacent to Caroline and Cook has returned with two coffees.

There is a tense atmosphere in the room as they wait nervously for the jury to file in.

Morgan spots the Mortimers at the far end of the room; Mr Mortimer is slumped over, his head in his hands as if trying to hide from what is about to occur; Mrs Mortimer is sitting bolt upright, staring anxiously into the room below, her eyes finally resting on the chair that Luke Fields has occupied throughout the trial. Morgan waves to them in greeting. Mrs Mortimer must have seen the movement out of the corner of her eye ad turns to look at him. She looks as if she has slept little and barely acknowledges him, producing only the tiniest of smiles.

Morgan allows his eyes to roam around the rest of the viewing gallery, seeking out any other familiar faces. As expected, Anna Jackaman is not present - she will be avoiding the throng of reporters who are waiting excitedly outside for the verdict. With the room perused, Morgan bends down and pulls out a newspaper from his carrier bag, which also contains a packed lunch made by Celia the previous night. It could be a long and very tedious day.

The jury spends the entire day deliberating, leaving everyone else waiting on tenterhooks. Half-an-hour before close of day, after which they would have yet again been sent home, the judge finally returns. The entire room watches in taut silence as Luke Fields is brought into the court and escorted to his chair followed by the twelve members of the jury who solemnly file back into their seats. The atmosphere is electric, dripping with anticipation. Morgan has never experienced such tenseness and feels a slight a flicker of fear that there could be trouble if the verdict does not go the crowd's way.

As the last of the jurors settles back into their seat, Judge Browne directs his gaze to the lead juror, whom he directs to stand. 'Have the jury reached a verdict?'

'Yes, we have,' the foreperson replies.

'And is this verdict unanimous?'

'Yes, it is, we're all in agreement.'

Judge Browne stares at the juror for a moment, as if trying to impress the seriousness of his next question. The entire court room is silent, no one daring to draw breath in case they miss the vital words that are about to be spoken. 'Do you find the defendant guilty or not guilty of the murders of Mrs Julia Fields and Ms Lucy Mortimer?' Judge Browne bellows, his voice filling the room.

Morgan perches on the edge of his seat, not able to tear his eyes away from Luke, who is wringing his hands together over and over again. Even the Mortimers are now standing up, trying to get a better view of the jury as they return their verdict. The foreperson clears his throat, before speaking in a loud, clear voice. 'We find the defendant guilty of the murder of Julia Fields and guilty of the manslaughter of Lucy Mortimer.'

Morgan hears a sharp intake of breath from someone sitting to his left. He can see looks of puzzlement on some of the faces in the public gallery as they try to digest what has just happened.

Judge Browne calls for order to placate the crowd, then addresses the courtroom. 'The jury does not feel there is sufficient evidence to convict Luke Fields of the murder of Lucy Mortimer, as the intention to kill was not unequivocal. A sentence hearing will be set for two weeks, so that I can further consider the evidence and decide upon a suitable punishment for Mr Fields. Until then, Mr Fields will be remanded in custody.'

All eyes turn to the prisoner as he is led out of the court room, a look of shocked disbelief on Luke Fields face. Cook too seems stunned by the verdict. He quickly composes himself though and heads towards the exit, where a group of journalists are waiting with their cameras and microphones to capture the first words from the victim's family. Morgan sees Phil Wattle amongst them but not Caroline. He must speak to her. Morgan pushes his way back into the court room to see if she is still there. She has gone.

Morgan strides back through the building and flings open the main door to find Cook standing on the top step, waiting for the press to quieten down so that he can speak to them without having to shout over the noise. Before Cook can utter a sound, the Mortimers' solicitor pulls out a pre-prepared statement and motions for the press to quieten down so that he can speak.

'We are of course disappointed that Luke Fields has only been found guilty of the manslaughter of Lucy but hope that the judge will set an appropriate prison sentence. We would like to thank Deben Quay police force for all of their hard work during the investigation and in securing the conviction of Luke Fields.' The solicitor folds the sheet of paper and replaces it in his coat pocket, then begins to fight his way through the crowd towards the car park. The Mortimers, who were standing to one side whilst their solicitor spoke to the press, also leave, ignoring the journalists who are shouting questions at them.

The throng of stunned journalists turn their attention instead to Cook, who is still waiting patiently on the steps in front of the court. Cook gives a brief statement to the journalists - assuring them that further details of the sentence will be shared with them in due course. He pushes through the crowd, ignoring the tirade of questions being hurled at him as he passes by, and heads off down the long busy street in the direction of the Eels Foot, where he has already arranged to meet the team. Leaving the car in the car park, Morgan quickly follows - it is obvious that Caroline has already left and in any case, the moment to speak to her has now gone.

Although the outcome of the trial is not quite what they had all hoped for, it is enough to ensure that Luke Fields will remain behind bars for many years and certainly warrants a celebration after the countless hours and sleepless nights that the team endured. Morgan runs to catch up with Cook just as he reaches the door to the pub.

Cook stands just inside the open door for a moment, a massive grin erupts across his face. A chorus of cheers and amiable cat-calling echoes across the room from the team, who hold up their drinks and toast their success. 'Speech! Speech,' comes a heckle from the back of the room.

Cook chuckles, then motions for the rabble to quieten down. 'Well, I don't think I need to say that we're all happy with today's verdict. We've all worked bloody hard, so tonight we're going to celebrate putting that bastard behind bars.'

'Hear, hear', a voice calls out. The sentiment is echoed by others in the room prompting Cooks' grin to widen. It has been a difficult case, particularly given that the nature of the crimes resonated through most of the team who have families – mothers, sisters and daughters - any one of them could have become the next victim of Luke Fields.

The team are more than a little merry by the time they leave the pub. The bar staff seem relieved when they finally go but wave cheerily at the officers as they file through the door one by one. Morgan makes a drunkenly apology to the landlord as he swings open the main door and shoos his team down the road ahead of him.

Cook sits on a bar stool and watches as the last of his team leave the establishment, chuckling at the thought that there will be a few sore heads the next day. He will of course overlook anyone coming into work late just this once; the team have worked hard and deserve to celebrate the successful outcome of the case. He pauses for a few moments, enjoying the quiet void left by the exiting of his raucous colleagues, then he smiles to himself as he pulls on his gloves and wraps his scarf around his neck; his team have done well and he is proud of them. Cook steps outside and breathes in the fresh, chilly air, watching as a flurry of snowflakes drifts down and settles on the path in front of him for a moment before melting into the ground. The road ahead is quiet as he meanders down the dusty-white street towards home.

Morgan is the first to arrive at work, eager to finish off the remainder of the paperwork resulting from the Luke Fields case. As he waits for Cook to arrive, he skims through the early morning paper, which he bought from a nearby corner shop on his way to the station. The front page is dominated by an article about the trial but also mentions the demolition of the tearoom, which seems to be rather timely considers Morgan – it is as if the Council have been waiting for the outcome of the trial before taking action.

THE SUFFOLK TIMES

Friday, 23 January 2007

Deben Quay Murderer Found Guilty
by Phil Wattle

Luke Fields has been found guilty of causing the deaths of his pregnant girlfriend and his estranged mother. The jury unanimously found him guilty of the murder of his mother Julia Fields and the manslaughter of his girlfriend, Lucy Mortimer. Ms Mortimer was drugged and subsequently drowned in the River Deben in February last year. Whereas Mrs Fields was strangled in her tearoom, which was also set on fire. The businessmen had serious financial problems and it is thought that he caused the deaths of the two women for financial gain. Mr Fields will be sentenced at a hearing in a few weeks, where he will learn if he will be given life sentences for both crimes.

Car Thefts Continue
by Leah Hart

Three cars have been stolen in the last week from the Pinewood area on the outskirts of Deben Quay. Two of the cars were found on the A14, but the other, a Skoda Fabia has not been located. Any information relating to these thefts should be given to Deben Quay Police.

Psychic Fair in Town
by Russell Carter

A psychic and spiritualist fair will be held in the town hall on Saturday. The fair will include palm readings, and the opportunity to purchase spiritualist merchandise.

Tearoom Demolished
by Leah Hart

Mrs Fields tearoom, which burnt down almost a year ago, was demolished yesterday. The building was at the heart of the investigation into the deaths of Lucy Mortimer and Mrs Julia Fields. A planning application was agreed by Deben Quay Council to demolish the listed building, as it was deemed dangerous and beyond repair.

Cherry Farm Shop
Locally grown and picked, fruit and vegetables, homemade jam and chutney. Locally produced meat and cheeses available.
Located on Deben Quay High Road.

Morgan finishes reading the paper and slaps it down onto his desk. No matter how hard he tries, the paper will always remind him of Caroline. He pours himself a coffee, which has just finished filtering and sips it as he waits for the rest of the team to arrive.

Despite more than a few hangovers amongst them, most of the team manage to turn up for the debriefing session, which affords them the opportunity for some closure on such a difficult case. Bennett arrives just after nine to congratulate them on their success, and joins Cook in thanking the team for their hard work over the last year. The last task that needs to be done, is for Cook to hand over to Fallow the numerous boxes of evidence that have been collated over the past year, so that they can be archived deep down in the basement. The case is now officially closed.

Chapter 33

News of Luke Fields suicide reaches Morgan in the early hours of the morning. A prison officer had found Luke hanging from his dressing gown cord, tied to a coat hook on the back of his door. To make doubly sure he would not be found alive, Luke also slit his wrists using a make-shift weapon fashioned from a razor blade, which he should not have had access to. Pools of blood congealing onto the vinyl floor beneath his body, had eventually seeped out underneath the cell door into the adjoining corridor, alerting a sleepy prison officer of the situation when he made his hourly checks. One look at the bloated, puffy face told the warden that there was little point in phoning a doctor but protocol needed to be followed and the prison doctor was duly summoned to certify the death.

The first thing Morgan sees when he arrives at the segregation unit are bloody footprints trailing down the length of the corridor in the direction of the hospital wing. Morgan cannot help but feel a little surprised at the apparent stupidity of prison administrators in allowing prisoners items with which they could kill themselves. He would have thought it obvious that the first year inside is critical in becoming adjusted to prison life and that greater care should be taken of those prisoners who are considered vulnerable.

As he makes his way down the corridor, Morgan is struck by how many of the cells contain multiple occupants and ponders on how it is that Luke managed to get a room by himself, especially being a newly convicted inmate. It is his understanding that new prisoners are not allowed to be in single cells as a suicide prevention measure. Morgan wonders if this rule is bent for prisoners who they know will cause problems, such as sex-offenders. He cannot imagine that many prisoners would be very pleased at sharing a cell with a paedophile.

There is a small voice in the back of Morgans head though that is nagging at him - the prison wardens will not be shedding any tears for the death of Luke Fields. His death will certainly solve a large problem for those in charge of the management of the wing where Luke was housed. He cannot help but wonder if the prison allows their inmates to resolve their own 'problems' without the need for costly and time-consuming interventions from staff. Certainly, the addition of a sex-offender in their midst, will not have been well received by prisoners and wardens alike.

Lukes presence on the high security wing would certainly have added to the already difficult conditions. The wing is based around a rectangular red-brick Victorian building that is ill-equipped to cope with the number of prisoners it currently houses, often seeing three inmates being squeezed into a tiny cell designed for one. It is a situation that has frequently led to friction between inmates and prison officers. On one occasion, the fracas even made the national news as several prisoners conducted a roof-top protest that lasted several days. The lifer's biggest grievance is usually over the basic and often dirty conditions in this particular prison, in comparison with fellow inmates at other more modern institutions, who at the very least have toilets in their cells, even if they too are on lockdown for much of the day and night. It seems to Morgan that little has progressed since the Victorian era. Perhaps the taxpayers hard earnt money might be better placed in rehabilitating younger prisoners to prevent this ongoing cycle of crime and abuse Morgan concludes, as he continues to walk down the corridor.

      Morgan follows the trail of bloody prints to the hospital wing, where Lukes body is lying on a bed in an otherwise unoccupied treatment room. The on-duty doctor is sitting at a nearby desk catching up on paperwork. As is the case for any unexpected death, a postmortem will be needed before a final cause of death is formally ascertained and a death certificate issued. Morgan wonders if the coroner will bother to investigate how Luke managed to commit suicide in a prison that has clearly managed to fail in its care of duty towards its' most vulnerable prisoners. Given that the senior warden of the wing is an old school friend of the coroner, Morgan thinks it unlikely there will be any comeback and that instead, blame for the incident will be firmly attached to the deceased. If any further culpability is required, the prisons chronic shortage of staffing will no doubt be duly highlighted.

Morgan stands at the doorway and observes how thin Luke Fields had become, noting some yellowing bruising to his upper arms that are uncovered by his short-sleeved t-shirt. He wonders how the other prisoners had been treating him. Now he will never know. His thoughts are abruptly interrupted by the arrival of two orderlies who are transferring the body to the morgue based at Hemley Hospital. Morgan assumes that Dr Bootle will be undertaking the examination but cannot imagine that anything other than suicide could be concluded. He watches as the body is zipped into a black bag and carried out towards the exit. Morgan follows it as far as he can, then turns towards the senior prison warden's office to collect Luke Fields belongings given that all of Lukes known next-of-kin are deceased.

Jim Turner spots Morgan in the doorway and motions for him to enter. Turner points towards an unoccupied chair located on the other side of the desk, then returns his attention to completing his phone call.

Whilst Morgan waits for the prison warden to finish his call, he allows his eyes to comb through the room, noting a number of certificates hanging on one wall and pictures of the warden with notable local dignitaries on another.

The warden at last concludes his call and replaces the receiver. He swings his chair around and turns his full attention to Morgan. 'We found this note amongst Luke Fields belongings, I thought you might like to see it,' Jim Turner says as he stretches out a short fat arm across the desk towards Morgan, the papers held tightly in his hand.

Morgan leans forward to take the articles from the once-muscular, bespectacled man, whose size even now is intimidating. He reads through the letter several times before looking up at the warden, who is waiting for a response.

---

12 November 2017

Luke,
The time has come for me to tell you the truth. It has been so long now that I do not know where to start. I did not die all those years ago, well not physically anyway. I could not take it anymore, it had to stop and it seemed the only way out at the time. I have not been far away from you though all these years. I have kept you close by and watched you become what our father was and I knew that you too must be stopped.

You may be wondering why I am writing to you after all this time. Well, I am dying and have nothing more to lose. I can die in peace now knowing that I have seen justice done for all that you did to me. You will of course by now have realised what I am telling you. It was me who left Lucy in the river, and it was I who set fire to mothers tearoom. The truth will never come out now, it will die with me and there is nothing that you can do to change that. I will see you in hell brother.

Your sister,

Charlotte

'His sister is alive?' Morgan says eventually, his brows creasing in puzzlement.

'It would seem so. You might also want to read the next note. I think you'll find this one just as interesting.'

Morgan takes the note from Jim Turners outstretched fingers and unfolds it.

> 17 February 2016
>
> Meet me at Deben Quay on Thursday at 11 pm at the bandstand. I have some information concerning your sister Charlotte. Don't tell anyone or you will never know what happened to her.

Morgan re-reads the note, shaking his head in disbelief, then sits back into the chair, closing his eyes. 'We got it wrong,' Morgan whispers, as if not wanting to hear the words. 'He *was* in Deben Quay on the Thursday, but not to see his mother, he was there to find out about his sister. She must have set him up.'

The warden smiles sympathetically at Morgan. 'If it's any consolation he wasn't entirely innocent, was he? He was still a sex offender.'

'But not a murderer,' Morgan croaks. He allows a moment to pass then stands up to leave.

He shakes the wardens outstretched hand and strides out of the office, turning his back on the place where Luke Fields has just committed suicide having been convicted for crimes that he did not do. Morgan heads towards the prison exit as quickly as his legs can carry him. How is he going to break the news to Cook that one of the most important cases they have worked was all a lie?

Fallow is sitting at his desk with his computer switched off, waiting for Morgan to return. When he sees the senior detective enter the room, he jumps up and ushers him excitedly into the small breakout area that the team share with the rest of the station.

  Morgan watches intrigued as Fallow glances behind him, checking that no one else can see what he is about to do. Fallow reaches into the top pocket of his pinstriped jacket and removes a folded piece of paper.

  Morgan leans around Fallow to pour himself a mug of coffee from the nearby pot, adding milk and brown sugar, before settling into a chair. It is only then that he takes the piece of paper from Fallow. Morgan looks at the white folded page for a moment, then hastily opens it.

  As Morgan reads the note, Fallow garbles, 'Phil Wattle came in when you were out. He found out that Caroline Woods was in the quayside the night that Lucy Mortimer died. She was caught speeding in the town centre - he found a speeding ticket in her desk when he was clearing it out. It was even reported in the Suffolk Times that a woman had been caught speeding on the Friday night. She lied to us about where she was.'

Morgan feels sick. He hands Fallow the two notes he has brought back with him from the prison.

Fallow reads them eagerly, his eyes lighting up as realisation hits him. 'Of course, he would have gone. People would do anything to find out the truth about the disappearance of a loved one. It's the not knowing that's the worst thing. The mud on his shoes, it must have been from the Thursday night. She's clever, I'll give her that,' Fallow says.

'I don't suppose you checked the CCTV footage from the boatyard from the Thursday?' Morgan asks.

Fallow shakes his head. 'I'll go and get it from the evidence room.' Fallow returns within a few minutes then follows Morgan back into the team office, where the video recorder is still wired up to the TV at the back of the room. Fallow flicks through the images until they reach the footage from the evening before Lucy was killed. They see nothing of interest until 10.45 pm, when they can just make out the grainy images of a woman walking past the boatyard in the direction of the bandstand. Fallow also had the foresight earlier to retrieve the sailing club records from the evidence room. Morgan scans through then again; the week before Lucys death, a Charlotte

Fields took out a kayak for two hours. She must have been working out where someone could enter the water and where they could end up, deduces Morgan as he slowly stands up from where he is crouching next to the TV. then walks out of the office without saying a word to anyone. Fallow calls after him but he does not look back.

Chapter 34

Morgans first thought is to try Carolines flat but she is not there so he drives to The Suffolk Times headquarters, only to find that her desk is empty. Rapidly he explains the situation to Phil Wattle and is given the address of Carolines holiday home at Eastleigh Point, a little over an hour drive from Deben Quay.

Morgan drives as quickly as he dares down the busy single carriageway, weaving past day-trippers who are returning from the beach. He turns off the main road and races along narrow winding roads that eventually evolve into a roughly made dirt track. Morgan slows a little to concentrate on evading the larger potholes, trying to avoid flicking up too many stones that could damage the cars paintwork. The track winds its way towards the sea for another quarter of a mile, eventually opening out onto the front garden of a small cottage located almost on the beach.

Morgan switches off the engine and sits in the car for a few minutes, listening to the caws of the seagulls as they flock over the incoming tide on the other side of the building. The soothing sound of the waves breaking onto the shingle beach behind the house, slows his racing pulse a little. Morgan takes a deep breath then pushes open the door before shutting it quietly behind him. The tranquillity of the isolated property is immediately interjected by a small dog who is barking frantically in the front garden, informing the occupant of the house that a visitor has arrived.

Caroline is standing in the doorway, watching as Morgan strides up the path towards her. Even from a distance, Morgan can see that she is very ill. Her wan cheeks are sunken, a crochet blanket is draped across her thin shoulders. Neither of them speak as she leads him through the doorway and into the front room of the cottage, where a fire is crackling and spitting out burning embers onto the hearth. Caroline offers Morgan a drink as he makes himself comfortable on the chair nearest to the fire.

'Your brother is dead,' Morgan says, eventually breaking the silence. He looks at her for a reaction but sees none, so returns his attention to the fire, which is now roaring. The flames are mesmerising and for a moment Morgan forgets about why he is here. 'I think you should tell me what's going on.'

Caroline face relaxes as if a weight has been lifted. 'Where shall I start?' She says, sitting down on the chair opposite Morgan.

'How about at the beginning Caroline…..or should I call you Charlotte?' Morgan replies, trying not to sound as angry as he feels at the betrayal of the woman he once respected and cared for.

Caroline lights a cigarette and sucks deeply on it a few times, then places it on the glass astray in the middle of the small side table next to her. 'It started when I was nearly six. My father would come into my room at night and cuddle me in bed whilst my mother watched TV downstairs. I never could bear to watch Coronation Street after that, the theme tune brought back too many bad memories.'

'It was not long before he began to touch me and made me touch him. I was eleven when he first raped me. He egged Luke on to join in, threatened him if he didn't. But he was so much older than me, he could've stopped it if he had wanted to. I couldn't.'

'Is that why you killed your father - to escape?' Morgan says, suddenly noticing that Caroline is smoking the same brand of cigarettes as her brother.

She nods. 'I didn't plan it. I just took the opportunity when it came. It was the day before my sixteenth birthday. He never was a very good swimmer. He only suggested going sailing with me as he thought it would mean he could spend some extra 'quality' time with me.'

'It was very misty. There were only few people about and certainly no one else brave enough to go out onto the water. No one saw through the fog when I hit him with the oar and pushed him out of the boat. When I close my eyes at night, just before I go to sleep, I can still hear the gurgling noise he made as he slipped down beneath the surface; still see the bubbles of his last breath rising up amongst the ripples. After he was gone, the boat capsized quite easily without anyone in it.' Caroline pauses for a moment to take another drag on her cigarette, carefully flicking the ash into an astray.

'I always loved swimming. I swam for miles that day; hours and hours until my arms ached and I could go no further. The river merged into another, so I swam up it until I found a good place to climb up onto the bank. It was freezing cold and I couldn't stop shivering. Luckily, I found a house nearby and stole some clothes off the line, slept in their summerhouse for the night. Once I had regained my strength, I hitched a ride into London and slept on the streets until I found a shelter and was eventually given a tiny bedsit.'

'I was fourteen weeks pregnant. It could have been either of theirs. I couldn't keep it. The life was sucked out of me in more ways than one. I had an infection after the… procedure, which left me infertile. After that I just got one with things as best I could. I was given the chance to work at a newspaper and that's what I've done ever since.'

'Why now?' Morgan asks softly.

'It was fate really. I saw him at a tube station near where I was working. I followed him back to Marham. That's when it started. I couldn't stand to see his perfect life when mine was so broken.'

'How did you meet Lucy?'

'I met her when I went to Marham, I often wandered around, looking for him, following him, finding out about his life. It was chance really. I started talking to her at a bus stop close to their house. She was on her way to the doctors to confirm the pregnancy. She was so excited. She said she was going to wait to tell Luke and I talked her into meeting me, said I would talk to her parents, let them know that she was safe. She wanted to see them again but didn't know how to approach them, how to handle the situation. She knew they wouldn't approve of Luke because of the age difference and because she was pregnant and unmarried. I arranged to meet her at my flat. We had dinner and I slipped a sedative into her lemonade. She was very sleepy and happy after that,' Caroline laughed then flicked her cigarette into the raging fire, where it was quickly consumed by the flames.

'But she wasn't dead though, was she? She was still alive when you pushed her into the river and left her to die.' Morgan spits, wondering who the person is, sitting in front of him. Whoever he thought Caroline was, had all been a fantasy, a mirage fabricated by his own imagination. She had become what he wanted her to be and until now, he had not seen who she really is.

'Yes, she was still alive. I parked her car on the slipway so that her tyre prints would be left there. After that it was easy - I led her down to the river and pushed her in. That weekend I used her keys to get into her house and wrote the suicide note on Lukes's computer. I knew he was going to be away, Lucy told me. Then I left the car somewhere I knew it would eventually be found.'

'But why kill her?' Morgan asks quietly, trying to stem the rising anger that is churning in the pit of his stomach.

'I did it to save the child from the life I had of course! He hadn't changed. He couldn't change from what he had become, what he enjoyed doing to little girls. What if the baby had been a girl?' Caroline says sadly, closing her eyes.

'Well, we'll never know now. You could have gone to the police. We might have been able to help?'

'No,' Caroline says, snapping open her eyes. 'It had to be this way. I had to see him suffer as I suffered. I knew he wouldn't last long in prison, he always hated confined spaces. Father used to lock us in the cupboard under the stairs. Sometimes we were there for hours. Sitting there in the dark not daring to move in case he was listening outside and would take us into the back yard and wrap his favourite leather belt across our backs. I knew when Luke learnt the truth it would finish him off. He always was feeble. Bullies are after all, just cowards.'

'What about your mother? Why did you kill her? And in such a violent way?'

Caroline laughs, throwing her head back, her eyes glinting with moisture. 'That wasn't her in the tearoom, she's here of course. I wanted her to be close to me. She's upstairs. Nutmeg is such a sweet dog, you must have seen him in the garden, we get on really well.'

'But…who was that in the tearoom then?' Morgan blurts out, finding it harder and harder to control his emotions.

'Just some old tramp who saw me and came into the building. She was begging for money. I was about to set fire to the tearoom to make it look as if Luke was after the insurance money, I couldn't allow there to be any witnesses to what I was doing, could I?'

'So that's why you killed Terry Smith. He could've reported that Betty was missing.'

'You catch on quick. I knew they wouldn't be able to identify the body without her teeth and I made sure her fingers were too badly burnt to print. Luke and I being adopted meant there was no one to match the DNA to, so the natural assumption would be that it was my mother's body in the tearoom.'

Morgan gets up from the chair and starts pacing up and down the length of the room, stopping next to the fire that crackles and spits as the logs are slowly devoured by flames. Morgan cannot help but wonder if that's how it was when the tearoom was set alight. 'What about us? Did it mean anything to you? Or were you just using me?'

'You mean as much to me as anyone can. I care about you a great deal, but I cannot allow myself to love you, that would be too cruel. How did you find out?' Caroline asks, looking up.

'You were caught speeding the night Lucy died. You told Phil Wattle that you were away that weekend and only got back on the Sunday morning. It was only when he cleared out your desk after the trial that he realised you'd lied to him.'

Caroline relaxes back into the chair, her eyes closing as she curls up into a ball. For a while Morgan thinks she is dead, as her breathing has become so shallow that he can barely see her chest move. Eventually though Caroline stirs. Gingerly she gets up from the sofa and puts on her shoes. Morgan watches as Caroline opens the back door and delicately walks towards the beach. A mist has crept up over the sand dunes whilst they have been inside. The swirling fog envelopes Caroline as she makes her way slowly across the sand bank peppered with grassy outcrops and onwards towards the shore. Morgan stands in the doorway, listening to the waves crash onto the shoal of pebbles at the shoreline. He knows that Caroline will not return.

Chapter 35

Later, Morgan could not recall how much time passed as he stood at the back door of the cottage, frozen by the shock of the events that had just occurred. Eventually Morgan realised that he was cold and needed to move again, so he retraced his steps back into the house and gently closed the door. The silence that descended was overwhelming as the heavy door shielded him from the sounds of the waves crashing onto the sand.

Solemnly Morgan walked through the tiny kitchen and back into the hallway, where he located the steep twisting staircase that led to the two upstairs bedrooms. The door to his right was open and he could see into the small, chintzy room that exuded Carolines taste in décor. From his vantage point on the landing, he could also see that the room was empty. The other door was closed. Morgan took a breath before tentatively opening the door, unsure of what he might find behind it. Caroline was right, Mrs Fields was upstairs in the bedroom and from the condition of the body, it was clear she had been there for some time; there was little more than a skeleton left, propped up in bed, a cold cup of tea was on the bedside table, a romance novel lying on the floral bedspread next to her. Morgan also did not later recall phoning the local police, but he must have done.

It had felt as if hours had passed before the emergency services arrived at the cottage. The unbearable stillness of the place only receding with the arrival of two local police constables, who were quickly followed by the SOCO team and Len Bootle.

After giving a brief recap of his conversation with Caroline, Morgan slowly drives back to Deben Quay, the radio playing softly in the background for company. As he approached the town, he remembered about his spare keys that Caroline had given him all those months ago. With a quick change of direction, Morgan turned into Maybush Drive and parked outside the familiar block of flats in the quiet, leafy neighbourhood.

Morgan parks haphazardly then races into the building and up the stairs, taking two at a time, until he reaches the top of the building. For a brief moment, the key sticks in the lock, as if the building is reluctant to allow him to enter. After some firm wiggling, the key eventually turns in the lock.

The flat is dark and musty, feeling unlived in. Unloved. Morgan supposes that Caroline spent most of the last few months at the cottage by the sea, seeking solitude in her final weeks. Morgan walks slowly into the hallway, the floorboards creaking beneath him as he moves, then shuts the front door behind him. There is an anticipatory stillness, as if a heavy weight is pressing down on Morgans chest, making it difficult to breath. It just feels wrong, being in Carolines home without her, creeping about it as if he is a thief. Morgan sighs heavily as he reaches the bedroom door, remembering another time where he was here. Gently he pushes open the door and steps inside.

Ignoring the feeling of guilt that is whelming up inside him at trespassing into someone else's life, Morgan rifles through the tall chest of drawers, followed by the oversized pine wardrobe that occupies most of one wall in the tiny space. Morgan does not know what he is looking for, but he does know that he has very little time before the flat is searched by the SOCO team, who are probably already on their way.

Morgan completes his search of the wardrobe and moves onto the bed that he shared with Caroline for just one night. He feels about under the metal bed frame and immediately comes into contact with a large box covered in a layer of thick dust. Morgan pulls it out into the centre of the room and flips open the lid, dislodging a cloud of dirt in the process. Inside are a stack of newspaper clippings dating from the time of the boating accident, as well as an out-of-date booklet on tides and rivers. Amongst the early newspaper clippings are ones relating to Luke Fields dismissal from the Deben Quay youth club. More recent clippings are from some of the church clubs that Luke had been part of over the years. The most recent article details Lukes's arrest for an alleged sexual assault of a fifteen-year-old whilst on a church camping holiday in the Lake District. Since Luke moved to Marham though there is nothing. Could it be that he had stopped? Or had Caroline simply stopped looking when she found out that she was ill? She had lied to him though, right up to the end. She hadn't simply bumped into her brother again, she had never let him out of her sight.

    Morgan still cannot grasp the fact that Caroline had hidden her illness from him all that time they were together. It certainly explains why she stopped working at the newspaper and gradually disappeared from Deben Quay. The last piece of paper in the box is a letter from a London oncologist, confirming that the cancer had spread to her brain and her condition was now classed as incurable. Morgan wonders if she endured any treatment for the disease or had instead decided to spend her time and energy in seeking revenge on her brother.

    Morgan places the papers to one side and finds beneath them, a small white plimsoll. He will need to check with SOCO of course, but he can only deduce that the shoe had once belonged to Lucy Mortimer; there are so many unanswered questions swimming about in his brain that it aches with frustration that he can no longer ask the one person who could have answered them.

Morgan carefully places the shoe back in the box, trying not to touch it any more than necessary. It is then that he sees it - a thin red book at the bottom of the box; Carolines diary. Morgan hesitates, then quickly quells the uncomfortable feeling of intruding on someone else's private thoughts. He opens the front cover and begins skimming through the pages:

21st February 2016

My head hurts. It often hurts these days, especially first thing in the morning and last thing at night. It feels as if there's a rat in my head, gnawing away at the soft tissue and bone, desperately trying to escape from its prison. I take another codeine and haul myself off the sofa where I slept last night, too tired to even to reach the bedroom. Exhaustion flows over me in waves, whispering to me to rest, tempting me to sleep, but there is no time to rest now. There will be plenty of time to sleep later. I have waited so long for this - for this time to come. I must make it happen, one way or another. I find it hard to keep myself in check, to trust that it will all go to plan. My thoughts are starting to run away with themselves, fantasising about the moment to come. The moment when I will at long last have my revenge. I savour the thought that I will soon be at peace; that this cycle of hatred will have gone full circle, back to the beginning again, finishing off what was started so long ago. What I should have finished back then.

I thought I could lead a normal life, forget the past, but I couldn't. It was always there and I can no longer fool myself that it will be any different. It is in my dreams, whether I am awake or sleeping. It has been so long since I allowed myself to have these thoughts and feelings. They have been locked away for an eternity, belonging to a different life, a different person. Seeing you again brought it all back to me. The evil, vileness of my former life. The fear you caused me, the hatred I felt for you. An anger I thought I had repressed has bubbled to the surface and split over into my life as it is now. I cannot control it any longer and have no wish to do so. The time has come. The end is near.

Saturday 28 February, 2016

I saw that old homeless man again today. I tried to be kind and give him a mug of tea but he told me to fuck off. Of all the cheek, talking to me in that way. He said he didn't know anything about the body found at the quayside but I'm not sure I believe him. He said he recognised me, so he must have seen something. He started asking for Betty, said she had gone to meet someone and never came back. He must know. It does not matter in any case. I went back later and left him with a nice bottle of gin to keep him company. He will sleep well after drinking that.

Monday 1 March, 2016

I saw him again today. The first time I saw him I liked him, perhaps even loved him a little. There is something honest about him, something pure. Something I cannot recognise within myself. I long for it, want to be a part of it. For it to become a part of me but I am afraid to let it in. To nurture this small shard of goodness within me would be cruel. It would give me hope for the future. But there is no future, not for me. I have to continue with the plan I have already set in motion. There is so much that has to be done and so little time to finish it.

I love watching him work, watching the wrinkles on his brow crease in concentration as he tries to work out the answer to the puzzle. My heart thuds with fear that my plan will go awry. I wonder how long it will take him to work it out. Will I be able to finish what I started in time? As much as I admire him, I hope that he will fail. He must fail. I will keep a close eye on him, make sure that he progresses in the direction he should be going in.

It is strange how we spend most of our lives wishing time away, wanting to get to the evening or the weekend, or perhaps a holiday we have planned. All I want now is time, something I can never have as it is slipping through the hour glass of my life. I have known for a while now that I do not have long left. My only wish now is to see my work completed.

Morgan takes a deep breath and slams the book shut. He cannot bear to read anymore. He traipses back to the car as if in a dream, not hearing the sounds of the birds in the nearby trees, nor the screeching of brakes as the police cars finally reach their destination. He does not remember Cook approach him and shove the morning paper into his hands before leading his team towards Carolines flat. Nor does he remember how he got into his car and drove the short journey home.

The house is still and quiet when he arrives. Morgan heads for the kitchen and pulls out a mug from the top cupboard, flicking on the kettle as he automatically reaches out for a canister of instant coffee. It is only then that he remembers about the newspaper that he is still clutching, as if it were the tattered yellow security blanket he clung to as a toddler.

It has not taken long for the press to get hold of the story. Reading through the front page seems to bring Morgan back to his senses again, the familiarity of the action soothing his frayed mind. He is shocked by the ease in which a journalist could gain detailed information about events from inside the prison, leaving him wondering if there were at least one member of staff at the prison who might be enjoying some extracurricular benefits.

THE SUFFOLK TIMES

Wednesday, 28 November 2007

Murder Accused Found Dead
by Phil Wattle

Norfolk businessman Luke Fields, who was convicted of the deaths of Lucy Mortimer and his mother Julia Fields, was found dead this morning at Feering Prison. The businessman had been found guilty of the two deaths in January and was sentenced to two life sentences, as well as ten years for sexual assault of two girls, a charge for which he pleaded guilty.

Mr Fields was also being investigated for the deaths of his father and sister, who died in a boating tragedy fifteen years ago. He may also have been linked to the death of local homeless man Terry Smith, who was dead found at the bandstand in February last year. The cause of death was thought by police to be accidental, but local residents believe the deaths were connected.

Former Teacher on Sex Charge
by Phil Wattle

Simon Morley, a former teacher from Hemley School was found dead last month after reportedly committing suicide at Seaton Park. Mr Morley was due to appear in court on two sex charges in December. The charges related to two separate incidents with the same girl who was a pupil at the school where he used to work. The girl, who cannot be named for legal reasons, was reported to have claimed that she and Mr Morley were having a relationship. Her parents decided to contact the police when they found text messages from Mr Morley on their daughter's mobile phone.

Snow Halts Traffic on Minor Roads
by Russell Carter

Heavy snow flurries stopped cars from going down minor roads yesterday as only major roads were gritted due to the fear of salt shortages. Several accidents reported yesterday morning during rush hour were due to the icy roads.

Seasonal Flu Vaccinations
by Leah Hart

Deben Health Centre are advertising that they have surplus 'flu vaccinations for anyone who wishes to purchase one. All those who are routinely vaccinated against 'fly have already had their vaccines.

Morgan discards the paper and picks up his coffee, which has now cooled. It is only then that it hits him. He will never again see anything in the paper written by Caroline. She has gone.

Chapter 36

Celia senses that something has changed. Her husband has been much more attentive recently, even taking her out for dinner at the Eels Foot, a place normally reserved for him to socialise with his friends and work colleagues. Even though they have not been blessed with children, this time of year always excites Celia, making her feel like a young girl again. James has planned to take some time off over the festive season and for the first time in years, they are planning to go away together - maybe a short break to Paris, Christmas shopping before the shops became too hectic to bear? It will be nice just to spend some time together. A simple pleasure that is often pushed to one-side, especially with her husband's demanding job. They have also decided to get a dog, hopefully this will give them something to bring them closer together. Celia is not sure why but she feels full of optimism for the future. It feels as if life is getting back to normal.

The sound of the newspaper being shoved through the letterbox jolts Celia from her thoughts. She pads across the deep pile carpet, opens the door and pulls the slightly shredded paper from the letter box. She takes it back to the kitchen and plonks herself down on one of the chairs where she unfolds the soggy pages to read it as she sips her morning mug of tea.

THE SUFFOLK TIMES

Friday, 5 December 2007

Shortage Due To Bird Flu Outbreak
by Russell Carter

An outbreak of Bird Flu that occurred on a Norfolk farm will have an impact on turkey availability this year. Trading Standards have confirmed that the outbreak has been contained but that all 120,000 birds on the farm will need to be culled. It is not known which strain of the bird flu was found, but it is not thought to be HN51 which is of high risk to humans.

Trading Standards will be visiting all properties in the area to test birds in near proximity to the farm and to advise those outside of the exclusion zone. Bird owners are advised to keep their birds indoors and follow precautionary advice from DEFRA.

Further information about bird flu can be found from the Suffolk Trading standards http://www.suffolkstandards.gov.uk

Christmas Fair at Wainmore Valley
by Leah Hart

A Christmas fair is being held at Wainmore Valley on Saturday 7 December. As well as local trade stalls there will be a Santa's Grotto and fairground. Entrance fees will be donated to the local Hospice.

Seasons Drink Drive Campaign Begins
by Russell Carter

Local police have announced a crack-down in drink-driving in the run-up to Christmas. Extra traffic police will be on hand to breathalyse any drivers suspected of driving whilst under the influence of alcohol.

Local Journalist Death Inquest
by Phil Wattle

An inquest has been conducted into the death of Caroline Woods, a former journalist who worked for the Suffolk Times. Ms Woods who drowned on 28 November close to her holiday home, had been suffering from cancer and had been given a terminal prognosis a few months before her death when she retired from working at the Suffolk Times. Colleagues at the paper were saddened to hear of the news and paid tribute to a hard-working and much respected journalist. Ms Woods only moved the Deben Quay just over a year ago but in that time had made a valuable contribution to the paper.

Celia folds up the paper again, drains the rest of her drink and places the mug into the sink to wash-up later. The paper is always full of such depressing news, she concludes, pulling on her coat. Then Celia heads down to the quayside so that she can sit by the river for a while and contemplate how lucky she is to have the life that she has.

ABOUT THE AUTHOR

J. D. Missen was born and raised in a small seaside town in Suffolk - the type of place that is overrun with tourists in the summer months and in the winter, an anticipatory quiet descends. She still lives in the town, with her two children and several rescue pets.

J.D. Missen was first inspired to write after studying First World War poetry at school and has had poetry published in several anthologies as well as publishing her own poetry book 'Love, Death and Madness'. This passion for writing soon developed into writing fiction and she quickly settled into the crime fiction and psychological thriller genres though she also has an interest in history, particularly modern and local history. J.D. Missen published her debut novel 'Confessions From A Fractured Mind' in 2024 and has also written two children's books; 'The Little Mole' and 'The Little Spider'.

Printed in Great Britain
by Amazon